Just Because You're Paranoid

Anne Louise Bannon

ISBN: 978-1-948616-27-0
Library of Congress Control Number: 2022919365

Healcroft House, Publishers, Altadena, California, United States of America

Thank you . . .

The reality of writing is that it does not happen in a vacuum. For example, a couple, three weeks ago, I was working on the exciting finish of the fifth Old Los Angeles book, when my friend and colleague Hal Bodner called to chat. Now, normally, this is the sort of thing that annoys the bejeebers out of me. But when I told Hal what I was doing, he kept it short, bless him, told me a little about why he called, cheered me on, then hung up. And I went back to work feeling renewed in spirit.

I am so very blessed to count Hal and a great many people among my support "staff." Carol Louise Wilde, my dear friend and amazing editor. Paula Bernstein, first my friend and now my medical consultant, who helped so much with the medical history of AIDS and what Sid and Lisa would have been dealing with.

And, as always, my dear husband, Michael Holland, who listens way more than he really wants to, and my wonderful daughter, Cornelia Ann Klarner, whose patience when I'm bouncing ideas off of her is not only amazing, her insight is incredibly useful.

Thank you, everyone.

To Gary Klarner, my ex-husband. I'm not going to pretend that we are friends. But you did give me the space back then to write the original Quickline stories. You read every one of them and offered some useful comments. And you gave me our wonderful daughter. Thank you.

October 5 – 6, 1985

I t happened as the result of a coincidence, one that was so bizarre and improbable that it could only have happened in real life. It even topped how my Mama and Daddy had met each other. They'd grown up in the same small city in Southern Florida but never knew each other, even though they'd gone to the same high school, only to finally meet in New York City at Columbia University, where they'd both gone to college.

Mama eventually said that she didn't think our coincidence was that weird. It's just how things are in South Florida.

It started when Mama arm-twisted Sid and me into going to my cousin Maggie's wedding. We weren't going to because we had decided not to invite Maggie and Jed Simons to Sid's and my wedding that coming spring. But then Grandma Caulfield called and let me know she wanted to meet Sid and our son, Nick, and that the wedding would be the perfect time to do it. Then Daddy told me Grandma Wycherly wanted to meet Sid and Nick and wouldn't the wedding be a good time to do it? We could come out a day or two early to visit with Grandma Wycherly, then Grandma Caulfield (Mama's mother), then go to the Maggie and Jed's wedding. Sid agreed it was probably worth meeting the grandmothers. We both made it clear that we did not want to go to the wedding. Yet that is exactly what we ended up doing.

We'd gotten into Miami airport late Thursday night. Friday morning, we met Grandma Caulfield, who was bowled over by Nick. Well, Nick, at twelve-years-old, was growing into his father's charm, but still had a happy, boyish energy. Sid and Nick look almost alike, with dark, wavy hair, bright blue eyes, and a sweet little dimple in their chins. Nick wears glasses, Sid wears contact lenses. Already, the top of Nick's head crested Sid's shoulder. Sid is not a large man, only three inches taller than me, and I'm average. Nick, I strongly suspected, would be taller than his dad.

Of course, Grandma Caulfield was in love with Sid even before she met him. Sid has money. Thanks to an inheritance and some shrewd investing, Sid and I are independently wealthy, which, as far as Grandma Caulfield is concerned, makes me the golden girl of the family.

Grandma Wycherly surprised us that Friday evening. We didn't expect her to get too excited about Sid's money. That side of the family is comfortable and has always looked down on my mama's side of the family because they aren't. It's one of the reasons we don't have too much contact with them. But Grandma Wycherly took one look at Sid, opened her eyes wide, then refused to talk to him. We had no idea why, although when we figured out about the big coincidence, it explained it some. Between Grandma's declining health and her odd reaction, it was one quick visit.

Saturday, though. What a miserable event it was. The rumor was that Maggie had pretended to be pregnant to get Jed Simons to marry her, then "lost the baby" after he agreed. As she walked up the aisle, she had such a look of desperation on her face that I shuddered.

Sid put his arm around my shoulders and squeezed me. "You're not her."

"I know."

With our own wedding on the horizon and a host of my fears about getting married, watching Maggie did not help. [I'm trying to remember. Weren't they divorced already by the time our wedding hit? That might have been one of your other cousins, but I know Maggie and Jed barely lasted a year, at the most. - SEH]

It was a secular wedding in a park, which had Grandma Caulfield up in arms. Mama's family is Catholic, but most of her siblings and all the cousins have left the Church. There was a receiving line at the end and Maggie gave me the stink eye as Sid and I greeted her. Apparently, I'd outdone her with a fancy, rich fiancé, and a wedding in Beverly Hills. But that's where Sid and I live, so there wasn't much to be done about that.

The reception was at a nearby Elks lodge. There were a head table and a tiny dance floor and a buffet featuring fried chicken and gravy, wilted lettuce, creamy salads, and some gray green beans. Tubs filled with ice, cans of beer, and wine coolers sat scattered around the room. There were sodas, too, for the younger kids, and pitchers of sweet tea on the tables. But I noticed a lot of the teens had wine coolers in their hands.

Sid and Nick kept getting a lot of odd looks from the adults in the room. At first, I thought it was because they didn't entirely fit in. Sid wore a perfectly tailored two-piece suit with a snowy white shirt and blue paisley silk tie. Nick had on a light-colored sport coat and dark slacks. Sid had helped Nick tie his bright green tie that morning. Sid was still wearing a cast on his right wrist from an accident we'd been in late the previous August. I didn't entirely fit in, either. I had on my favorite green shirtwaist dress, with big shoulder pads and a button-up front, and cute high heels. But then, I realized there was an undercurrent to the looks that was oddly speculative.

Maggie and Jed and the wedding party got to go through the buffet line first, and we all watched them eat as we waited in line for the food.

"I'm beginning to think you were right about not having a head table," Mama said softly to me as we stood in line. She's small and pert and a force of nature, and at that time, driven by planning mine and Sid's wedding. Both Sid and I were working overtime to keep her from going crazy.

"Thanks," I said without enthusiasm, looking around the room for my son. He'd been running around with some of the other kids, and I needed to warn him about the wine coolers. "Nicholas!" I signaled, and he ran over.

"What's up, M—" He choked. His voice had just started breaking and usually did at the most inconvenient times.

"See those bottles with the B and J on them?"

"Those are disgusting!"

"They're also a poor excuse for wine, so be careful."

Nick made a face. "There's wine in that? Yuck!"

"And it will make you pretty sick pretty quickly."

Nick does like wine. Sid and I let him have a little at dinner when we have some. We're hoping that by not making alcohol a forbidden fruit and by us setting a good example, Nick won't go overboard when he gets to high school.

"Okay." He ran off again, only to be summoned by his father, who was sitting with Daddy at a table near the door to the room. It looked like Sid shared the same concern I'd had, because Nick rolled his eyes and pointed at me.

"Did you see the baby pictures set up next to the presents?" Mama asked. "Isn't that the sweetest thing?"

"No. Absolutely not. No way, no how. No baby pictures. Sid doesn't even have any."

"Why on earth not?"

"I don't know. I guess his aunt didn't take any."

Sid was raised by his Aunt Stella.

Mama looked perplexed. "Didn't his mama take any?"

"I don't think so. And she died when he was two."

"Oh, that's right. I forgot."

We finally got to the food, and Mama and I filled plates for ourselves and for Sid, Daddy, and Nick. I put a plate with a chicken breast, some limp salad, and some green beans in front of Sid.

"I'm sorry, sweetie," I told him. "It's the best I can do."

He sighed. Sid is a health freak, and while he will give way sometimes on how and what I eat, the wedding had put him in a pickle.

"Well, hello there!" One of my two uncles ambled up to the table, a beer can in hand. Both are not overly tall, but big around and older than Mama. The problem is my Uncle Steven and my Uncle Leonard are identical twins, and I can seldom tell them apart.

"Hello, Leonard," Mama grumbled. She can tell her brothers apart.

Uncle Leonard was Maggie's father. He held his hand out to Sid.

"So, you're the fella that's going to make an honest woman out of our little Lisa," Uncle Leonard said, laughing.

"I couldn't possibly," Sid said with a tight smile as he shook Uncle Leonard's hand.

"What's that?"

"How can I make Lisa that which she already is?"

It took Leonard a minute and he still couldn't parse that one out.

He belched. "'Scuze me." He swallowed some beer. "The big question is, where you been hiding that boy of yours, Lisa?"

"With my first mom," Nick said, digging into the food on his plate. "Lisa's my second mom. She's adopting me."

"Oh." Leonard nodded. "I didn't know you was married before, Sid."

"They weren't," Nick cut in. "I didn't even know Dad until I was eleven."

Sid looked fondly at his son. "It's worked out well, though."

"Must run in the family," Leonard said and wandered off.

"Sorry about that, Sid," Daddy said around some chicken. "Have to say, though, if Lisa's relatives haven't scared you off of her, you must really love my daughter."

Sid laughed and gazed sweetly at me. "I must really do."

"Run in what family?" Nick asked.

Mama and Daddy looked at each other, then Mama patted Nick's arm.

"You and your daddy just look a lot like some people we knew in the area."

Nick's eyes opened wide. "You mean, like his dad? Is that why everybody is looking at us funny?"

"Not my father, Nick," Sid said, scraping the skin off his chicken breast. "Our features come from my mother. I showed you that picture I have of her."

"Your mama, Sid?" Mama looked curiously at him. "What was her name?"

"Sheila Hackbirn," Sid replied. "I don't know if that was her real name, but it's the one on my birth certificate. My aunt had already changed hers when her sister came to live with her. And I guess my mother took the same name for some reason."

"And what's your daddy's name?"

"Unknown." Sid chuckled.

"Oh." Mama looked at Daddy again, who shrugged.

"It doesn't bother me, Althea." Sid smiled at my mom. "You know I'm shameless."

Mama looked at him. "Don't you ever wonder, though?"

"Not really." Sid thought for a second. "Maybe a passing thought or two. But in the environment in which I grew up, I was hardly the only kid who didn't know who his father was. If anything, it was more unusual to have a dad."

Daddy looked at him. "I don't understand."

"I was raised with a bunch of beatniks, communists, and later, hippies." Sid smiled softly. "It was all about free love, and conventional societal mores were the kiss of death for relationships. I didn't even know what conventional societal mores were until I went to high school."

"Will you folks excuse me?" I said, getting up. "I'm going to see if I can find a soda."

"We've got some sweet tea right here," Mama said.

"Mama, soda has less sugar than that tea."

Mama shrugged as she poured herself some of the iced tea that was so sweet it would have made my teeth ache. I don't know if Sid told them that he and his aunt had been estranged since he was nineteen and drafted into the U.S. Army. It was one of those sore spots he had, understandably.

I found a tub that had a can of generic cola in it and bent to get it. As I straightened, I saw that my cousins Darlene and Miranda had flanked me.

"Hi, guys." I smiled but felt no warmth.

Darlene was short, like most of the women in Mama's family, but Miranda was about my height. Both had their blond hair teased out and sprayed into place.

"Well, Lisa," Darlene said, taking my arm by the elbow. "How did you get that man to marry you?"

"I asked him to." I tried to edge away from them and couldn't.

"Oh, come on." Miranda giggled. "We want to know how you snagged him. Landsakes!"

"I didn't snag or trap him," I snarled. Both Darlene and Miranda were still married, but I'd heard the clock was ticking on Darlene's marriage.

Darlene laughed. "Oh, don't be shy, Lisa. Something that delicious ain't settling down without some serious motivation."

"We love each other." I finally pulled away. "That's motivation enough."

I walked away, feeling really steamed that no one in my family thought I was attractive enough on my own to get a husband without resorting to chicanery. Perhaps it was because most of my female cousins had done exactly that. I was going to return to the table but changed my mind and went to visit the ladies' room, off the front foyer, instead. As I went in, I could hear Aunt Amanda (who was married to Uncle Leonard and Maggie's mother) and Aunt Marie (Uncle Steven's wife) talking to each other in the stalls. I closed myself into one and tried to relax a little.

"Well, I'll tell you, that little boy of his is a caution," Marie said.

A toilet flushed.

"Cute as a button, too." Amanda added. The other toilet flushed. "Leonard told me just now that the boy said his father never married his mother."

"Sounds just like you-know-who." Marie lifted her voice over the water running in the sink.

"Wait. I wonder." The water in the sink stopped and a paper towel dispenser thunked several times. Amanda laughed. "You know, *she* looked like both him and his daddy. You think...?"

"You think we should call...?"

"I do believe we should." Amanda cackled. "Course, she ain't going to be terribly happy to find out."

Marie cackled, as well, and the two left the ladies' room. As soon as I could, I grabbed my soda, washed my hands, and hurried out.

Sid was waiting for me.

"Sid, I just heard the most amazing conversation." I tried to go back to the reception hall.

Sid held me back. "I don't care. I've had it. We're leaving."

"But—"

"Nick got sick." Sid's eyes blazed. "One of your idiot cousins spiked his soda and talked him into chugging it."

"My poor baby!"

Mama came up. "He's alright, Sid. Bill's helping him rinse out his mouth now."

I looked back at the reception hall. "I don't want to stay either."

"Then don't," said Mama. "Bill and I better stick around a while longer, though."

"We'll head to the airport from here." Sid sighed. He took Mama's hands in his. "Althea, you are a lovely person to know, and I consider it a privilege to have you as my mother-in-law. But I cannot stand your family."

"I can't stand them either," Daddy said, his arm around Nick, who still looked a little ashen. "The only folks worse are my family."

"We should never have come back to South Florida," Mama said.

My parents own a resort in South Lake Tahoe and spend the warmer months there, then go down to the motel they bought in Homestead, near the Everglades, during the winter. They'd gotten tired of the snow and Grandma had raised a stink about not having her only daughter living near her.

There were hugs and kisses goodbye, then Nick, Sid, and I went out to the rental car in the parking lot. When we got to the airport, we discovered that the soonest flight to Los Angeles wouldn't leave for another five hours. Nick, fortunately, had mostly bounced back.

"Dad, there's a flight to New York in half an hour. Can we?"

Sid looked at me. "Honey? We can spend the night and get a late flight out to L.A. With the time change, we won't be back too late."

I put my arm in his. "You know, that sounds like fun."

We had a lovely time. New York, with its reputation for never closing, had plenty to offer us, and we happily walked the streets and took a carriage ride through Central Park. We spent the next day ambling along Fifth Avenue. Sid stopped us as we started past Tiffany and Company.

"Son," he announced. "Your mom and I are about to get goopy-eyed, so just deal with it, okay?"

Nick's eyes rolled, but he still had a grin on his face.

Sid looked at me and folded his arms across his chest. "I seem to remember that I made a promise to you standing outside this door once."

I flushed. I did remember, but looked away. "That's one I'm not holding you to."

"Ah, but I think the time has come." He gently took my arm and ushered me inside, Nick at our heels. "I have never broken a promise to you, and I never will. Hands in your pockets, son."

Nick sighed.

We looked around the glittering room. Sid had promised me he would drag me into the store at some point when I no longer had an excuse to protest and twist my arm into telling him what I liked, and he would buy it for me.

"Now, what do you like?" Sid asked. "And don't try fibbing."

I sighed. "All of it. None of it. It's just so overdone."

We looked at some flatware. Since we were rebuilding our house, we would need a set. We'd been collecting some beautiful antique sterling, but we needed something for everyday use. Nothing there was right. Sid had me look at necklaces and earrings and I finally found a lovely, but simple necklace with a fine, gold chain and a pendant of two wavy crossing lines set with small diamonds.

"Perfect," Sid said, and waved at the sales lady. "She'll wear it out."

The sales lady took his credit card and wrapped the opal necklace I'd been wearing in the familiar blue box. Sid had bought me that necklace, too. This time, the purchase was more of a gesture, though. The winter before, Sid and I had merged all our money and assets into a business partnership, and now we co-owned everything, including the house. As Sid often noted... Well, I did, too. We were, for all intents and purposes, already married. The church ceremony to come was about the Sacrament of Matrimony, which was important to me since I am a practicing Catholic. Sid's an atheist, but he appreciated the way I felt about it and was happy to go along.

Nick was bored out of his mind, but didn't get too fidgety for a change. That's one way he and his father are very different. Nick is hyperactive. I couldn't imagine a fidgety Sid, no matter how hard I tried.

It was close to ten, California time, when the shuttle from the airport dropped us off in front of the condo building on the corner of Wilshire Boulevard and one of the side streets in the area. We'd had to move out while our house was being rebuilt and had bought the condo directly across from the one owned by our friends Kathy and Jesse. Once upstairs, Sid and I kissed Nick goodnight, then went to get ready for bed ourselves. I stripped and Sid put on a pair of tight jeans. That was the one shadow in our lives.

Until the previous spring, Sid had slept around. A lot. We didn't know it at the time, but the AIDS epidemic was just getting into the straight population right around when Sid stopped sleeping around. We had even thought he'd been exposed to the virus by one of his girlfriends. His test had come back negative, which was a good sign, and it had been long enough since he'd slept with the girlfriend in question that she probably had not given it to him. The problem was any one of the many women he'd slept with after that could have passed on the virus, and it had only been a little over six months since the last time he'd had sex with someone. Given that we didn't know how long it took after exposure for the virus that caused AIDS to show up in the bloodstream, we were waiting for Sid to get tested again.

For a while, he'd been reluctant to even kiss me, he was so worried about potentially infecting me. But I'd pointed out that if saliva carried the virus (which was by no means certain) and if he had the virus (again, very unlikely), then it was already way too late for me. Yeah, we'd been deep kissing even before he gave up on other women. Eventually, we got pretty involved in some extremely heavy petting, you might say, which is when we started sharing the old waterbed we'd brought over to the condo from the house. Sid wore jeans to keep me safe from any of his bodily fluids. We could have used condoms, but Sid didn't trust them. He had a point. He'd been wearing one when he conceived Nick, and didn't want to take any chances.

Sid slid up behind me and softly kissed my shoulders. It felt so nice, but we were both exhausted.

"I love you, Sid," I said as I blinked and rolled over to kiss him.

"I love you, Lisa."

We kissed again, snuggled, and fell asleep.

October 11, 1985

It was a nice, normal week. Sid and I worked at our free-lance writing business and only got one drop to make for our side business. Nick went to school, which made it easier for Sid and me to get frisky. We do get a little on the loud side [A little? - SEH] and it did sometimes wake up Nick because of the thin walls in the condo. Wednesday, Sid got his blood drawn for his AIDS virus test. Thursday, he got the cast off his right hand, but still had to wear a brace.

Sid was also taking a couple music classes on Tuesdays and Thursdays through a small arts college in the area. It was a special program for working adults that would provide credits but wasn't entirely degree focused. Sid had wanted to enroll in a formal Master of Music program, but attendance was going to be a problem since we often traveled thanks to our side business. He was also taking private piano lessons again on Saturday mornings. I was so glad.

One problem he'd had when he'd stopped sleeping around was what to do with himself, since he wasn't going out four to six nights a week to get laid. That he'd settled on exploring his first love, music, made both of us happy.

Between the lessons and his theory and his composition classes, he was almost as busy as I was with bible study, teen bible study, teaching confirmation class, and the Friends of the Los Angeles Public Library. We spent time at our gym, too, working out on weights, and practicing martial arts. We both played racquetball, though not with each other. Sid is way too good for me.

Friday morning started out nicely. We were expecting the results from Sid's AIDS test sometime that morning and we were expecting them to be negative - it really wasn't likely that Sid had the virus, even with his risk factor, and he didn't have any symptoms, which helped even though we knew it could be years before any showed. That meant that night we would fully make love for the first time. Sid wanted to romance me and make it extra special, too. He teased me all morning, which almost made Nick late for school. The plan was to take Nick to spend the weekend with my sister and brother-in-law and their kids in Pasadena, then go out to dinner, then come home and let nature take its course.

Then Sid got called out for a pickup. He didn't look entirely happy about it.

"The drop used kind of an old code." He looked pensive. "But it hasn't been deprecated."

"What line?" I asked.

"Yellow. And there's no addressee."

"That's odd."

"Not if it's coming to us."

I shrugged. It was always possible.

I should probably explain. Within the structures of the FBI and CIA are several smaller shadow groups that are so top secret that mostly only their members know they exist.

Sid and I are members of one called Operation Quickline. Our primary mission is to move information around, although we do sometimes do investigations and other chores.

Sid left at nine. Shortly after that, my friend Kathy Deiner came over from across the hall.

"I'm told tonight's the night," she said.

She's a tall, elegant woman with closely cropped hair and skin the color of dark chocolate. For some reason, around the end of September, she'd resigned her position at the accounting firm she'd worked at as a CPA and had started her own accounting business.

"We do have to wait for Sid's test results to come back," I said.

Kathy laughed. "I'm not talking about you."

"Huh?"

"Frank and Esther." They were our other friends. "Jesse told me this morning that it's all set to go for tonight." Jesse is Kathy's husband.

"Holy crud. I completely forgot about that."

Frank and Esther had been best buddies as long as I'd known them. The catch was the two of them had fallen in love with each other and had been in denial about it longer than Sid and I had been about our own feelings. Esther Nguyen was an engineer at a defense plant down in the South Bay. She'd basically been supporting Frank, who was a wonderful musician, but he'd had a horrible time trying to make a living at it. Esther had finally confessed to Kathy and me that she was in love with Frank but couldn't see him being in love with her about the same time Frank had confessed to Sid and Jesse that he, Frank, was deeply in love with Esther, but couldn't see Esther loving him the same way.

"Sid set it up with a limo, dinner out, and tickets to some concert downtown," Kathy said. "I told Esther over the weekend that she'd better 'fess up and that tonight would be the perfect opportunity to. Jesse told me he told Frank the same thing the other night."

I crossed myself. "This could go either way, you know."

"I know. But what else are we going to do?"

"Not much," I sighed, then winced. "Kathy, are we doing the right thing, interfering like this? I remember a time when I would have been really angry if someone had."

"Yeah. I know." She shook her head. "But you and Sid had his whole sleeping around thing to get past. Frank and Esther have been trying to figure out what to do about each other for months now."

"True."

Kathy shrugged. "Hold on a second. What's this about tonight being your night?"

"Sid's AIDS test. The results should be in today. If they're negative, and the odds are good, then we're cleared for takeoff."

"Aren't you already doing that?" It wasn't as though Kathy hadn't heard the noise at one time or another. "I mean, you can use a condom."

"Limited to really heavy petting." I sighed. "Sid doesn't trust condoms. He was wearing one when he conceived Nick. If I'm still a virgin, it's only on the technicality of no penetration."

Kathy burst into laughter. "And you're making that much noise with just oral sex?"

My face went vermilion. "He is fantastic at it."

"I do not want to hear the two of you when you get it on all the way. And he's just as bad as you are. Wait. You aren't doing oral on him."

I whimpered a little. "No. We have other ways of satisfying him."

Sid came back by ten-fifteen, his three-piece suit a dusty mess, and his language turning the air blue.

"It was a bad one," he told me between swear words. "I was set up in a parking lot. A car came straight at me. I was just lucky I heard it revving up and scaled a fence into the vacant lot next door."

"Are you alright?" I asked anxiously. "How's your wrist?"

Sid flexed his right fingers. "It's fine."

"Oh, thank God!" I grabbed his face and kissed him.

He put his arms around me. "It's okay. I'm alright."

We didn't get a chance to get more involved, though. The phone rang. We were in the living room of the condo, where we'd squeezed our two desks in facing each other. There was a couch in there, as well, and just beyond that, in front of the tiny kitchen, a dining area that also doubled as my sewing space.

Sid answered the phone, then put it on speaker.

"Okay, Dr. Kline," he said, looking warmly at me.

"Well, Sid, I'm afraid there's a problem." Dr. Kline, a woman, had a fairly deep, but soothing voice.

"What?" Sid's face turned pale.

"No, no. We just need to get you retested. The lab screwed something up and three samples got combined or something. The problem is the test came up positive. We just don't know who the positive person is."

Sid's backside sank onto the desk's edge, and he cursed.

"Sid, it's still unlikely. If it's the sample I think it is, then there's a far more likely candidate. It could even be a false positive. I've seen a few of those. I've already sent the orders to the lab. Just get your butt in there today and get your blood drawn."

"Okay. Thanks, doctor." He slapped off the phone and looked at me. "Well, there goes our evening."

"It's okay. Why don't we still send Nick over to Mae and Neil's and still spend the weekend playing with each other?"

Sid chuckled lecherously. "Yeah, that sounds like fun. Tell you what. Why don't we pack an overnight bag? Not sure where or if we'll go, but it might be nice to keep the option open."

"Okay. Meilin said she was going to be at the house today. We can go over right after you get your test done, then maybe lunch, and then pick Nick up from school."

Sid smiled. "Now that sounds like a plan."

Meilin Chu was the architect working on the house. Sid and I hadn't been out there in a couple weeks, and we were both getting excited about it. I changed into jeans and a nice knit top and vest, then packed a skirt that would look nice with the top and a pair of heels, along with some extra underwear and tops, into a carryon bag. Sid exchanged his suit for a pair of his tight jeans and a nice sport shirt and sweater. He added a couple extra pairs of jeans, under-shirts, and silk boxers to my carryon and put a clean suit and shirt in a garment bag and added our toiletries bag. Then I got Nick's bag that he'd packed for the weekend.

We drove out to the doctor's office near Cedars Sinai and got Sid's blood drawn reasonably quickly. From there, we went to lunch, then out to the house.

The exterior construction was finally done, and it looked great. Sid and I had settled on a Tudor look for the place, with brickwork on the bottom of the walls, and white plaster and dark half-timbers above. The new second floor towered over the rest of the house as we pulled into the driveway that afternoon. Inside, however, a lot of work still needed to be done. All the studs were exposed, wires were everywhere, and the plumbing contractor was having an animated discussion with Meilin as we came in.

Meilin was a tall woman with long, dark hair and bright brown eyes. She grinned at us and sent us upstairs to check out the soundproofing on the new workroom. Both Sid's music and my sewing stuff were going into the huge space. I had no idea how he was going to practice playing the piano while I was running my sewing machine, but that's the way he'd wanted it. He'd been practicing at the condo while I'd been sewing, so I guess it wasn't as big a problem as I thought. [It wasn't. - SEH]

Meilin joined us in the bedroom space.

"Did we talk about soundproofing in here?" Sid asked.

"What do you need soundproofing in your bedroom for?" Meilin asked.

I flushed a deep red. "Um. We just need it."

Eventually, Meilin showed us to the front door. Then she paused.

"One other thing." She handed Sid a piece of paper. "I found this pinned to the front door yesterday. I don't know what it means, but thought you guys would want to know."

"Okay. Thanks."

Sid and I walked outside to the car, then looked at the paper.

"I am coming for you," someone had scrawled on a sheet of typing paper.

"That's creepy," I said.

Sid cursed. "This is not our day." He sighed. "We have to take it seriously." He checked his pocket watch, which he had tucked into his jeans. He couldn't wear a watch on his right wrist yet and didn't care to write around one on his left wrist. Sid's left-handed. "We've got time to get over to Henry's office, then get Nick. If we're going to be late, we'll call from Henry's."

I nodded.

Angelique Carter, who is as much a friend of ours as Henry is, wasn't at her desk that afternoon. She's Henry's secretary. Henry was in and less than enthused about the note, especially after the bad pickup that morning. He's a tall man with a really red face.

"Why don't you two try and trace the pickup?" he said, then took the paper. "I'll see what our lab guys can do with this. This was at the house, not the condo, right?"

"The house," said Sid. "The architect found it pinned to the front door yesterday."

"Increases the odds that it's a prank," Henry said. "Anything Quickline related wouldn't go there. It's not clear which of you it's aimed at, either. And let's face it, you two have pissed off quite a few people over these past years."

I sighed. "We know."

Henry shook his head. "Well, the first thing I'd do would be to get you out of the house, but since you're already out, I'm not going to do that. The problem is, I've got a major job for you two starting Monday, and we cannot put it off any longer."

"Alright." Sid shook his head. "We've gotta get Nick and head out to Pasadena. Thanks, Henry."

We got to Nick's school right on time. It's my parish's school. We joined the line of cars winding through the parking lot, picking up other students. As we slowly pulled in front of the school buildings, Nick burst from the pack of kids and ran to the Beemer.

"Hey, Mom, Da-a-a-ad." His voice suddenly squeaked. Groaning, he tossed his day pack into the back seat, followed it, then shut the door.

"Buckle up, son." Sid gently rolled away from the front building.

Nick got his seat belt on and took a deep breath. "Hi, guys. Why are both of you here?"

"We're taking you out to your Aunt Mae and Uncle Neil's," I said. "Don't you remember?"

"Oh, yeah." He looked at us and his face fell. "Are you guys working this weekend?"

"Not at all," said Sid, glancing at him in the rear-view mirror.

"Well, something's up."

"Nothing we have to think about until Monday," I said. "In fact, we'll be safer not being around."

"Okay."

The poor kid. Having lost his first, or birth mother, the summer before, he still worried a lot when Sid and I had to take off for our side business. And he always knew. He'd been with us on a couple jobs since that summer and knew how dangerous things could get. The last thing Sid and I had wanted was to dump that on him, but there had been no way around it. So, we were slowly training him.

As we pulled into the narrow driveway at Mae and Neil's house in Pasadena, their kids came streaming out the side and front doors. Darby was Nick's age and also dealing with a voice that wouldn't work when he wanted it to. He's a redhead along with his younger twin brothers Marty and Mitch, who were five. Ellen, seven years old, and Janey, nine years old, are both brunettes, and Janey had inherited my dad's and my round eyes. [Those gorgeous cow-eyes were, and are, my biggest weakness. - SEH] In fact, Janey's sweet nature and special insight make her Sid's particular favorite.

Darby hugged me as Nick got his overnight bag from the trunk, then he and Darby ran upstairs almost immediately. The other kids had to get hugs and kisses from both Sid and me. We followed them into the house. The twins suddenly decided that a wrestling match with Uncle Sid was the most important thing in the world, and their sisters stayed in the living room with them to referee. I went on in and found Mae at the back of the kitchen, folding clothes from the dryer. She's a full-time mom. The washer sat at an odd angle because both washer and dryer did not fit into the slot made for them.

"Hey," I said.

Mae's smile was lackluster. "Hey, sis."

"Where's Neil?"

"It's his practice day."

Neil had recently taken a post as an associate professor at the USC dental school, but that meant he also had to maintain a part-time practice as a dentist.

"You okay?"

"Okay enough."

"Mae, what's going on?"

She looked up, then fixated on my neck. I put my hand up and realized I had my new necklace on.

"Where were you this weekend?"

"At Maggie's wedding. I told you that."

"I know. But Mama told me you left early on Saturday and when I called you Sunday, you weren't answering your phone again."

"You could have left a message."

Mae folded a pair of socks in on itself. "What good would that have done?"

I sighed. She had a point. I didn't always answer my messages from her. Usually, I was trying to cover up that I was out of town. Sid and I couldn't call attention to our wanderings.

"I'm sorry," I said, reaching over to help her fold.

"I can take care of this!"

"Mae, what's going on?"

She squeezed her eyes shut. "I'm pregnant."

I'm not sure which was more disturbing. The way my gut clenched at the news or the fact that this was obviously not the happy announcement it had been before.

"Oh," I said simply. "How are you doing?"

"I'm fine." Mae sniffed. "I know I should be happier about this, but I'm just not this time. Worse yet, I'll be showing by your wedding."

"I don't care about that."

"But you made that lovely top and skirt."

"The skirt's gathered. We can let it out. As for the top, it's the only one I cut out. You'll just have a nice top for after the baby's born."

Okay, I was fibbing. I had cut out the tops and skirts for not just Mae, but Esther and Kathy, who were my other bridesmaids. The only reason I hadn't cut out the top and skirt for Janey, my final bridesmaid, was that she was nine and likely to have grown by March. It's the reason I seldom sewed for my nieces and nephews. They had a nasty tendency to grow out of what I was making before I finished the project.

Mae took a deep breath. "I'll be fine, Lisa. It's just hard." Her eyes flitted to my neck again. "That's new, isn't it?"

"It wasn't that big a deal. Sid and I celebrated the date we met."

As if that would help. Neil did not have Sid's ability to find just the right gift. I remember the time Neil wanted to buy Mae a necklace that said, "Number One Mom." I tried to convince him that while Mae loved being a mom, she would have rather been Neil's Number One Lover. While I didn't think either Neil or Mae remembered what date they met (they had barely noticed each other initially), it sure looked like Mae wished her husband would.

"Sweetheart?" Sid called.

"I'll be right there, love," I called back. I looked at Mae. "Are you going to be okay?"

"I'll be fine."

"I love you, Mae."

Her reply was just a touch mechanical. "I love you, too, Lisa."

I was somber as Sid backed the Beemer out of the driveway.

"Airport?" he asked.

"Sure."

He looked at me. "Are you okay?"

I winced. "Reasonably. Where are we going?"

"Haven't made my mind up yet. Any thoughts?"

"We do San Francisco a lot. I'm feeling like I want to do something different."

"Sounds good. Let's see what flight we can get." He steered down the street, oblivious, as always, to the speed limit. "Is it just everything today or is there something else? You seem a little upset."

"So-so." I made a face. "Mae's pregnant and she's not happy about it."

"That's not surprising. Well, the pregnancy is. But I can't imagine she'd be that thrilled about another eighteen years of active duty."

"You're right. I'm sure that's part of it." I blinked my eyes. "She's also really jealous of me."

"We can't help that."

"I guess not."

"Lisa, I am not going to reduce my standard of living to make your sister feel better."

"As if patronizing her that way would help in the least bit." I shook my head. "It just stinks is all."

The funny thing was, I couldn't quite tell him what else I was feeling. There was a part of me that suddenly realized that I wanted to carry his child. The problem was Sid had gotten a vasectomy years before, and it had been long enough ago that a reversal would probably not work. We'd already talked about that. At that time, I really was perfectly fine not having a baby. I couldn't figure out why, suddenly, I wanted his so badly.

October 13 – 14, 1985

S id and I ended up in Las Vegas, and while we passed the Graceland Chapel (where the Elvis impersonator performed your wedding), we decided we could wait until March to be officially married.

We got back to Pasadena on Sunday at mid-afternoon. Mae's mood seemed to have lifted. The kids had been told that they had a new sibling on the way and were ecstatic. Neil just smiled. Sid got on their piano and played as we all sang. Even Sid sang. He never used to, with one exception. But that September Nick had talked him into singing, too, and Sid had decided he liked it.

Nick had to ask the tough question as soon as we were in the car and headed back to the condo.

"Mom, Dad, are you guys going to have a baby?"

I looked at Sid, who, for possibly the first time in his life, looked guilty.

"We can't, son," he said quietly.

"Why?"

"I had surgery a number of years ago to prevent that from happening." Sid looked over at me.

Drat him. He'd seen the look on my face and realized what I was feeling.

"It's okay, Nick," I said. "I wouldn't mind having your father's baby, but I knew that wasn't going to be possible early on, and I still want to be with him. You're pretty much it for me, and I'm happy to have you."

"Cool."

"Yeah. It is." I smiled because I was happy to have him.

Sid didn't question my feelings for Nick. But he wasn't convinced that I was entirely fine with not having children and, if I'm honest, I couldn't blame him. Sid waited until Nick was in bed to challenge me about it.

"Do you want a baby?" he asked as we sat on the couch cuddling.

"I know what I said before," I said, wincing. "And I was being honest then. I really was okay with not having kids, especially with how guilty I feel every time we have to do something that makes Nick worry." My eyes started blinking again. "It's just that when Mae told me she was pregnant and she wasn't happy about it, all I could think was how happy I'd be if I could get pregnant." I shut my eyes. "I'm sorry, Sid. It just kind of snuck up on me. I'd probably make a terrible mother, anyway."

"You are a wonderful mother," Sid said, squeezing me even more tightly into his arms. "You are exactly what our son needs. And, yes, I mean ours. Nick and I may have the genetic connection, but you are his mother because you want to be. You know I was never entirely sure that Stella wanted me, so it means a lot to me that you love and want Nick as much as you do."

"Thanks." I wiped my eyes. "I'll get over this. It may even be the usual expectations creeping in."

Sid stroked my face. "Let's not downplay it, honey. Truth be told, and I can't believe I'm saying this, I wouldn't mind having a baby with you. But like with the AIDS thing, I couldn't have seen this coming." He sighed. "I don't generally regret the choices I've made in my life, and I don't regret the vasectomy. I just feel bad that it's making you unhappy right now."

"Sid, I'd rather have you and no baby than not have you. Okay? I knew what I was getting in for, and, until now, I've been pretty relieved that I don't have to think about diapers and terrible twos and all that. I don't know why it's suddenly getting to me."

"Maybe it's that we've been talking a lot about what makes a family lately." He nuzzled into my hair.

"Or it could just be that latent rebellious streak I've got. Tell me I can't do something and what's the first thing I want to do?"

Sid chuckled. "There's a reason I love you so much." He kissed my ear and got up. "Come on. Let's make sure Nick is really asleep, then go make each other happy."

Monday Sid put his contacts in before running. He doesn't usually, even though he almost never wears his glasses. But that day he drove the three of us and Motley, my springer spaniel, to another part of the neighborhood to do our run. After getting dressed and breakfast, Sid drove Nick to school, while I went over the plan for the week in terms of our writing business and took a couple phone calls. The first was from Henry, and puzzled me a little, but since he was coming over, I knew I'd find out soon enough. The second call was especially odd.

"Is Mr. Sid Hackbirn there?" asked the voice of a middle-aged woman with a Southern accent.

"May I ask who's calling?"

The line went dead.

Sid returned close to eight-thirty and fifteen minutes before Henry knocked on the condo door. I answered it, diving and catching Fritz, the gray tabby kitten, as he made yet another break for freedom. Besides Motley, we have three cats. The fall before, Nick had befriended and named Long John Silver, a one-eyed gray cat with a mangled ear, only to find that Long John was a she and pregnant. We'd kept two of the four kittens. Viola and Chin-Chin lived at Kathy and Jesse's condo across the hall. Blueberry and Fritz were ours. Long John, who loved sitting in Sid's lap, stayed with us.

Sid shooed the cat off his lap, then got up from his desk and invited Henry to sit on the couch while I pulled over two of the dining room chairs.

"Let me guess," Sid said as we all got settled. "That big job you mentioned."

"Yep." Henry handed Sid a nine by twelve manila envelope.

Sid looked at me, then opened the envelope and pulled out the sheet inside.

He swore. "Are you serious?"

"Deadly serious," Henry said. "We need personnel. The Yellow Line is just barely back up and functioning and we're still trying to rebuild the Green Line."

The lines are different courier routes, with a bunch of stops where information gets transferred from one courier to another to make it easier to lose a tail. All the stops on the routes are close enough together that a courier can get to the next stop and back home within a day, so it's a lot easier to look like a normal person. The Yellow Line, however, got decimated the summer of 1983, and the Green Line had taken a serious hit early in 1984.

I looked at the sheet and gaped. "Yeah, but them? How could you do this to them?"

"He wants to."

Sid and I gazed in wonder at Henry.

Henry sighed. "About five years ago, Jesse White applied to the Central Intelligence Agency. He passed all the tests for potential operatives but failed the interview. Given that he's Black, I have to assume that was behind it."

Sid muttered another obscenity, this time directed at The Company, which was how we referred to the CIA when we weren't using ruder terms.

"But Kathy, too?" I asked.

"He told me he wouldn't do it without her." Henry sat up. "I haven't given them any details, of course. I decided to check Jesse out after you'd been kidnapped, Lisa, last spring. I saw it happen. You put yourself between the kidnappers and their target. Jesse moved the target further away. The perfect move. So, I researched it and found Jesse's application. I approached Jesse that week you two were in Sunnyvale after Nick's mother died. He talked to Kathy about it. I'm not sure how enthusiastic she was, but a few weeks later, Jesse called me and said they were in."

"So, that's why Kathy quit her job," I said.

"I assume so," Henry said.

"What took so long?" Sid asked.

"A variety of things. Paperwork. Waiting for your wrist to heal. Making sure we could re-route some of your work so that you can focus on getting them trained."

"Alright." I looked down at the adoption paper I had in my hand. "So, we need to start twenty-four-hour surveillance, right?"

"That won't be necessary this time." Henry smiled.

It was when I'd been recruited, which was why Sid had me live at his house when he hired me. I had my own room because my religious principles did not include free love, and Sid had respected that, even if he didn't understand it. I could have moved after I found out about Quickline, but Sid had Conchetta Ramirez as a housekeeper even then, and I hate housework.

I looked at Henry, who chuckled then looked at Sid.

Sid sighed. "We were having a lot of trouble finding the right associate for me."

"Usually, when we recruit, we ask our operatives to find a likely candidate among their friends," Henry said. "This gives them a good visible reason to know the other operative, and usually friends have similar qualities, among them the qualities that make a good operative. The problem was Sid didn't just need an associate. He needed a partner, someone who could work closely with him. His male friends didn't have the right attributes and the few women who did, they didn't last very long."

"Two weeks." I laughed, gazing at Sid fondly.

Sid shrugged. "You know the problems I had sustaining a relationship back then. But that's what made you so perfect. Because there wasn't going to be any sex, I didn't have to worry about a relationship. Or so I thought. By the time I knew better, it was too late, and we were stuck with each other." He reached over and took my hand. "I'm glad I was, honey. If we hadn't been, you would never have been able to push me into communicating with you. And you would have been gone, too."

"I almost was," I said with a soft smile. "I'm only glad I thought I was stuck. But why did I need to be under surveillance?"

"You were an unknown quantity," Henry said. "You'd checked out okay on paper, but we didn't know how you'd react, if you could do the work, if you were even interested in it. We were testing you."

"You turned out to be a natural." Sid chuckled and looked at me proudly. "The way you kept ditching those tails and snooping and asking questions, and we didn't even know what a sharpshooter you were."

I looked at the paper in my hands. "So, now what?"

Henry looked over at the front door. "Are they there?"

"I think so," I said. "Why don't I go find out?"

I went over and knocked on the door to Kathy and Jesse's condo. I could have just walked in, and in fact, we used to until Jesse accidentally walked in on Sid and me during one of our more intimate moments.

Kathy opened the door. "What's up?"

"Can we come over for a few and talk to you and Jesse?" I asked. "He's here, isn't he?"

"He is." Kathy looked a little puzzled. "Come right on in."

"I'll be right back."

To be honest, I wasn't at all sure how I felt about re-cruiting Kathy and Jesse into our side business. I hated that Nick was involved, although we could hardly keep it from him. And now, my dearest friends were about to be exposed to the same dangers and risks that Sid and I pretty much took for granted. It was not a comfortable feeling. Sid and I loved the work we did most of the time, but it had its downsides.

When Sid and Henry had joined me, I knocked and walked into Kathy and Jesse's condo. It was almost the mirror image of ours, only their living room looked like an actual living room and was significantly deeper with sleek fifties modern furniture and African prints on the walls. They also had three bedrooms instead of two. Jesse used one of the extra bedrooms as his dark room, and the third room was a combination TV and guest room. Jesse saw Henry and suddenly grinned, even if he wasn't sure what to make of it that Sid and I were there.

Kathy got us settled on the couch and chairs, then Henry smiled.

"Your adoption has finally come through," he said to Kathy and Jesse.

Jesse grinned. "About time."

Kathy looked somewhat less enthused, but I could tell it thrilled her that Jesse was happy.

"Sid and Lisa will give you the particulars on our organization," Henry continued. "They'll also be your immediate supervisors and your training team."

Jesse looked at me, then Henry. "Lisa too?"

"What do you mean, 'Lisa, too?'" I asked indignantly.

"But you got that problem with corpses," Jesse said.

I have a phobia of stiffs, and it makes things awkward at times.

"Don't sell Lisa short, Jesse." Henry said, standing. "She could whup your backside without thinking about it."

I flushed.

Henry headed for the door. "I'll leave you four to take care of things."

He left. Silence followed.

"You're our supervisors," Kathy finally said. "I mean, we figured you were up to something and when Henry talked to Jesse about joining some secret group, that at least Sid was part of it."

"I've been doing intelligence work for over sixteen years," Sid said. "And, yes, I hired Lisa intending that she would work as my partner." He smiled fondly at me. "She caught on pretty quickly, and, Jesse, she can whup your backside."

"Not that I'd want to," I said.

"We'll see how long that lasts," Jesse said, laughing. "So, we're really doing this."

"Yes, you are." Sid sighed. "It's a whole different way of life, Jesse. Everything you do from now on will be about keeping your secret."

"We don't wear monograms or anything that might give an enemy a clue to our identities," I said. "We don't use each other's names in public. Even how we wear our hair and what bras I wear are based on being able to hide something, anything, that could help us get out of a dangerous situation."

"What about Nick?" Kathy asked.

I blinked back the tears. "He knows we do intelligence work and that he's now part of it."

"We're training him because we have to," Sid said. "It's not something we wanted to do. But it was either that or abandon him, and I couldn't live with abandoning him." He shifted. "Within the structures of the FBI and CIA are several smaller organizations so secret mostly only their members know they exist. We are part of one called Operation Quickline. Our primary mission is courier work, but we will train you to handle investigations, break-ins, surveillance, and a host of other chores. We work under the FBI since we are a domestic division."

"Oh." Jesse looked a little crestfallen.

I smiled. "Jesse, you are far too nice to be part of the CIA. Those guys are total jerks."

Sid added his usual obscene version of the acronym.

We went into an extended discussion on keeping physically fit, plus all the things we'd need to teach them to help them stay alive.

I finally had to break away to get Nick from school, and Jesse asked to go with me. We went down to the garage and got into Sid's BMW. As I backed out of our one and only parking space, Jesse looked at me.

"I was wondering about you a year ago," he said.

"You mean when George died." My gut clenched, and I knew what was coming.

George had been Jesse's roommate and best friend, and my fiancé.

"I'd seen the exchanges," Jesse said. "In the middle of the night, behind George's studio."

"George said something about that. He said you'd seen a kidnapping."

Jesse shrugged. "That's what I called it. Maybe I shouldn't have."

I focused on getting us onto Wilshire Boulevard without an accident.

Jesse looked straight ahead. "He called me that night and said he saw your truck."

I pulled out, sighing. "He did see it."

"Sid lied when he said it wasn't your truck?"

"I'm sorry, but yes. He had to." I blinked, trying to stay focused on the traffic in front of us.

"What happened?"

I knew why Jesse was asking. It had been a miserable experience for both of us, made the worse because at that time, I couldn't tell Jesse what I knew.

"It was a prisoner transfer," I said, feeling oddly relieved, even though it had been one of the most horrible things I'd ever seen. "Sid and I had just gotten him out of the truck when George came running up. The prisoner popped his cuffs. It's like Sid says, you can always hide something. Anyway, he got Sid's gun and shot George. Sid got George's camera, got me into the truck and we got out of there. We had to. The other team wouldn't come in until we were clear, and George wouldn't get help."

"Did they ever get the guy?"

I thanked God we had stopped for a red light.

"Yes." I swallowed. "I killed him. I didn't want to. He was about to shoot Sid and I didn't have time to aim."

"Right before camp that year."

Our church puts on a week-long retreat at a Christian camp on Catalina Island.

I nodded. "The day before we left."

"I thought something had messed you up."

"Yes. It did." I glanced at Jesse as the light turned green. "It was the first, and so far, only time I've killed someone. I still have nightmares about it."

Jesse cursed. "This isn't going to be easy for Kathy."

"I know." I glanced over at him. "I get that you're on board with this. I am a little worried about Kathy. It just seems so unfair to dump this on her."

Jesse sighed deeply. "I almost backed out because she was worried. She didn't think she could do it. Then that Sunday when Maryann Dreyer got on your backside about being with Sid, Kathy dropped your pix in your purse, and you didn't see it until she told you it was there."

A pix is a special container for blessed hosts. I'm a Eucharistic Minister at my church and bring communion to several shut-ins, as well as serve at mass. That Sunday, Maryann Dreyer had made a stink because of Sid, and I'd backed off serving at mass. Kathy had gotten the communion hosts that I needed for my shut-ins and had dropped the pix into my purse in a perfectly smooth drop.

"I was impressed," I said. "That was a beautiful drop."

"And when you said so, she knew she could." Jesse shook his head. "I don't know if she thinks she can handle all the rest of what you two were talking about today."

I thought. "I'll bet she can. Henry's no fool. If he had any doubts about her, he would have done something about it."

"Did you want to be a spy?"

I shrugged. "It wasn't in my life plan. But then, I really didn't have much of one when I met Sid. I wanted to be a college professor, but I'd lost my teaching job and when I couldn't get another, it made me really wonder if I was cut out for academia."

"Hm."

I looked at him. "I do like what we do. Yeah, it's dangerous, and it creates some barriers between me and my family and other people I care about. But there are compensations."

"Oh, I know that. Just please remind Kathy, will you?"

I smiled. "I will."

Nick was a little surprised to see Jesse with me when we picked him up.

"What's going on?" he asked as he buckled his seat belt.

"It's a long story, Nick," I said, pulling the BMW out of the parking lot. "It looks like Kathy and Jesse are joining our little side business."

"Oh." Nick suddenly grinned. "So, I can talk about it with them?"

"Anytime, dude," Jesse said.

"As long as he has Need to Know," I said firmly.

Nick rolled his eyes and groaned. Jesse laughed.

"Mom," he stopped as he croaked. "You hate Need to Know."

"Yes, I do. But it is a fact of our lives sometimes."

"Jesse, are they going to let you do anything cool?" Nick leaned forward as far as his seatbelt would allow. "They don't allow me to do squat."

"We'll see about that," said Jesse.

Dinner that night was a weird experience. Sid and Kathy made it at their condo, and that's where we ate because there was no room in Sid's and my condo. We ended up skipping the Teen Bible Study because it was more important to talk about what we were dealing with. Sid and I had never been able to talk about our side business and seldom did even with Henry for obvious reasons. But Kathy and Jesse needed to know what they were up against and Kathy, in particular, needed reassurance. So, after Nick got sent to bed, the stories started coming out. Sid and I skipped details where we could. That sort of thing is practically a reflex with us. But there was fear. There was laughter. There was the reality that Sid and I were not alone anymore. That should have been reassuring. It was a lot harder to deal with than I would have thought.

October 15 –18, 1985

That Tuesday, Sid and I had a fair amount of writing work to get squared away, although we still found time to get Kathy and Jesse signed up at our gym and at the martial arts dojo. Then Sid put them to work on learning various codes and ciphers while I started on the writing work.

I got to a point where I could stop, then went to check on Kathy and Jesse. Jesse was looking a little cross-eyed, but Kathy was in her element. I felt for Jesse. Codes were my weak spot, too. I got Jesse straightened out, then went back to our condo. Sid was just hanging up the phone.

"Who was that?" I asked.

Sid sighed. "Dr. Kline. The good news is that my test was negative."

"Oh, wonderful!"

He winced. "Yes and no. They're still not sure exactly how long it takes for the virus to show up in the blood-stream, although Dr. Kline is mostly sure I'm clean. She's just not absolutely sure. So, we'll test again in another six months."

"Six months!" I groaned.

"Lisa, this is a deadly disease we're dealing with here. You watched your friend Rick die of it. Do you want that to happen to you?"

"But six months? That will be after our wedding."

He shrugged. "Okay. I'll get tested right before. Honey, I'm sorry. You have no idea how badly I want to ditch the jeans. On the other hand, I don't want to take the chance."

"Aren't you overreacting just a little bit?"

"Possibly. Probably. But I'd rather overreact than take a chance on infecting you." He sighed. "Look at it this way, you'll make it to the altar a virgin."

"Only on a technicality."

"That's something, isn't it?"

All I could do was groan. Yes, I know. As a religious person, I wasn't "supposed" to be having sex with Sid. And I do believe that sex works best within the commitment of marriage. It's just that Sid had given up sleeping around for me. I figured the least I could do was be more flexible on the definition of marriage, and as I have pointed out already, Sid and I were already married for all intents and purposes. What we'd been doing was great, but it was also occasionally awkward.

"Alright," I sighed. "Can you forgive me if I'm a little on the petulant side? I was really looking forward to ditching the jeans, too."

Sid chuckled, then came around his desk and pulled me into his arms. "I can forgive you, my dearest, if you can forgive me. We'll find a way to make it through."

Okay, so maybe some of the writing work didn't get done. I was in a slightly better mood by the time Sid had to leave for his composition and theory classes late that afternoon. Kathy drove me to the Single Adults Bible

Study that night. Jesse elected to stay home with Nick and the codes. Nick was kind of on the border of being able to stay by himself, especially since Sid's later class usually let out by eight and he was home by eight-thirty or so. But we didn't like doing that. Nick's first mom, who had only passed away a few months before, had been prone to leaving him alone while she worked odd hours as an emergency room doctor.

I have no idea why we still referred to the bible study group as Single Adults since the vast majority of the group was married, most of them to each other. However, that was how the group started out. Frank and Esther were among the few singles left. Frank wasn't even there that night.

"He got wedding gig," Esther told Kathy and me at the beginning of the study. "He has to meet with the bride and groom tonight."

Kathy and I would not begrudge him that. Frank is a terrific musician. He plays flute and guitar and directs the new Guitar Choir at ten-thirty mass. He also has the worst luck of any human being I've ever known, which is why he'd been having such a hard time making a living as a musician.

We started the study with an announcement from Sarah and Dan Williams.

"We're expecting!" Sarah said, her face glowing with joy.

I smiled, but my gut clenched. She was far from the only expecting mom in the room. In fact, Irene Sanchez was due within another month. Erin MacArthur had her third on the way. I would never be able to make that announcement. I tried to remind myself that it was for the best and that I did have a perfectly wonderful son in Nick. The thought almost soothed me.

As the study went on, Kathy and I realized Esther was not her usual boisterous self. In fact, when she only made one off-color remark that night, the rest of the group may have been relieved, but Kathy and I were worried. So, after the study ended, we talked her into coming out with us to our favorite bar for a nightcap. I paged Sid with one of our special codes to let him know that Kathy and I would be home late.

"What's going on?" Kathy asked her after we'd ordered our drinks.

"What do you mean?" Esther asked, almost defensively.

I looked at her. "Sid said he got billed for two bottles of Champagne in that limo."

Esther shrugged. "You know me. You know Frank. You can put two and two together. It was very nice."

"What?" said Kathy.

"It was very nice." Esther sighed. "Okay. We're a couple now. Only we don't know how to do that."

"I get that," I said. "You just don't seem all that happy."

"I'm happy." Esther smiled. "I am. Frank is really happy." Her smile almost got goopy at that point. Then she frowned. "We just don't know how to be a couple."

"Does that really matter?" asked Kathy. "You two are who you are."

"I know that."

I reached over and put my hand on her arm. "It is weird, isn't it? Sid and I went through the same thing."

"You did?" Esther looked at me curiously.

"Oh, yeah. It was really tough, at first. I mean, we knew we loved each other. He'd finally been able to say so. But then he had all this time on his hands and…" I made a face. "I didn't want to get married."

"But you're getting married now," Esther said.

"Yes. It's about the Sacrament more than anything else."

"Oh." Esther thought that over. "Frank and I want to do the same, but we don't want wedding."

"I'm with you on that one," I said.

"Oh, come on," Kathy said, patting my back. "You're doing fine." She looked at Esther. "You and Frank will figure things out, just like Sid and Lisa did."

"Oh, I know," Esther said. "It's just weird right now."

Back at the condo, Sid was very curious about Esther's reaction after I'd told him why Kathy and I had come home so late.

"She's trying to figure it out," I told him. "It's not all that far off what you and I went through last spring."

"Did she say what happened?"

"She said we could put two and two together."

"I think they did." Sid grinned.

"She only said it was very nice."

"Hm." He made a face. "Not much we can do about it right now." He suddenly smiled. "On the other hand, I can guarantee Nick is soundly asleep."

I couldn't help giggling.

The next day, the phone rang, and I got it before Sid did.

"Is Mr. Sid Hackbirn there?" asked the middle-aged female voice.

"May I ask who's calling?" I said.

There was a pause this time. "Mrs. Carla Caponetti."

"Please hold while I see if he's available." I pressed the hold button, then looked at Sid. "Carla Caponetti?" I frowned. "The name sounds familiar."

"Doesn't ring any bells with me." Sid thought, then pulled out his address book. "Nobody in here." He flipped another couple of pages. "Not even under K."

I pressed the button for her line. "Mrs. Caponetti, Mr. Hackbirn doesn't recognize your name."

"That's impossible!"

But then the line went dead. Sid looked at me as I hung up the phone.

"She hung up," I said. "That was weird."

"Except that we have somebody coming to get us. Or me."

I sighed. "Right. We need to take Kathy and Jesse to the gun range, and Nick needs some practice."

"Why don't you bring Kathy and Jesse over and I'll get Nick from school and meet you there."

"Sounds good."

The good news was neither Kathy nor Jesse was terribly excited about learning to shoot guns. Kathy almost gagged when I handed her the Smith and Wesson Model Thirteen revolver she'd been issued. Still, they had to learn. They were a little freaked when Sid showed with Nick and Nick took his turn on the firing range. I couldn't help being proud. The boy was turning into quite a decent shot. Kathy and Jesse almost went slack jawed when they saw me putting a clip of bullets into the shoulder of the human silhouette I was aiming at.

"Don't worry about what I did," I told them. "You want to aim for the largest target, which is the center of the body."

Jesse did okay. Kathy did somewhat less so. Jesse, Sid, and Nick rode home in their car. I drove Kathy in the Beemer.

"How do you do it?" Kathy asked.

"You get used to it, I guess," I said. "And I'm good enough that I can put it in the shoulder more often than not."

Kathy shook her head. "I know I'll get it eventually. But I gotta say, it doesn't seem all that likely after today."

I smiled at her. "It took me a while to get used to it, too."

After we got back, Sid took plaster casts of each of their feet and got a cast of his own. The casts were for a very special bit of equipment, our armored running shoes. They look like normal running shoes, but you can pull the sole off the body and there's a hidey hole for all sorts of tools and goodies: transmitter and batteries, stilettos, screwdrivers, bits of spring steel. Even some of my fancier dress shoes have bits and pieces hidden in the soles or heels. As Sid says, you can always hide something. I also got both of their measurements and cut out a pair of pants for each of them.

Kathy watched with a puzzled frown. "What are you making?"

"Break-in pants," I said, frowning as I laid the pattern pieces on the black twill. "You'll need these eventually. They make life a lot easier when you have to break into someplace you aren't supposed to be."

"I thought you told us we weren't going to be doing anything illegal."

"It's not illegal." I winced. "We don't go anywhere we're not authorized for. But local law enforcement might not see it that way."

"Oh, dear Jesus, have mercy!"

"The trick is not getting caught." I grinned.

As if that would reassure her. Still, Kathy took it better than I would have thought. I glared at the layout again. Half the fabric was rolled up because there wasn't enough room on the dining table where I had my sewing stuff. That made it harder to get it all straight. I really missed the huge cutting table I'd had in the old house.

Thursday morning, Sid, Nick, and I returned from our morning run to find two Beverly Hills P.D. detectives at our door. Sid made sure Nick was in his shower before he let the detectives talk to us. What they had to say was nerve-wracking, to say the least. We took Nick to school together, then went out to the house. The beautiful Tudor exterior was still mostly intact. Too bad all the windows had been shot out, not to mention all the bullet holes in the white stucco.

"This is bad," I said softly to Sid as we gazed at the damage.

"It is."

"What do we do now?"

"That, my darling, is a very good question."

We went straight from the house to Henry James' office at the Federal building in Westwood. Henry was less than thrilled about the situation.

"I have no idea where this is coming from," Henry said, drumming his fingers on his desk. "Have you talked to the Dragon about that bad pick up?"

Sid and I looked at each other. The Dragon was, as far as we knew, the head of Quickline.

"It may have slipped our minds," Sid said, slowly.

Henry cursed. "Why haven't you?"

I glared at him. "Oh. Let's see. What happened Monday? We recruited our best friends into a business that could easily get them killed, and we get to train them. We've been a little preoccupied."

Henry sat back. Sid held his hands out.

"We'll call the Dragon when we get home," Sid said, getting up. "We'll need a couple more rifles."

"I've got them in the car." Henry got up as well.

"Why couldn't you have recruited Angelique?" I got to my feet.

Henry paused. "She's going to have a different position."

Sid and I looked at him.

Henry shook his head. "Neither of you, nor she has Need to Know yet."

Sid winced and squeezed my hand. It probably wasn't fair of me to get mad at Henry, but I couldn't help it.

I was grumpy as Sid drove us home.

"Sid," I suddenly asked. "When you were looking for your eventual partner, why didn't you try to recruit Angelique? I mean, she is a friend."

"I was afraid you were going to ask that," Sid grumbled. "Okay, she was and is a friend. Henry wouldn't let me. I used to think it was because he was worried about Angelique getting her butt killed. But if I'm honest, I think he was more worried about me hurting her."

I sighed. For a long time, Angelique had been in love with Sid, but it never went anywhere. I mean, yeah, she'd move in every so often for the requisite two weeks, then leave with a broken heart because Sid really couldn't sustain a relationship outside of his bedroom. They'd become better friends since he'd stopped sleeping around. She'd figured out on her own that she deserved better and stopped sleeping around long before Sid did.

"You did hurt her, you know." I said, probably out of my pique at Henry.

"I know." Sid glanced at me. One of his favorite rationalizations for his lifestyle had been that he wasn't hurting anybody. "She seems to have gotten over it."

"She got over it long before you woke up."

"Then that's all to the better." He looked over at me again, thoughtfully. "How is it you don't worry about the past women in my life?"

"I've lasted longer than two weeks. I've lasted over three years with you. I know it's gross, but honestly. How many of even the live-ins saw you use the toilet? Or shared your toothpaste tube?"

"Good point." He turned his eyes back to the street.

Sid made the call to the Dragon when we got back. I went to quiz Jesse and Kathy on codes and ciphers. When I got back to the condo, Sid's face was grim.

"What?" I asked.

"The Dragon knows nothing about the pickup."

"Really?" I made a face. "I thought everything went through her one way or another."

"That's what she said. She thinks somebody with past access may be behind this."

"Goody. Who do we know that qualifies?"

Sid smiled. "Far more than you know. It doesn't seem to be directed at you, as well. At least, not so far. And I've got a lot more years of this under my belt."

I frowned. "Who's Carla Caponetti?"

"I have no idea."

"Then maybe we should find out. The name does sound familiar. I just can't place it."

"Sure. Why not? When we get the time."

I sighed. "Good point." I raised my eyebrows. "So, we're doing rifles this afternoon?"

"Yep. That's your bailiwick."

In my youth, I won fourth place in the Tahoe Regional Skeet Championship. The three ahead of me went on to international competition. I'm darned good with rifles and shotguns. After lunch, I changed from business wear to jeans and a sweater, then went to get Jesse and Kathy.

The funny thing was, Jesse got into this competitive thing with me. I had way more experience and I am good at shooting. But Jesse wanted to be, as well. I took that as a good sign and enjoyed kicking his backside at the target range. Kathy just sighed and rubbed her right shoulder, which was getting sore from the kickback of the guns.

"I did not think for better or worse meant sniper lessons," she muttered to me at one point.

"Yeah, but just think. You'll really be able to mess with someone now." I grinned at her. "Why don't you think about putting the bullet between Maryann Dreyer's eyes?"

Maryann Dreyer was a mutual nemesis.

"There is that." Kathy chuckled, then went and nailed a few targets.

The next afternoon, Sid's pager went off and mine didn't. That was a little weird. We mostly got paged together. When Sid called in, we found out why. The operative wanted a male to drop to.

"And it's an older receiver code," Sid said with a frown. "But it hasn't been deprecated."

"That doesn't mean it's bad," I said.

Our group kept receiver and caller codes around longer than we probably should have because sometimes operatives from overseas needed access and didn't have the more recent codes.

"Who's the addressee?" I asked.

"New York, mostly on the Yellow Line."

New York was where things got routed to Langley, Virginia, which, of course, was CIA headquarters. Oddly enough, the Company didn't want things routed to their HQ, but that was the CIA.

Sid left. I went back to doing some writing work after checking on Kathy and Jesse and their code work.

An hour later, the phone rang.

"Hello?"

"Ms. Lisa Wycherly, please?"

"May I ask who's calling?" I was barely paying attention to the call as I scanned over my latest rough draft of an article.

"This is Nurse Jen Harding at Broadway Memorial Hospital. Your fiancé is here. He has a gunshot wound."

"Oh, my god!" I gasped. I didn't have to fake it, either. "Is he alright?"

"The doctor is with him now."

"I'll be there as fast as I can."

"Thank you." She hung up.

I blinked back tears, then called Nick's school. Cissie, the secretary, picked up.

"Cissie, it's Nick Flaherty's mom. I need to pick him up. His father's in the hospital." I winced. It wasn't as though Cissie didn't know who I was.

"Oh, dear. I'll get him. How long before you're here?"

"Maybe ten minutes?"

"I'll have him ready for you, Lisa."

"And please be gentle. He's been through enough trauma."

"He'll be fine, dear."

I could only hope we could say the same of Sid. I took Kathy's car - she offered, and she and Jesse had two of the treasured parking spaces in the condo complex. Well, they did have a larger condo. Sid and I only had one, which was why my truck was in storage. I got to the school in eight minutes. Okay, I have a lead foot and that day, more reason than most to be driving as fast as I could. Nick was just coming into the office as I hurried in. He took one look at me, and his face went a queer sort of green.

"We have to go to the hospital," I told him. "They just called and your dad's there. They said the doctor was with him. I'm hoping that means good news."

"Uh-huh." Nick blinked and swallowed.

"Come on, sweetie."

We hurried out to the car. Nick looked up the hospital in the Thomas Guide map book, and I went hell for leather there. When we got to the emergency department, Nick told me what to tell the nurses. His first mom had been an emergency physician, and Nick knew his way around the E.D. Sadly, they weren't going to let Nick back into the treatment area. He was too young. I left him in the waiting room.

I found Sid in a curtained cubicle, his left bicep bandaged, and a damaged suit coat in his lap.

"You're alive!" I gasped.

"Yeah. He just winged me." Sid winced as he got off the bed. "It's a little sore, but I'm fine. I've just got a new stripe on my arm. Lost another suit, too."

I grabbed his face and kissed him for all I was worth. He started grinning lasciviously when I yelped.

"I've got to tell Nick!"

I ran from the room.

Nick looked terrified as I hurried into the waiting room.

"He's okay!" I almost hollered.

Nick sank into himself in relief, and I grabbed and held him.

"He's fine, sweetie," I repeated. "It was really minor. He's okay."

Nick let go of me long enough for me to get back to Sid. Sid, however, was already heading our way. I put his right arm over my shoulder and walked him out to the waiting room. Nick slammed into him with a deep hug. Sid winced and laughed at the same time.

"Where's the Beemer?" I asked.

"How'd you get here?" Sid asked.

"I took Kathy's car. Now, where's the Beemer? And are you okay to drive?"

"Well enough."

We got back to the condo in good time, and I got Kathy's car back where it belonged and the keys back to her. Nick and I put Sid to bed immediately. While Nick tried to adjust the pillows on the waterbed, I looked at Sid's blood-stained and torn shirt and suit jacket.

"Oh, dear. These are ruined," I groaned.

"Easy, Nick," Sid said. "It's our life, Lisa. I have more suits and shirts."

He did. For all Sid is a nudist at heart, he is also a clotheshorse.

"Nick, can you get me some water, please?" Sid asked.

Nick scrambled off the bed to get the glass. Sid winced as the bed rocked.

"It was a bad pickup," Sid told me once the boy was gone. "Aiming right at me."

"Oh, no."

"The good news is he missed."

"What about the cops?"

Sid shrugged. "Couldn't avoid it. Someone called it in right away, and I was in no condition to get out." We usually tried to avoid getting the police involved when we were working, but it couldn't always be helped. "I made the report on scene, and they didn't spot my weapon." Sid shifted. "Can you call the Dragon?"

"Sure. I'll do it as soon as Nick gets back." I looked at him. "Caponetti?"

"It's as good a guess as any." Sid kissed me softly. "Any landing you walk away from, right?"

I smiled. "Right. What was the old code, specifically?"

Sid gave it to me. We're good at memorizing that kind of ephemera. We have to be.

The Dragon was not happy when I called. "I did not send a pickup through for you two."

"It was an older caller code," I said, repeating it. "It hasn't been deprecated."

"Well, it will be now." She sighed. "I'm going to have to talk to Marissa in Systems. I suspect with all the new personnel, whoever had past access sneaked it past her."

"Systems? I knew a kid there."

"You know Marissa."

"Then she's pretty sharp. How could somebody get past her?"

"It's complicated. Oh, by the way, do you have your list of invitees for your wedding?"

That had been another shocker. We're not supposed to know anybody else's real names, apart from a few logical exceptions. But the Dragon kept telling Sid and me we were going to have to get used to working under our own names.

"Um. Yeah. Do you want me to send them upline?"

"Why don't you just tell me now? I'll send the correct information to you."

I sighed. "Believe it or not, you're on the list."

The Dragon chuckled. "Thank you, darling. And who else?"

I gave her the five names we had, then we hung up.

October 19 – 29, 1985

One of the problems Sid and I have when Sid and I feel stressed is that we get nightmares. That Friday night was not a good one. Sid usually talks in his sleep, so it's easy to tell when he's having one, and his nightmare woke me up first. We cuddled and calmed down, and then I had mine. Which meant that neither of us felt that cheerful the next day. I got through teaching my confirmation class, then after class, Dan Williams, who's our youth minister, caught me and put in a request. Kathy reiterated it when I got back to the condo.

"About the Halloween dance next week," I told Sid as we ate lunch. Nick was playing guitar in his room.

"What about it?" He was seriously less than enthused.

"I'm going as Cleopatra. Maybe you'd want to go as Caesar or Mark Antony?" I tried to wriggle suggestively.

He lifted an eyebrow. "I might be interested in being the asp. She put it to her breast, right?"

"Seriously, Sid. We need another chaperon."

"No."

I tried blinking twice. "Pretty please?"

He wouldn't even look at me. "No. No way in hell. Absolutely not."

"Why not?"

"It's noisy and it's boring. I swore I would never chaperon a teen dance again, and I will not."

I went over to Kathy and Jesse's condo. Kathy looked at me hopefully.

"No way in hell," I said.

Kathy sighed. "He meant it when he said never again."

"Yep."

"Now what?"

"I have no idea."

Sid was still a little grumpy that evening when he, Nick, and I ate dinner together at our place. Kathy and Jesse had decided they needed a night to themselves, and I was all for it. Nick, however, found a way to tease his dad out of his ill-humor. Finished with cleaning up after the meal, I went back to sewing break-in pants, and grumbling about the cramped space, and Nick talked his dad into playing piano and singing with him. Nick practiced the bass line of the theme from the Peanuts specials, with Sid playing the treble. Then Nick got his guitar out, and the two played tunes from Billy Joel, Tears for Fears, including Nick's ongoing fave, Everybody Wants to Rule the World. Nick had the riff down on his guitar. I sang along, too, where I could, as I pinned and ran the sewing machine.

Finally, we each kissed Nick goodnight, then I went back to work.

"Peewaddles," I grumbled, as I tried to get a pocket flap to sit straight over the pocket. "Frickin' pain in the patootie."

Sid laughed. He finds the sort of curse words I use when I'm sewing highly amusing. He turned on the piano bench, flexing his right hand.

"How's your wrist?" I asked.

"Fine."

"And your arm?" I looked at him a little severely.

"Also fine. I'm taking requests."

I smiled and put down the pair of pants I was working on. "Do we have the Ain't Misbehavin' book here?"

"Yeah." Sid went through the box next to the upright piano. "Here it is."

"How about Two Sleepy People?" I got up and went over to him.

He smiled. "Are you suggesting a duet?"

"Yes. I am." I sat down on the piano bench next to him. "I love hearing you sing. I don't know why you never did before."

He made a face. "I don't think I have that good a voice. But if it makes you and Nick happy, then it doesn't matter." He opened the book to the requested tune, kissed me softly, then started playing. "Oops. Too high." He played a couple chords, transposing the tune down a bit.

We went through the tune, instinctively finding just the right lines to sing solo and when to sing together. When we got to the line, "And built this cozy nest, to get a piece of—" Well, the next word is rest and I emphasized it because Sid was about to sing something else. He stopped playing.

"What?" I asked.

"I'm resting." He grinned.

I groaned. He meant a musical rest, as in a pause in the tune.

"That is really bad, Sid."

He began playing, and we finished the song, but then he started playing other, more familiar chords. You and

Me Against the World is kind of a weird tune for a love song, but it is ours. It reflects a lot of the feelings we have, the isolation we feel because of our side business. For the first time, Sid sang along with me. Again, we instinctively found the few solo lines, then finished the final chorus together. The last chords had barely melted into the air when we held each other and kissed, soft sighs escaping us.

Sid pulled away a little. "How badly do you need that chaperon?"

I sighed. "I don't know. It would be nice to have you there."

"I really don't want to go."

"Then don't. You do plenty at that parish and you're not even technically a member."

"Thanks."

I got up. "Let's go see if Nick is asleep."

"Let's." He got up and kissed the side of my head. "But we really need to work on keeping it down. We woke him up the other night."

"Again? Oh, the poor kid."

The poor kid, indeed. He woke up the next morning, stuffy and coughing. I dosed him with my grandmother's homemade cough syrup and skipped mass. I didn't want to be serving the Eucharist to parishioners if I was contagious. It was a good thing I did. By that evening, I was stuffy and coughing. Sid woke up that Monday stuffy and coughing, and went straight to Dr. Kline, who pronounced it a cold and not the first sign of AIDS.

"Didn't we just do this last month?" Sid grumbled that evening as he poured hot water into three mugs with more of Grandma's cough syrup, a blend of honey, lemon juice and Grandma's home-distilled corn liquor.

"Those were ear infections," I said, blowing my nose. "Did you ask Dr. Kline about it?"

"She said it's because we have a new kid in the household and he's at a new school." Sid coughed. "He's picking up new germs and bringing them home to us."

"Come to think of it, I remember when Darby first went to nursery school, Mae and I were getting sick all the time."

I'd been living with Mae and going to college at that point.

Having colds made training a little difficult, but there was always more code work to do, not to mention writing work. We also had to write up the monthly newsletter for the parents at Nick's school, which Sid did with a great deal of cursing and grumbling because it had to be typed using mimeograph paper rather than run on the computer.

We got another call from Carla Caponetti on Wednesday. Sid was napping, and when I tried to take a message, she hung up again.

Nick was mostly over his cold by Thursday. Friday, Sid's cough was lingering, but much better. We got a legitimate call through, and Sid had Jesse make the actual pickup and drop, although Sid stayed close by.

I was still sniffling on Saturday, but it didn't matter. That darned dance needed a chaperon, and I was going as Cleopatra. Nick dressed as D'Artagnan and looked very dashing, although he had a couple problems manipulating the fencing foil we'd gotten for the costume. Sid got a few pictures of us before we left. As we shut the door to the condo, I could hear him working on his composition class final, which was, of course, composing a piece of music.

The church hall was dimly lit. I'm not sure who was the DJ, but I knew it wasn't Frank when a gorilla ran past and hoisted me over his shoulder.

"Frank, put me down!" I hollered.

He did. "How did you know it was me?"

"Who else?"

He laughed, then looked around and pulled me aside. "Listen, can you talk to Esther?"

"About what?"

"I don't know. I mean, it's been good, but it's been weird, too, these past couple weeks. She doesn't want to tell anybody about us."

I rolled my eyes. "And I know three incredibly good reasons why not. Janet Weinstock, Sylvia Perez, and Maryann Dreyer."

Frank cursed. "Dreyer."

Janet and Sylvia were part of the Single Adults Bible Study who were among the first to get married and had decided it was their mission to make sure everyone not only got married but had Janet's and Sylvia's idea of fun doing it. They were just pests.

Maryann Dreyer was a full-on problem. Back when I'd first come to work for Sid, she decided that my living with him was immoral, never mind that it was obvious there was nothing going on. She had since decided that I was in a state of sin and a scandal to the parish. Our pastor and my personal confessor and friend, Father John, had reassured me he knew better and that his only interest in what Sid and I did was if I felt guilty about it. Maryann really had it in for Sid. But Frank and Esther were also in her sights, since they shared Esther's condo, never mind that Esther's cousin also lived there. If Frank and Esther were "just friends," Maryann had a much harder time carping about it.

"Yeah, her," I said.

Frank's eyes blinked through the gorilla mask. "Still. I'm worried about Esther. I know it's all part of figuring us out, but..."

"Shouldn't you be talking to her about this?"

"I'm trying to, but it's not easy. We've got a bunch of cross-cultural issues to work through. Plus, Esther is totally out of her element here. She's never even had a boyfriend, and the last guy she dated was gay. She's totally convinced that she's blowing it."

I sighed. "I'll see what I can do."

Esther was keeping an eagle eye on the punch bowl. Because the teen dances drew a much bigger crowd than the Teen Bible Study, there were usually a few kids there looking to make trouble, including spiking the punch. Esther wore her usual traditional Vietnamese dress.

"How are you doing?" I asked her.

She shrugged. "Okay."

"Frank's worried about you."

"I know." She looked at me with a frown on her face. "It's just a big problem, is all. My father wants Frank to move out of the duplex and stay away from me. He wants me to marry Vietnamese."

"So, why haven't you told Frank this?"

Esther blinked her eyes and looked away. "I don't want him to move. I want him to stay. But I also have to honor my culture. I know how my father feels, and I understand it. It's not easy."

"I don't doubt. Are you afraid you're going to come down on your father's side?"

"Oh, no." Esther got a sweet, soft, and happy smile on her face. "I love Frank. I just have to find a way to honor my culture and love him, too."

"Well, maybe you ought to stop trying to do that all by yourself. If you love Frank, he should be part of this, don't you think?"

"You're right. I just don't want to mess this up."

"I think he loves you enough that the only way you will is if you shut him out."

Esther nodded.

I bit my lip. "I think maybe we shouldn't have set you guys up."

"That was a good thing!" Esther grinned. "Even if I'm pregnant."

"What?" I gaped, my stomach twisting at the same time.

"I'm not quite late, but I'm a little worried." She shrugged. "It may be a good thing. Father can't say no if I'm pregnant."

"Don't, please." I sighed. "I've got an entire group of cousins doing the same thing in South Florida and it's not working out well for them."

"You're sad."

I winced. "I don't know why the whole pregnancy thing is getting to me."

"Because you can't have babies with Sid? I can understand that." She snorted. "Here I am, dealing with possible pregnancy I don't want, and you can't have pregnancy you do want." She shrugged. "We'll figure it out."

"You just make sure you talk to Frank, okay?"

When Nick and I got home, Sid was waiting for us, wearing a pair of jeans and nothing else. Nick was very enthusiastic about what a fun time he'd had. Sid waited for him to go to bed, then helped me out of my costume.

"You're sad," he said, putting the wig I was wearing on the chest of drawers.

I made a face and went to the bathroom to get my makeup off. "Yes and no. It was a weird night, is all. Frank and Esther are having a tough time coming to terms with her culture's expectations, and Esther thinks she might be pregnant."

"And that got you thinking about not getting pregnant."

"Sid, I just have to find a way to deal with it, is all." I smeared eye-makeup remover over my eyes. "I'm not going to skip marrying you just because we can't have babies. And we do have a perfectly lovely son in Nick. It's all the other feelings that I have to work with."

"You don't have to do it by yourself, sweetheart." He slid up behind me and just held me.

"Thank you, lover." I leaned into the embrace.

Monday, it was mine and Kathy's turn to make her first pickup and drop. I made the call, though, set it up for a drug store near Century City, and took Kathy with me.

"Priority and Code are on a five-point scale," I told her as we drove to the store. "Priority One is pretty easy to figure out. They're also pretty rare. Code is the level of contact allowed, with One being absolutely none and Five, go ahead and chat for a while. This one is a Priority Two, Code Two. You may or may not see your contact, but she'll probably be around to make sure you get it."

"Why behind the tampons?"

I giggled. "It's sort of a joke, but it is true most guys won't touch feminine products."

Kathy laughed.

Once Kathy got the pickup, I had her make the call to Red Light, and we took off for San Bernardino. Red Light was at the lunch counter at the truck stop. Kathy walked by, and even though I knew she was doing it, I almost didn't see the envelope land in his jacket. Red Light, a youngish fellow in a plaid cowboy shirt, with a straw-colored mullet and an overfull mustache, sat up and looked around. He spotted me. I nodded and his eyebrows went up, but he found the envelope.

Kathy and I met in the parking lot.

"Well?" she asked.

I grinned. "That was a thing of beauty. I am impressed."

"Thanks. I needed to hear that." Kathy smiled.

There are some days when from the first moment you wake up, you know you haven't got a chance. Tuesday, I have no idea why I was so sleepy that morning. I could only hope that Nick hadn't brought home yet another bug. I felt like a zombie as we ran and then through breakfast. Later that morning, the letter-quality printer kept jamming. Sid and I got into a snit over something so trivial neither of us could remember what we'd been fighting about five minutes after we calmed down. Kathy and Jesse were snipping at each other, too.

I didn't really notice that only my pager had gone off right before noon. The caller code was current, though, and it was for a Priority One, Code Three pickup at an address on Edgemont Street, going up through the Yellow Line.

"Lisa," Sid said when I told him what was up. "I've got a bad feeling about this one."

"It's a current caller code," I told him.

"Still, only your pager went off, it's the Yellow Line again, and it's outside on the street. Let me call the Dragon first."

"It's Priority One and I've got less than fifty minutes to get across town."

He made a face. "You're right. Wear some jeans, your running shoes, and your ankle holster. It'll be tight, but you should be able to make it. I'll make the call, then page you."

"Alright." I went and changed clothes and got out of there, missing lunch completely.

Traffic was miserable, but I hit a couple clear patches along Sunset Boulevard and got to the pickup only a couple minutes late. I parked the Beemer around the corner of the address and ran around the block, only to run straight into a young man holding a very large automatic handgun on me. He grabbed my arm, and I began plotting ways to wrench away and knock the gun from him.

"Nice to see you, Miss Wycherly," he said. He had dark brown hair and soft brown eyes and was about average height.

I kept my face straight and somehow managed to keep plotting.

He pulled me off the street and into a nearby street-level apartment. After he patted me down and took my ankle gun, he shoved me into the back room. It was bare and there were bars on the window. I tried the fire escape latch right away, to no avail. I heard my captor pick up a phone, punch in a number, listen for a minute, then hang up. Okay, so he was waiting for instructions. That gave me a little time. I popped open the space between the top and sole of my shoe and picked out the stiletto. Snapping the sole back, I slid the knife up the sleeve of my sweater.

A minute later, my captor opened the door and leaned in the doorway.

"What's going on?" I asked, far more casually than I felt.

"Can't get through. You're not a bad looking babe."

"You're not so bad, yourself," I said, flashing what I hoped was a sexy smile. [I'm willing to bet it was very sexy. - SEH]

"I hate it when they get chicks involved."

"Involved in what?"

"Not saying."

"What difference does it make? You're going to waste me, anyway."

"I don't do the wasting. They don't pay me enough."

"So, I'm bait for a trap."

"Dunno. I was just told to get you alive if I could."

I looked him over appraisingly. He had a shoulder holster over his dark shirt, although it was empty, and possibly another holster in the back of his jeans. I smiled again, thinking I might be able to play on his sympathy. Turning away, I rolled my shoulders and rubbed the left one. I looked back at him.

"Sorry. Spastic bursitis," I said with a wince. "I get it every now and then."

"It looks like it hurts."

"It does." I made a face. "But all I can do is rub it."

"Why don't I rub it for you?"

"Nah, don't bother."

"Well, if it hurts..."

"It's not going to help."

"Aw, come on. I give good back rubs."

"If you insist."

His touch was gentle but firm. I leaned into it, moaned a little, then shifted to the side. I half-closed my eyes, looked down, groaned happily again, then whacked him hard where it hurts. [Ouch. - SEH]

He gasped as I whipped around and knocked him in the head. I didn't want to do what I did next, but I needed to keep him out of commission long enough to get around the block. I quickly drew the stiletto along the outside of his right arm. He howled and sank to his knees. I knocked him forward, then grabbed the gun from his back holster. In the other room, I found my ankle holster and quickly strapped that back on my leg. I put the other snub-nose into the back of my waistband, then grabbed the cannon he'd been carrying.

I got out the door without problem, but another man spotted me from the end of the complex driveway. There was a fence at the other end. I ran and scaled it right into the backyard of another small complex like the one I'd been in. Turning, I got the huge automatic aimed and took out the man running toward me with a shot to his shoulder.

I went running along the backyards of that street, scaling fences into yard after yard, until I landed in the yard of a lone small house between the apartment buildings. A very pretty, but very large German Shepherd growled at the other end of the yard. I stood firm and glared at it. It backed down, obviously a pet and not a trained guard dog. I moved carefully toward the front gate, opened it, and got outside.

"What a good boy!" I hissed at it, and it came running up for a pet.

But then I had to hurry to the car. As I got out of there, I checked my pager. I'm not sure when Sid had paged me, but I had not felt it go off. I stopped at a service station and called the house.

"I'm okay," I told him.

"Good. Meet me at Henry's office as fast as you can."

"Should I pick our kid up first?"

"Nope. Jesse will get him."

Henry's secretary, Angelique Carter, waved at me as I arrived at the office.

"How's it going?" she asked. She's got full, brown hair and a model-thin figure.

"Crazy. What else? You?"

"As always. Hey, I want to show you this. It's the latest pic of my nephew and nieces."

I took the framed photo. "Oh, they're adorable."

"And guess what? I told you my brother got re-married last August?"

"Yeah."

"His wife's pregnant. I get to be an auntie again."

My smile froze. "That's great."

"Uh-oh. What's going on?"

I sighed. "It seems like everyone around me is getting pregnant."

"And Sid's fixed. Oh, dear. I'm sorry."

"No. Ange, it's fine. I just have to deal with it, is all. Anyway, Sid has a question for Henry, so I'd better..."

Angelique looked puzzled. "He's already in there."

"Then why did he ask me to come by? I'd better go on in."

Sid and Henry both had seriously grim looks on their faces.

"It was another bad one, right?" Henry asked as I flopped into the other chair in front of his desk.

"Oh, boy, was it," I said. "He addressed me by name. He's on somebody's payroll. And there was someone else coming to waste me. I asked if I was bait and he said he didn't know."

"So, is this just directed at Sid, or is it directed at both of you?" Henry looked at us.

I shrugged. "It's not the most reassuring thought, but if it's directed at both of us, it does narrow down the suspect list."

"That's assuming you weren't being used as bait for me," Sid said. He shook his head. "Henry and I have been going over it. Since you've been with me, there are three people who are still alive."

"That's it?" I made a face.

Henry sighed. "And none of them have previous access to Quickline codes."

"What about...? You know, from when the Yellow Line leaked?" I looked back and forth at them.

"Nope." Henry shook his head. "Dead."

I was confused. "But those two Brits said extradition papers had been signed."

Henry shrugged. "Their own peculiar version of extradition, I would imagine. As the Dragon says, those two can be very medieval."

"I thought that went through way too quickly." Sid sighed.

I frowned. "There was that guy in Tahoe. He could have gotten access to codes."

"He's in prison," said Henry.

I looked at both of them again. "So, now what?"

Henry drummed his fingers on the desk. "All calls, no matter what the priority, are to be verified with the Dragon. In the meantime, live your lives. You've got a pair to keep training, too. Given the attack on your house and the fact that no one has the condo address, I think you'll be reasonably safe there. Even your old phone numbers are linked to your house."

Sid and I looked at each other. It wasn't the most encouraging news, but there was little else we could do.

October 31 – November 4, 1985

T hursday, or Halloween morning, when both Sid's and my pagers went off, we both looked a little nervously at each other. Nick, thank God, was already at school. We verified it with the Dragon, but it was a legit pickup, a Code Five at a coffee shop near LAX.

"Odds it's payroll?" Sid asked with a glint in his eye.

"Darned well better be," I grumbled.

Trust me, we do not do this for free. We get paid. The catch is the paychecks don't always show up with the same regularity one gets on a normal job. We still get our full compensation, though. Sid and I decided to have Kathy and Jesse join us. They'd need to know this stop. And I don't think they realized there was money for them involved. Why, I have no idea.

It turned out to be rather celebratory. Sid explained the Code Five situation on the way. I was stoked when we got there. Chicken fried steak was on special. They do an amazing chicken fried steak at the coffee shop. Sid sighed but let me go. Okay, Sid is very picky about what he eats. No red meat, refined sugar, caffeine, artificial anything, limited fats, and I do have to be decent about it. His system can get tetchy. Me? I have a cast iron stomach and the kind of metabolism that lets me eat whatever and however much I want and not gain weight.

But there weren't just paychecks in the drop (although it was very gratifying to see both Jesse's and Kathy's jaws drop when they saw the amount on the checks from Amalgamated Paper Company). There were two pagers, one for each of them.

"You guys are getting there," I said with a smile.

"It's a relatively new system," Sid explained.

Okay. We shouldn't have, but we also explained how Sid and I used the pagers to keep tabs on each other.

"I thought that was just for the fun of it," Jesse said.

"Well, it's entirely possible that we're using these for personal use in addition to strictly official," Sid conceded. "They're damned useful. However, we have another exercise to practice this afternoon. Ditching tails."

Sid went over a lot of the evasionary tactics we used whether or not we thought we were being followed. We didn't tell Kathy and Jesse, but we had a secret weapon waiting for them when we got into the "field," as it were. Namely, the Westwood Village. Sid had sent them on ahead. We stopped and got Nick from school. I'll give Kathy and Jesse points. They spotted Sid tailing them. They spotted me in my blond wig tailing them, although they didn't realize it was me. Nick didn't get spotted, even though Kathy and Jesse knew him. Okay, who's going to suspect a kid of doing that kind of espionage work? But Nick really has a talent for tailing people. Call me a proud mom if you like. I don't care. He's good at it.

To Breanna, 10/19/00

Today's Topic: Parental Pride

My Darling -

Thanks for pointing out that Mom was a little down when we went for drinks last night. I really appreciate that you spot things like that. Mom doesn't always make it easy to see what's going on with her. I talked to her this morning, and whoo-ee, she was not happy.

It was the meeting she had to go to before we met with her and Dad. It wasn't Liturgy Committee. She likes those folks. Anyway, there were a bunch of moms there and they all got into a whole brag fest about how wonderful their little darlings were, and how this one got that scholarship, and that one got that award. So, they look at Mom and she just says that I'm continuing work on my dissertation, and one bitch just smiles and says, "Still?"

The problem is, she can't talk about a lot of the things about me that she's proud of. She's proud of my articles and my dissertation work. But she's just as proud of the way I can tail people and not get made, not to mention the explosives stuff. In fact, she said that all she could think of was that I could follow their little darlings for a week without being seen, then break into their places and leave them hogtied, and blow up their cars for good measure. Well, I suppose I could. Not that I would.

But if people found out that I can do all those things, it could get me into some serious trouble, such as The Company taking an interest in me. That's the last thing Mom wants to happen, and it could. A biochemist with explosives certification and excellent surveillance skills? Oh, yeah. If they knew about that, those rat bastards would be peeing their pants.

Sid and I both took Nick to his friend Josh Sandoval's Halloween party that night. Nick wore his D'Artagnan costume again, and I couldn't help but smile at how many of the girls at the party went ga-ga over it. Nick was less than enthused by all the female attention, which both puzzled and relieved his father. It also puzzled me.

"What's going on?" I asked Nick during the middle of the party. "You've got all these girls going nuts over you and you don't seem to care."

Nick rolled his eyes. "Laney's okay, I guess. But most of them? They're, like, totally stupid. I tried talking to Erin about tide pool eco-systems. She, like, smiled, then said something about kissing."

He shook his head and sighed. I tried not to laugh.

Sid spent the party hanging with Josh's father Reuben, who's an orthopedic surgeon in the area. I hung with Lety, Josh's mom, and some of the other moms. It was a little weird because they were mostly older than me and had raised their kids from infants. On the other hand, it was kind of nice to learn that Nick's hit-or-miss approach to personal hygiene was pretty normal for a kid his age.

"I was never that way," Sid insisted once we got back to the condo.

"Please," I said around the soap on my face. "I certainly was. I remember Mama yelling at me for putting lipstick on without washing my face first. It's part of the learning process."

"But he used conditioner and forgot to shampoo. That makes no sense." Sid went back to flossing his teeth.

"It's also been a heck of a long time since you were twelve."

"Possibly. Probably." He looked in the mirror and sighed. "We grow out of it, don't we?"

"Apparently, we do."

The next day, after All Saints' Day mass, Sid took Kathy and Jesse to do tailing exercises. Me. I had a date with my sister.

I met Mae at Union Station, downtown. Admittedly, it had gotten frowzy, but it was still a neat place and there was parking. I drove the Beemer from there down Los Angeles Street. Mae held her breath as I steered the car around and through the traffic.

"Lisa, be careful!" she yelped.

"This is Sid's car. Believe me, I'm being careful."

"I swear, Lisa. You never used to drive this way."

"Enough with my driving habits, okay?"

"I'll try. So, where are we going?"

"The Garment District. They have a bunch of great fabric shops down there. We've got to get new tops for the bridesmaids' dresses."

"Oh." She looked crestfallen, even as she kept a death grip on the door cushion.

"Mae, it's okay."

"Sure, it is."

"What else are we going to do? I can't find that lace that I have for the other tops. I don't mind starting over."

"You shouldn't have to."

I rolled my eyes. "For crying out loud. It doesn't matter."

"You're the one who doesn't have to worry about getting pregnant."

"I just wish like hell I could!"

Mae looked out at the traffic and sniffed. "Maybe I'm not being fair to you, Lisa. But I can't help wondering if the reason you want to get pregnant so badly is because you can't."

That stung.

"You always get what you want," Mae continued.

"No, I don't. There are lots of things I want that I don't get." Like not having to worry about my work killing my son and my friends. But I couldn't tell her that. "There are lots of things that you have that I won't and will never have, like five, going on six, beautiful children. I'll trade a big, fancy house for that any day."

Mae hung her head. "You're right. I'm sorry. It's just hard. Money is tight. The kids are getting on my nerves, and Neil doesn't seem to notice. Or maybe he does. He just seems to think he knows what's going on with me better than I do."

"It's alright, sis." I pulled into a parking lot. "Anyway, if you don't mind, I need to focus on bridesmaid dresses or Mama will skin me alive."

"Skin us both," Mae sighed. "She really liked those other tops."

"Well, she's going to have to learn to like whatever new ones we come up with."

We found a lovely polished-cotton print. The background was the dusty rose we'd chosen as the secondary color, with navy blue and white roses and green stems. Mae was a little skeptical that I'd be able to adjust the pattern from my wedding dress for the tops, but I didn't see why. I'd done the same thing for the former bridesmaid tops, only with a waist. We went on and picked out laces and buttons and ribbons and, okay, maybe I found a couple other fabrics, including a gorgeous blue print that matched Sid's eyes for a sport shirt for him. I could make dress shirts for him, but those are rather boring, so I leave those to his tailor.

Mae and I ate a late lunch at Olvera Street, which is right across from the train station, where she'd parked, then I returned home.

Sid was not thrilled when he saw my bags.

"Why did you buy so much fabric?" he groaned.

"We were at the Garment District," I explained. "You can't count on going back and finding something. You have to get it when you see it. Which is why I bought extra in case I need more."

"What about these other fabrics? You don't need those."

I held up the print I'd bought for him. "This was only a buck a yard and it will really make your eyes pop."

"Yes, it looks nice." Sid sighed and waved at the crowded living and dining room. "But where are you going to put it? We don't have room here for the stuff you've already got."

"Well," I looked around, sighing. He was right. I put the bags on a stack of small boxes in a corner of the dining area. "This will work for the time being."

"Honey, can you please put the brakes on new fabric or yarn until after we move back into the house?"

I glared at him. "Are you going to put the brakes on your sheet music habit?"

Sid folded his arms across his chest. "My sheet music doesn't take near the room your fabric does."

"And yet it somehow keeps blocking the utility cupboard." I pointed at the two boxes next to the upright piano. The piano also had piles of sheet music neatly stacked across the top. It wasn't great for the sound, but there was literally no place else to put it. "At least my fabric doesn't get in your way."

"Except when you're laying something out." He sighed. "I can't wait to get out of here."

"How far behind are we?"

Sid made a face. "That shooting put us back, but only a week. Maelin says the drywall will go up this week, then another round of inspections, and then they'll be able to start the interior work. We should be in well before Christmas. So, about the fabric?"

"I'll do what I can. Okay?" I looked at him. "The sheet music?"

He sighed. "I will, too."

At least Nick had some space in his room, but it was beginning to overflow as well.

It wasn't just the space being a problem, though. Sid and I were both tense, wondering where the next attack would come from. We'd talked to Henry and there was something of a plan in place for when we got the next bad call, but it didn't really help since we had no idea when, or if, the call would come.

Nick had picked up on the tension and was getting worried. It was really hard to know what would worry him more, not knowing about the bad drops and that someone appeared to be coming after us or knowing about it and wondering when we were going to get killed. His primary fear was that he'd say goodbye to go to school or to bed and never see us again. Unfortunately, with his first mother passing away and having seen some of the work his dad and I did, it wasn't all that unreasonable a fear.

After Nick went to sleep that night, Sid and I went around and around and still couldn't come to any real conclusion about the best way to handle it. It was certainly not something most parents dealt with. The one advantage we had was that Nick knew that we usually couldn't tell him what we were working on. Other times, we simply did not want to burden him with the knowledge, which was why we hadn't told him about Sid's AIDS tests.

Sunday afternoon did not help my mood any. I almost didn't go, but I'd already promised Esther I would. Kathy drove to the party at Sarah William's apartment for Irene Sanchez, whose baby was due in a week or two.

"Are you going to be okay?" Kathy asked me.

I shrugged. "You know how much I hate showers."

"Yeah, but this is a baby shower and I know you're feeling it."

"Well, I may as well get used to it. People aren't going to stop getting pregnant because I can't."

Kathy rolled her eyes but didn't say anything more.

If Esther wasn't entirely her usual boisterous self, it had nothing to do with Frank or her own worries.

"Sarah made me promise to be good." Esther made a face. "It's boring!"

I'm not sure what was worse. Listening to the three-quarters of the room swapping horror stories about how miserable it was to be pregnant and teasing Sarah about her morning sickness, or the three incredibly inane games. I couldn't believe I'd won a prize - a baby bottle filled with candy. Of course, Sylvia Perez, who was about four months along, herself, came up just then to tell me I could save the bottle for when my little ones started coming along.

"Why do you assume we are just like you?" Esther asked her loudly in front of everybody.

The room quieted, and I flushed.

"I mean it," Esther said. "First, you and Janet bug Lisa about getting married. Now, you're bugging her about having babies. Why do you guys get to decide that and not Lisa? Huh?"

Kathy came up. "I agree. You have no right to make assumptions about any of us. But that doesn't seem to stop you. And I know for a fact those assumptions have hurt people before."

Irene blushed, then somehow smiled. "Thank you, Kathy."

I looked at Irene but didn't say anything.

"In fact," said Kathy. "I think we can call this party done. How about you, Esther?"

Esther grinned. "About time."

Kathy turned to Sarah. "It's been a lovely party. I'll stick around and help clean up."

Sarah caught something in Kathy's eyes and nodded. "Thanks, Kathy. I appreciate it. Who wants to take home cake?"

"But...," said Sylvia. "Presents...?"

"Boring," said Esther, and I knew she meant it.

"I'm with her," I said. "Sarah, what can I do?"

The other women slowly filtered out of the room. Soon, only Irene, Sarah, Kathy, Esther, and I were left.

"I'm so sorry!" Irene sobbed from the couch.

Kathy and I flew to her side.

"Why?" I asked. "Sylvia was the one being obnoxious."

"It's just that my blood pressure's going up." She looked at the rest of us. "I have Type One diabetes. It's not usually that big a deal. I'm good about keeping it under control. It's just that there are complications, and I shouldn't really be pregnant. It was an accident. Kathy caught me crying in the bathroom just now. It's not that I don't want my baby. I'm just so scared that I won't make it through the birth. I don't want to open presents I'll never get to use."

"Oh, Irene!" I put my arms around her, as Kathy did.

"I didn't want a shower," she sniffed. "But Janet and Sylvia were so sure I did, and we need the presents. I couldn't tell them no."

"Well, somebody's got to start," Kathy said, glancing at me. "Not everybody wants to share their health issues with everybody else."

"Or other problems," said Esther.

Sarah reached over and patted Esther's arm. Esther grinned.

A little later, as Esther and I packed presents into Irene's car, I pulled her aside.

"How are you doing?" I asked.

Esther grinned. "Oh, fine. I was just late."

"Whew!"

"Yeah. Tell me about it."

"What about you and Frank?"

Esther shrugged and smiled. "We're talking. He has a friend who married a girl from China. It's not the same culture, but a lot of the issues are the same. So, we're talking to them, and it helps. Father is still not cooperating." She blew out her breath with a snort. "You think your dad hates Sid. Father really hates Frank. But he better get used to him. Frank is going to be around for a very long time. It helps that Frank learned Vietnamese, but not much."

"Well, that's good."

Esther held me back. "Lisa, I told Kathy what's going on. And Father John because we had to because we are getting married. We just don't know when. But it will be a very small wedding. So, we're not telling anybody else."

"No problem, Esther."

I looked at Kathy as we drove home. "You okay?"

"Okay, enough." She shook her head. "I am pretty fed up, though. You. Irene. And remember Donna? God only knows what's going to happen if those two get their hooks into Esther. We've got to stop them from running roughshod over everybody."

"Well, you showed them today," I said.

"How are you feeling?" Kathy looked at me.

I made a face. "Fine, I think. Irene did remind me that giving birth can be dangerous. Way back when, it was a major cause of death for women in the childbearing years. I just pray to God she's okay."

"We both do."

When we got back to the condo, Sid had made dinner for Kathy and Jesse, as well as us, and we ate together, enjoying the company and relaxing. Kathy and I decided not to ruin the peace by talking about Sylvia Perez.

The next morning, I went into Nick's room to get him to go running.

"Mom?" he said from the top bunk, as if he was having a really hard time saying it. "I don't feel good."

"What's the matter, sweetie?"

"My throat hurts."

I touched his forehead. He had a fever.

"Alright. Go back to sleep. I'll be back in a bit."

Sid lifted an eyebrow as I left the room. He was ready to go in his warmup suit. I shook my head.

"He's sick," I said.

Sid's face fell. "Again?"

"Fever. Sore throat. Good odds it's strep. I'll call Dr. Kline as soon as it's eight."

Dr. Kline doesn't really do pediatrics or family medicine, but she has some sort of clearance that means when there are gunshot wounds involved, she doesn't ask questions. As it turned out, she did want to see Nick. Nick, for his part, was exceptionally unenthused about getting up and going to the doctor's. More than that. He started crying as I helped him off the top bunk.

"What's the matter, my sweet guy?" I asked.

He winced. "When I got sick like this, my first mom would just call my pediatrician, then go get the prescription." Rachel, Nick's birth mother, had been an emergency room doctor. Nick took a deep breath. "I miss her."

"I know, sweetheart. It's okay." I held him next to me, his fever radiating through to my skin.

He cried for a couple minutes more, then got dressed. The poor thing. He was feeling just plain awful on top of his grief. It hadn't been that long since he'd lost his first mom, and I really felt for him.

Dr. Kline took one look at his throat, felt for the glands under his chin, then smiled comfortingly at him.

"You, young man, have probably got strep throat. We'll take a throat culture just to be sure, but in the meantime, I'll write up a prescription for you."

He nodded and winced as he tried to swallow.

When we got back to the condo, Sid had taken Kathy and Jesse on tailing practice. I put Nick to bed.

Sid got back around four.

"Well?" he asked.

"It's strep," I said. "Dr. Kline just confirmed it. He's on his second dose of antibiotics and sleeping now. I've laid in plenty of Haagen-Daz and chocolate pudding until he can get something else past that throat."

Sid rolled his eyes. "Fats and sugars."

"And smooth and creamy and soothing, which is what he needs right now. I also called Conchetta. She said she'll bring by some chicken soup tomorrow."

"How did we end up here?"

"The condom broke, darling."

"Right."

November 6 – 7, 1985

The first call that Wednesday morning came through while Sid was taking Nick to school. The boy had bounced back quickly, even if he was still taking antibiotics.

"Is Mr. Sid Hackbirn there?" The voice was familiar.

"Is this Ms. Caponetti?" I asked, even though I knew it was.

"Yes, I need to speak with him right now."

"He's not in. I can take a message."

The line went dead again. I was about to call Henry about it when Sid came into the condo with a grim look on his face.

"Did you get paged?" he asked, shutting the door.

"No." I swallowed.

He didn't look any happier. "I better call the Dragon, then."

It turned out the pickup request had gone through her, but there had been something off about it. I heard Sid telling her about the plan we'd cooked up with Henry and she liked the idea. So Sid made the call and arranged things for around four that afternoon. I called Lety Sandoval and asked if she'd mind picking Nick up from school along with Josh that afternoon. Lety not only didn't mind, she thanked me profusely.

"One of Josh's brothers has a soccer game this afternoon," she explained. "Last night Josh decided he'd rather eat broken glass than watch his brothers play soccer. Maybe Nick can keep them both entertained."

"I'm glad it's working out."

Lety laughed. "Yeah. This adolescent thing is making me crazy. I mean, Josh has been pretty good, but he still gets that attitude going and I just want to bounce him out of the house on his ear. Worse yet, I totally sympathize with him about watching soccer. Thank God, Josh was never the little jock his brothers are."

I volunteered to call Cissie at the school to let Nick know who was picking him up, profoundly grateful that Cissie would be the one telling Nick and not Sid or me. Nick could always tell when we had something going with the side business, and I hated how he worried about us.

Sid was in the middle of talking to Henry when I hung up. That conversation, however, did not last long.

"He wants us to bring Kathy and Jesse," Sid said when he'd hung up.

"Terrific." I glared at my desk. "They're still pretty green."

"They're going to have to get used to it sometime."

"I know. There are just so many ways this one could go bad."

"Well, let's see what we can do to mitigate that."

I took a deep breath. "Should I take lead on this? I'll be above everything."

"Sure. Makes sense."

I shook my head to clear it, then got some tracing paper from my sewing stuff and unrolled the 36-inch-wide sheet onto the table. I opened up our Thomas Guide map book and looked at the page.

"According to the Thomas Guide," I said, using a pencil to sketch in some blocks. "We've got the building here, fronting on Melrose, with the alley alongside and curving behind it. Apartments here, across the alley, and if what Henry said is true, a fire escape on this side of the main building."

"He said that the middle unit in the building is vacant, so you should be able to get in and to the roof through there." Sid pointed to the drawing. "Jesse should be able to set up there."

We made sure everything was laid out, then went and got Kathy and Jesse. Kathy was not happy, but there was little we could do about it.

Around two, Kathy and I took off in Sid's Beemer. We were wearing our black break in pants and light-colored shirts with dark sweatshirts on top. We did not bring masks. I found a parking space on one of the side streets and the two of us casually walked to the building on the eastern end of Hollywood, in the unfashionable section of Melrose Avenue. I had a dark daypack on one shoulder. The building was white-ish, had two stories, and a flat roof. As we approached it from the side street, I scanned the rooftop of the two-story tan stucco apartment building across the alley.

"See anything?" I asked Kathy.

She also scanned the area. "Nothing."

We went to the back of the building and the center unit. There was a door there. Henry had sent us the keys earlier that day. I got my gloves on and the keys out of my pants pocket.

I nudged Kathy. "Gloves."

"Oh, right." She quickly put her gloves on.

"Any time you are someplace you shouldn't be, you wear gloves." I got the door open, and we stepped into a dark hallway.

I shut the door and blinked several times to adjust to the darkness. The smell of mildew was almost overpowering, but didn't entirely mask something else that smelled even worse. I couldn't tell what. I decided I didn't have Need to Know on that one. The roof was a little scary, with multiple soft spots, but there was a waist-high rim wall around the edges. Kathy and I slid over to the rim overlooking the alley and laid down behind it.

I switched on my transmitter. "We should be hearing from the guys any time now."

Kathy nodded, and sure enough, half a minute later, we heard a grunt and peeked over the rim. Across the alley, Jesse had scaled a wooden fence and was hiding under an awning belonging to an office at the back of the apartments.

"Red Dawn, I have eyes on you," I said softly.

"Thanks, Little Red." Jesse kept his voice low, but he came in loud and clear through the receiver parked on my ear.

"Red Sky and I are in position."

"Copy that."

Kathy swallowed.

We had almost an hour and a half to wait. It felt like eight. All three of us kept the chatter to a minimum. Kathy, who was the principal lookout, did sweep after sweep with her binoculars and didn't find anything. I slowly assembled the rifle I'd stashed in the daypack and made sure I had a full clip in it, as well as a couple extra to hand. My neck was getting a little sore, but there was nothing I could do about it. Kathy did yet another sweep and didn't see anything.

"Check the rooftops?" I asked her.

"Especially there. Nada."

I did not find that at all reassuring. Someone had to be watching. I didn't say so to Kathy, though. She was nervous enough.

About twenty minutes before the scheduled pickup, Henry's voice broke into our ears.

"Red Team, this is Red Knight. Everyone in position?"

"In position, Red Knight," I said.

"You ready to go?" Henry, however, was not addressing us.

"Let's get it done," said Sid, his voice slightly taut.

I think it's fair to say that this was not a plan that I supported. There just seemed to be few better options for capturing whoever was after Sid, and possibly me. I rolled over and got my rifle mounted. Sid, wearing jeans, a nice sport shirt, and a windbreaker style jacket, walked into the alley just a little ahead of the appointed time, found a space between two dumpsters and crouched between them. Kathy lay next to me, scanning the alley and roof tops.

"Nothing," she muttered. "Wait. Suspect approaching from the side street."

I looked. He was too far away, but... My heart in my throat, I yanked the binoculars from Kathy, and looked down at the suspect. It was the young man who'd held me the week before.

"We're hot!" I said, my voice rising with worry.

I gave the binoculars back to Kathy and followed the young man with the sight on the rifle.

"Second suspect approaching from the alley to Melrose." Jesse said. "And he's armed and ready."

I didn't quite curse, but quickly let off a couple rounds at the first young man's feet, then scanned the alley for the second suspect. He was almost on top of the dumpsters. I sent three rounds his way.

We were trying to take the suspects alive. Aside from the fact that Sid and I really hate killing people, we wanted them alive in the probably vain hope they'd tell us who'd hired them, or maybe accidentally offer us a clue.

A gun shot sent a spray of stucco into Kathy's face from the wall rim, and Kathy screamed.

"Are you alright?" I ducked.

She whimpered, but I didn't see any blood.

"Get down!" I scanned the rooftop directly across from us. The shooter had also ducked, but a minute later, I saw what looked like a middle-aged woman aiming a rifle at us. At least, she had blondish hair poufed and glued into place around her head. I ducked.

Gunfire erupted in the alley below us, and I heard bullets pinging off metal.

I mounted the rifle and rose over the wall rim, shooting at the apartment building across the alley. The young man was face down in the alley, but still moving. I couldn't see the other suspect. Kathy burst into tears. I ducked again.

"We got one of them," Jesse said. "Big Red? You got him?"

There was no answer. Kathy cried.

"It doesn't mean anything," I told her softly, never mind that I was just as worried. "I need you to crawl over to the fire escape. Stay as close to the wall rim as you can. I'll cover you as you go over."

"But—"

"Sh! Now go."

She stayed put.

"Damn it!" I snarled. "Go!"

I reached over and pulled her arm in the right direction. She looked at me, utterly terrified. I blinked back tears. I'd been where she was once.

"Go! Now!"

Somehow, Kathy started crawling toward the fire escape at the end of the building. When she got there, I slid up again, firing wildly at the apartment across the way. Kathy stayed on her tummy, too frightened to move. I ducked.

"When I start shooting, you get onto that fire escape and get down or I will shoot you myself!" I snarled.

From the look on her face, I knew she'd heard me. I popped up again, firing wildly, and Kathy got over the rim and down the ladder. I slid below the wall rim, then swapped out clips. More bullets rained down and Kathy screamed.

Okay, I came awfully close to cursing. I got the extra clip loaded and the empty clip into my daypack. As I swung the bag onto my shoulder, a shot from the apartment across the way tore through the pack. I popped up again, firing wildly, only this time, I somehow got to my feet and ran for the fire escape. I'm still not sure how I made it, but I felt the bullet in the air above my head as I scrambled down the ladder. Kathy had gotten to the ground safely. Jesse held her. I lowered myself from the end of the ladder and dropped. Sid trotted up from the street end of the alley, breathing heavily. I blinked with relief.

As I'd thought, Sid's transmitter had merely died. It happened, and given Sid's dusty appearance, he'd obviously dived for cover and knocked the transmitter out of commission.

"Looks like that second guy took one," Sid said. "Feds are on him."

"Red Team, please clear the area," Henry's voice said in my ear.

"We've gotta get out of here," I told the others.

Kathy and Jesse already knew that. Sid just nodded.

I let Jesse take Kathy and took Sid with me around the long way to where I'd parked.

"You hear anything on the other guy?" Sid asked as I dumped the daypack and rifle into the Beemer's trunk.

I shook my head. "Last I saw, he was down, but still moving."

Sid let me drive. I told him about the other sniper.

"A middle-aged woman?" he asked.

"I'm pretty sure. Could it be Carla Caponetti? She called this morning while you were taking Nick to school."

Sid shrugged. "Could be. We'll have to ask Henry."

Sid asked to make one stop, and I was glad. One thing Kathy really loved was good bourbon, as did Sid. We stopped at one of Sid's favorite sources and got something extra special, not for any celebratory reason. This was medicinal.

Once we were parked in the one measly space we'd been allotted at the condo building, we double checked to be sure no one could see us. Then I broke the rifle down and hid it back in my daypack. We went upstairs to our condo first. I dumped the daypack in our bedroom and quickly changed my break-in pants to jeans in case Nick came home. Then I went to the back corner of my closet and pulled out three tattered wire-bound notebooks.

Sid had finally seen the collection of notebooks and binders filled with binder paper when we were packing our things before leaving the house for the condo. He was pretty angry at first. But I let him read the first set, and the one after that, and then he understood.

When we got to Kathy and Jesse's condo, Kathy was still sobbing on the couch, with Jesse's arms around her.

"I almost got you killed!" Kathy wailed when she saw me.

Jesse was also trembling, but working really hard to be strong for Kathy. Sid got four water glasses from their kitchen and poured generously from the bottle we'd just bought. I took two of the glasses, the notebooks still under my arm. Sid put the other two in front of Kathy and Jesse on their coffee table.

"You didn't get us killed," Sid said slowly, accepting one of my two glasses. "We survived. It doesn't have to be pretty. We just have to do it. Any landing you walk away from is a good landing."

We sat down in the chairs that flanked the couch. I reached over and patted Kathy's knee.

"Kathy, sweetie," I said. "It's okay. It was your first encounter with violence. That's pretty scary."

"I'm never going to get this," she sobbed. "I can't get this."

"Yeah, you panicked," I said. "But you got over it and did what you needed to. That's the important thing."

"But it's going to happen again."

"And you'll be in better shape to deal with it," I said.

"I'm never going to get this!" Kathy leaned against Jesse.

"Yes, you will," I said firmly. "You'll get used to it."

"And how do you know that?" Kathy glared at me.

"Because I did." I put my notebooks in her lap. "You're good at the R-four cipher."

Kathy looked at me, then opened the cover on the top notebook. "'My name is Lisa Wycherly. I live with my boss...'" She looked at Sid and me.

"Go ahead," I said, not entirely sure I wanted her to. "Read it. I hope it helps."

I got up, took my glass of bourbon, and went across the hall to Sid's and my condo. It hadn't bothered me when Sid had read my journals. He'd been part of it all. He already knew. [I didn't know what all you'd been feeling. - SEH] That someone else was reading them, even someone I loved as much as I love Kathy. That was harder to take, but it was the right thing to do.

Sid showed up several minutes later. I called Lety Sandoval and asked if we could pick up Nick. She said she'd bring him over, adding that the afternoon had been a spectacular success. When Nick got home, he agreed he'd had a good time, but then took one look at Sid and me and knew our afternoon had not gone nearly as well.

"We had a good landing," Sid told him. "That's all that counts."

Nick rolled his eyes, then asked what was for dinner and if Kathy and Jesse were eating with us. We told him we were letting Kathy and Jesse have some time to themselves. Nick helped Sid make dinner, and soon we were eating, with

Sid and I still sipping the bourbon. It was a darned good bottle.

Nick had homework to do, so we sent him off to do it. Right before nine, Sid checked it, then we gave him his last dose of antibiotic for the day, kissed him goodnight, and sent him to bed. I checked him a half hour later, and he was asleep. It felt good watching him, so still, but breathing freely, in his top bunk. Sid came up behind me.

"Hard not to love him, isn't it?" he whispered.

"Impossible. He's such a sweetheart."

"Kind of makes the rest of it all worth it."

"Yeah."

We watched our son sleep for several minutes more, then made our way to our bedroom. Sometime later, I lay on my back, still unable to sleep. Sid snuggled up to me.

"What are you thinking about?" he asked.

I sighed. "That one really bad fight we had. The one in DC after I totally messed up."

"Kind of like today."

"Yep." I looked at him. "I said some really horrible things to you."

He chuckled. "You also quoted the Hitchhiker's Guide to the Galaxy."

"But it was pretty unforgivable. I had no idea how low I was hitting."

"You had no reason to." Sid squeezed me gently. "I'd made sure of that. And, yeah, it really hurt. But I'm... Glad you did. Lisapet, you know what I was like then. Only a full body blow was going to move me, and if you'd known how hard you were hitting, you would never have done it. Which means we wouldn't have what we have now." He gently kissed my shoulder.

I held him and kissed his forehead, then drew back.

"What?" he asked.

"How are you feeling?"

He thought about it. "My throat's a little sore."

I kissed his forehead again. "I think you've got a fever."

"No."

It was. When he woke up the next morning, his glands were swollen, and he couldn't swallow. When I called Dr. Kline, she asked to see him right away, and one look in his throat confirmed it.

"I'll take the culture pro forma," she said. "But you've had one case in the household. You've obviously picked it up."

Sid tried to swallow and sighed. I got him home, then back into bed, then went to get the prescription Dr. Kline had phoned into the pharmacy. Fortunately, there was plenty of ice cream and chocolate pudding left from Nick's bout with strep throat. Sid balked when I brought him the first bowl of chocolate ice cream.

"It's Haagen-Daz," I told him, sitting on the edge of the waterbed.

"Fats and sugars," he said, wincing.

"Smooth and creamy and soothing. And you've got to get something on your stomach so you can take your antibiotic."

Sid let me give him a spoonful of ice cream. "It feels like Conchetta has been in there with a scrub brush."

"I know, sweetheart. Try another spoonful."

He did. "How come you don't have this?"

"I have no idea. It's entirely probable I'm next."

As it turned out, I dodged that bullet. Sid was both glad and annoyed. Later that night, I held him close to me.

"Your fever's down," I said. "How are you feeling?"

"A little better." He swallowed. "It's not hurting as badly."

I kissed his hair. "You seem pensive."

"I never thought I'd like being mothered." He squeezed me again. "It's watching you take care of Nick, then how you take care of me. And I can't help thinking about how Stella would take care of me when I was sick as a kid." He swallowed again. "She was never very maternal. But that somehow changed when I caught the flu or some other bug."

"So, why are you thinking about her now?"

Sid and the aunt who raised him had been estranged for years and he seldom talked about her.

"I don't know. I just am."

I kissed his hair again. "Then it's all to the good."

November 12, 1985

I t was insanely annoying that after nearly getting several of our backsides killed, we still didn't know who was trying to kill Sid and probably me as well. The suspects had been closed mouthed, according to Henry. I'd told him about the middle-aged woman I'd seen and pointed out that Carla Caponetti sounded middle-aged. The problem was Caponetti checked out on paper. No connection to anything espionage-related, and it seemed clear that whoever had set up the bad pick up had access to a lot of Quickline information. That didn't mean Caponetti didn't have some way of accessing Quickline, but it made it unlikely.

So, Sid and I went back to living our lives. There really wasn't much else to do.

Kathy and Jesse didn't say much about my journals. They just returned them with sincere thanks and said they'd helped a lot. I was profoundly grateful. We had a few legitimate pickups and drops, and they pulled them off without a tremor. Sid got over strep in only a couple days, although he was on the antibiotic for a full week.

The Tuesday after the shootout, though, was not entirely a good one. It started relatively early, when Mama called right after I got back from taking Nick to school.

I took the call from my desk, with Sid across from me, working on some edits.

"About your wedding invitations," she said.

"We're still working on that, Mama."

"I was thinking we could use just a simple, straightforward traditional card."

"Okay." My tone was guarded, at best. "I sort of like that idea, but I really hate the traditional wording."

"What do you mean?"

"Mr. and Mrs. Wycherly invite you to see Lisa Jane married to Sid Hackbirn. It leaves my last name off and I don't like that."

"Well, honey, you're going to be changing your name."

"No, I'm not, Mama. I'm keeping my name."

"Oh. What does Sid think about that?"

"It's irrelevant. It's my name."

"Oh."

I sighed. "Mama, um, give me a few days. We'll come up with something."

"Honey, your daddy and I want to do the inviting. We are paying for the wedding."

"Something you don't have to do. We are indulging you on that one."

"Still, we are paying for it. We get to do the inviting."

"Okay. Fair enough. Let me work on it, okay?"

Sid's eyebrow raised as I hung up the phone. "The invitations?"

"Yeah. We've got to fix the wording on them. Mama and Daddy want to do the inviting, which is fair, but I don't want my last name dropped."

"I got that."

"She asked me how you felt about me not taking your name."

"It's irrelevant. It's your name."

I sighed. "Still, it only seems fair to take you into account."

"Why?" Sid sat back in his chair.

"Social expectations." I frowned.

"I couldn't care less about those. You know that." He paused and thought. "I'm not even sure I want you to take my name. It's mine, damn it. It's not yours."

I laughed. "It's like Nick being excited because none of us has the same last name."

"Sounds about right."

"Sid." I sat up, suddenly remembering something. "You know Mama's old boyfriend, the one she said looked just like you?"

"So?"

"I think his name was Caponetti."

"I got my features from my mother."

"Still..."

"Whatever. What about the Bolton profile? Do we have enough interviews to write it?"

I looked at my notes. "I think so. We could get some clarification from him on his opinion of table cover counts, but it's a pretty minor point."

"I agree."

We went back to work and spent a very pleasant morning and early afternoon not thinking about weddings or espionage or anything but the various assignments we had and how we were going to get the next assignments. Around two-thirty, I got up to go. It was my turn to get Nick from school.

But Nick wasn't waiting as I pulled into the school pick-up area. Cissie, the school secretary, had me pull further into the parking lot and come into the office.

"There's been a fight," Cissie told me once I was there.

Sister Maria Campos, the school principal, opened her office door and Nick came slowly outside. He wore the school navy-blue cardigan over his light blue uniform shirt, which was coming untucked. He almost winced when he saw me.

"Nick, why don't you sit out here while I talk with your mom?" Maria asked.

Nick sighed deeply but nodded. Bewildered, I went into Maria's office. Now, Maria and I are friends, but that doesn't always help Nick.

"What's going on?" I asked, as Maria shut the door to the office. "There was a fight?"

"One punch thrown. Unfortunately, Nick was the one who threw it." Maria sank into her desk chair and rubbed her eyes.

I sat down in the chair in front of her desk. "What happened?"

Maria has dark black hair, bright brown eyes, and a rounded figure. "It was Jason Dreyer."

Jason, the son of my nemesis, Maryann Dreyer.

"Oh, no," I groaned.

"There were several other kids who saw and heard it all, luckily for Nick. It started with a couple eighth graders, I'm not saying who. They were teasing Jason and Nick stepped in and told them to back off." Maria gave me a weak smile. "Your little guy can be a pretty tough customer. He's been very good about protecting not only Jason, but Josh Sandoval and some of the girls. Only Jason did not react well and started taunting Nick. According to the other kids, Nick endured more than mortal boy could be expected to endure before punching Jason." Maria shook her head. "I had to call him on it. He threw the first punch. But he told me what Jason had said, and so had the other kids, and frankly, Lisa, I would have punched the little jerk, too. I have to suspend Nick, but I'm only giving him one day and I'm not putting it in his record."

"Still, he shouldn't be punching people," I said.

Maria sighed. "Go easy on him, Lisa. Jason was the one who was out of line. You're right. Nick shouldn't have punched him, but I can hardly blame him."

As we left the office, Maryann Dreyer stormed into the outer office, dragging Jason, sullen and slightly corpulent, behind her. Maryann's blond hair remained poufed and glued in place, never mind how her pinched face shook with rage.

"What are you going to do about this?" Maryann demanded of Maria, pointing to Jason's red nose and rapidly blackening eye. "I demand that you expel that boy!"

"I'm not expelling anyone," Maria said calmly. "Now, why don't you come into my office, and we'll talk this over. I'm convinced that Jason has told neither me nor you the truth."

Maryann suddenly noticed Nick and me. I put my arms protectively around Nick.

She drew herself up. "You'd better tell your boss what his boy did."

She was about the only person left in the parish who referred to Sid as my boss.

I pulled Nick closer to me. "I've been told that my son was defending yours until your son got nasty."

"Hm!" Maryann swept into Maria's office.

Nick was on the edge of tears as we rode back to the condo.

"I didn't mean to hurt him." Nick's voice broke into a squeak.

"We'll talk about this when we get home."

"Is Dad going to be mad at me?"

"He will take everything Sister Maria told me into account."

Sid actually did more than that. When we got back to the condo, I had Nick go to his room.

"What's going on?" Sid asked.

I told him everything Maria had told me. Sid lifted an eyebrow.

"Well," he said finally. "I'm glad that Dreyer kid finally got what was coming to him and that it was my kid that gave it to him."

"Sid, he punched Jason Dreyer!"

"Who has been repeatedly running both of us down in front of Nick. You have no idea how much Nick has been holding back. And he has been standing up for Jason almost since he got to that school."

"Excuse me, we are big enough to handle a few insults."

"That's not the point, Lisa."

"Then what is?"

"Sometimes, you just have to stand up and fight. It's not fair to Nick to ask him to stand down and let some little worm walk all over him."

Um, Sid may have used a few other epithets. [I did and then some. The little shit. - SEH]

"I thought we were trying to teach him to behave like a civilized human being."

"What's uncivilized about knocking the snot out of somebody who seriously deserves it?"

"Violence is not an answer, and you and I know that better than most."

Sid looked away. "Sometimes, it is the answer, and we both know that, too." He looked back at me. "Honestly, Lisa. I am this close to working over Michael Dreyer. I don't care what he says about me, but you are, in fact, innocent, and he has been harassing you."

"I don't need you to defend my honor. And I don't think we need to be encouraging Nick to haul out and punch anybody who's annoying him."

Sid sighed. "Okay. You're probably right. We don't want to encourage violence. But I'm sorry. I find it really hard to bust Nick when he has been pushed to his limit. He held out a long time."

"I didn't know it was that bad." I looked at him. "Why didn't you tell me?"

Sid's frown was a little guilty. "Nick asked me not to. He didn't want your feelings hurt. Lisa, I don't even want to think what you'd do if you knew Jason had been calling Nick names."

I pressed my lips shut. Sid had a point. I had gotten rather nasty a month or so before when a shopkeeper at one of the local malls had insisted that Nick had been shoplifting when it was obvious that he hadn't.

Sid put his hand on my shoulder. "Tell you what. I'll go in and talk to him. I will point out that violence is only the very last resort, okay?"

"Okay. He is suspended tomorrow."

"We'll figure that out." He went first to our bedroom, then into Nick's.

To Breanna, 11/14/00

Today's Topic: Describe a time when your parents made you feel safe.

Hey, Sweetheart -

That little journaling book you have has some damned interesting questions. Okay, maybe this one has a different spin on it simply because of what my parents were (and are). Oddly enough, I always felt safe with Mom and Dad, even when things got really, really dangerous. I guess this gets more into how protective we are of each other.

I remember when I was twelve, and one of the kids at school, Jason Dreyer, used to call Mom and Dad names. It drove me nuts. But I kind of figured it had to do with Jason being picked on all the time, which is why I stepped in when some of the other kids would tease him. Only there was this one time.

It was right after school and a couple of eighth graders were pushing Jason around. I told them to back off, and they did. But then Jason started yelling at me and calling me AIDS boy.

"Your dad's got AIDS," he sneered.

I shook my head. "My dad is straight."

"He still sleeps with whores. And that makes your step-mom a whore."

And that's when I punched him.

Mom was mad, but Dad came into my room that after-noon.

"Good job, Nick," he said, then put up his finger. "I'm supposed to be reminding you that violence is only to be used as the very last resort."

"It was, Dad."

"I know. And I'm proud of you."

I was still upset. "He keeps calling me AIDS boy. He says you have it."

Dad sighed. "Nick, it is very unlikely at this point, but yes, there is a possibility that I was exposed to the virus. We didn't want to tell you until we knew for sure. You've been through enough with your first mom asking you to keep quiet about her leukemia, not to mention our side business. I've been tested at least twice, and both times, the test came up negative."

"Negative meaning you got it?" Of all the times for my voice to break. I hated it when that happened.

"No. Negative means it hasn't turned up."

I couldn't help but worry again. "But you and Mom. You're doing it, aren't you?"

"In a limited way." He smiled. "How many details do you want?"

"Yuck."

"We're taking precautions. The last thing I want to do is infect your mother, and again, it's not likely that I have it."

"Because you're straight?"

"Yes. It is possible to get it through heterosexual contact, but it's not as likely."

"I thought only gay guys got it."

Dad shook his head. "It's getting into the straight population, and unfortunately, because I slept around, it increased the odds that I came into contact with it." He took a deep breath. "That's the biggest reason I'd really rather you didn't sleep around."

"I don't like girls. I mean, I'm not gay."

"I couldn't care less either way."

"I'm just not into girls yet. They're kinda stupid."

"That can change pretty quickly, Nick."

"Really?"

"Right after I turned thirteen, I woke up one morning not the least bit interested in sex. By that afternoon, I couldn't get enough." He sighed, then handed me a strip of condoms. "That's why I want you to start carrying these on you. We'll make sure to keep them fresh. You may not be interested now. But with AIDS out there, I absolutely do not want you to discover that you are interested and not be able to protect yourself. You know your mother and I don't agree on a lot of things regarding sex, but we both agree on this."

So, I guess that made me feel safe, too.

That night, as Sid and I got into bed, he slipped over and snuggled.

"Um, during my talk with Nick, we got into my AIDS status."

"Is he okay?"

Sid made a face. "I think I was able to reassure him. But I did talk to him about sleeping around and that I'd rather he didn't. Also... Lisa, there is a box of condoms in my bedside table. I've been keeping them for us just in case we can't help ourselves."

"Nice to know."

"I still don't trust them." He sighed. "However, I opened it today. I had a feeling my status might come up, so I got a strip out just in case before we had our talk. I gave the strip to Nick."

"We both agreed he should use them if he's going to have sex."

"I know, and he's definitely not into girls and that stuff. But I'd rather he has them and not need them than be caught without."

I looked at Sid. "I agree."

He still looked guilty. "I didn't want you to find the open box, knowing that we hadn't used them."

"I would have asked you about them. There are plenty of legitimate reasons why you'd have an open box."

"But you would have wondered."

"Maybe. On the other hand, you haven't given me any reason to."

"And I am doing my damnedest to never give you any reason to doubt me."

"I appreciate that." I smiled and rolled onto my back. "What did he have to say about the fight?"

"Not much."

I debated pressing the issue. Somehow, I didn't think I'd get much out of Sid. Or Nick, for that matter. For all I'd protested about them defending my honor, I knew it wasn't about that. They simply didn't want to see my feelings hurt in much the same way I didn't want either of theirs to be hurt.

"He does get that it's a last resort, right?" I asked instead.

"He knew that even before today." Sid noticed that I was watching him. "I know you're not exactly thrilled about my reaction this afternoon."

"No, I'm not, but I'm more surprised. You don't usually like violence."

He laid on his back and stared at the ceiling. "I don't, but even growing up among a bunch of pacifists, we boys were usually tussling over something. Then when I got to high school, it was fight or get beat up, and I did not like getting beat up."

Sid's early education had been irregular, to say the least. He'd gone to a series of freedom schools, mostly places where his aunt had taught music, then had ended up in a regular public high school starting his freshman year. It had been quite the culture shock for him.

"It seems like fights are a normal part of growing up," he continued. "I'm glad that Nick knows how to defend himself and is standing up for even a little jerk like Jason Dreyer. That takes a lot of guts, Lisa. I'm very proud of him for that."

"I'm glad, and I am proud of Nick for standing up for his friends." I made a face. "I just worry about us keeping that... What did Mae call it? That united front thing going. We don't always have the same values."

"Nick's always known that. He's better able to parse that out than you think. And we're aligned on enough things that I don't think he's going to be able to play us against each other."

"I hope not." My eyes blinked. "I sometimes wonder if he's so enthusiastic about me adopting him because he still has the out that I'm not his real mother."

Sid rolled onto his side and kissed my temple. "As someone who was raised by a woman who did not give birth to me, I can tell you motherhood does not have that much to do with bearing children. If what I've been told is true, it's not likely that the woman who did give birth to me would have been much of a mother. I told you. I was almost aborted and the only reason I'm here now is because abortions were illegal, and it would have been too easy to get butchered." He sighed and looked thoughtful.

"The funny thing is, as distant as Stella could be, there was something between us. There were times when I wondered if there was another reason behind her talking my mother out of that abortion."

I looked at him. "Sid, you've been talking a lot about your aunt lately. What is it? Are you regretting walking out on her?"

"I've regretted that since my first day in boot camp."

The reason Sid and his aunt were estranged was because he'd allowed himself to be drafted instead of going to Canada.

He looked at me. "It's probably a lot of what you and I are trying to build with Nick. A real family. I see you and Nick together and wonder if I could have had that. Probably not. Nick is very different from me that way, and you are nothing like Stella. She wasn't cold, just emotionally distant. And in many ways, I was the same. You, on the other hand, wear your heart on your sleeve, which is exactly what I need, and more to the point, exactly what Nick needs. Thanks to you, I finally learned that affection is not automatically tied to sex, and because Nick is learning that, maybe he won't be as loose as I was."

I curled up and laid my head on his shoulder. "Do you think that's why you slept around? To get the affection?"

He chuckled. "There were other compensations. But, yeah, having sex was about the only time I got any affection. Until you came along. I swear, Lisapet, there have been times when I needed one of your hugs more than I needed sex."

"Good," I whispered. "I love you, Sid."

"I love you, Lisa."

November 15 – 16, 1985

Racquetball and weights. Classes. Gun range practice. Martial arts practice. Piano practice. A legitimate drop that we sent Kathy on solo, and she managed perfectly. Tailing and evading tails. Kathy was also showing some genuine talent for tailing, and Jesse could spot one even faster than Sid could. He even made Nick once.

Writing work continued. Sid went to his orthopedist and was told his wrist was healed and he no longer needed his wrist brace. Nick went back to school and Maria told me later that he'd been hailed by some of his classmates as a hero. As much as I despised Maryann and Michael Dreyer, there was a part of me that felt sorry for their son, whose popularity had sunk to an all-time low. I was so proud of Nick for not letting the other kids bully Jason in spite of Jason not accepting it well.

It was, admittedly, hard trying not to wonder when and where the next attack would occur, but there wasn't much we could do about it. Even Carla Caponetti had stopped calling. The frustrating thing was that our best shot at finding who was out to get us would be when that person attacked again.

That Friday, right after lunch, Sid got frisky, and we got so involved, I was afraid I'd be late getting Nick from school. Jesse and Kathy had tickets to see the Lakers play the Clippers with Jesse's cousin and his wife. So, the two took off early to go to dinner before the game. Calling Kathy and Jesse Lakers fans is kind of understating it, and they'd been a little peeved that they'd already missed a few games that season, thanks to their training. As Sid and I cleaned up, he suggested we go out for the rest of the day and relax a little. So, I put on my favorite jeans and a turtleneck and vest, then got Motley on a leash and a pair of jeans and a t-shirt for Nick while Sid finished shaving and put on tight jeans, a blue sport shirt and his windbreaker-style jacket. It was more like a Members Only one, but his tailor had designed and made it specially for him. Nick was thrilled to see us and changed in the back seat of the car as we left L.A.

We took advantage of our early departure and drove up the coast to Santa Barbara, missing the worst of the traffic, and ate dinner at one of the outdoor restaurants on the pier there. Nick talked us into a walk on the beach, despite the November chill in the air, then went on an extended monologue about how oil spills in the area had affected the local sea life. He was a little disgusted by how much tar we found on our shoes and on Motley's paws when we got back to the car. We left Santa Barbara after nine and Nick and Motley promptly fell asleep in the back seat. Sid got off the 101 freeway as we left Oxnard and took California 1 (aka Pacific Coast Highway) even though it would take longer to get home.

"What are you thinking about?" he asked, glancing at me between swerving around cars.

"Oh, just wishing we could have stayed all weekend in Santa Barbara." I sighed as I looked out the window. "It would probably be safer and certainly more relaxing."

"I know. But we've got the trauma center fundraiser tomorrow night."

I made a face. "Oh, goody. Just what I want to do, go to a big gala to stand around and smile at strangers."

"Okay, I get that they're not that much fun for you, but they are important." Sid smiled.

"I know. That's why we're going." I blinked back tears.

Sid gets invited to a lot of fundraising galas. Before we became a couple, I'd get a few invites here and there, but I happily and quickly turned them down flat. The only event I went to was the one for the Los Angeles Public Library foundation, and that was mostly because I usually volunteered to help coordinate.

Sid, on the other hand, is the darling of the fundraising set. He is a very generous man, and he not only buys tickets, he sponsors tables, bids up silent auction items, and otherwise spends money like there's no tomorrow, which gets all the other guys at the event donating like crazy.

"They're not that much fun for me," Sid said.

"Not anymore," I grumbled.

"Honey, they never were."

I just looked at him. That previous June, when I'd brought Sid with me to the library wingding, I found out there was another reason why he was so popular.

He chuckled guiltily. "Okay, they had their fun moments." He glanced at me again. "Are you afraid I'm going to start offering my former usual inducement to donating?"

Which involved a lot of bored women with money and the kind of fun he and I were usually having at night.

"No." I half-chuckled. "It's just being at a gala. I mean, it was funny last June when Patricia got all excited when you showed, then got upset when she realized you weren't doing the inducement thing anymore. But I was still bored out of my mind and nervous and all that. And I'm sorry, Sid, but last September did not help."

That one had been just awful. Sid had promised the previous winter to be on the coordinating committee for the event supporting music in public schools, another cause he supports heavily. He'd told the organizers later that summer that he was bringing his fiancée and would not be up to his usual antics, and the organizers were, as it turned out, fine with that. The female donors were not.

Worse yet, Sid had talked me into wearing my red-sequined formal. It has a turtleneck and long sleeves, but it is backless, and for some reason that dress gets him even more steamed up than usual. [How could you have missed how amazingly sexy you looked in that dress? And even now you still don't see how sexy you are. – SEH] It was bad enough having to be social with a bunch of people I didn't know. But then all these nice society matrons kept looking daggers at me.

I shuddered at the memory.

We were coming into Malibu, so Sid pulled into a parking lot overlooking the beach and the black ocean dotted by white caps here and there, glinting in the faint light of the new moon and the stars.

"What?" I asked.

Sid softly opened the driver's door. "Come on. Let's talk this out where we don't have to worry about waking Nick."

"But..." I nodded toward the back seat.

"We'll stay where he can see us if he wakes up."

I slid out of the car, softly shutting the door, and met Sid at the car's nose. He pulled me close to him, the wind whipping around us, whistling as the waves crashed on the sand and the salt air filled our noses.

"Now, what's going on?" he asked me. "It's just a party."

"I hate big parties." I blinked back tears. "All those people I don't know that are probably judging me because that's what people at big parties do, especially the people at galas. I've always hated small talk. I'm not any good at it and I'm always afraid I'm going to say something stupid. Worse yet, I get so bored smiling at people and listening to speeches. I don't have your grace and style."

"No. You have your own."

"I suppose."

"My darling, sweet Lisapet." Sid squeezed me even tighter. "Did it ever occur to you that the reason I was up to my hips in hanky panky at those galas was because I was just as bored and tired of small talk?"

"You're a lot better at hiding it than I am." I shrugged. "I mean, I'm getting to where I can tell when you're putting up a front. But, honestly, Sid? You've always had that kind of easy self-confidence, as if you don't have anything to prove."

His chuckle sounded rueful. "Oh, I've had plenty to prove in my time, especially when you consider how small I am."

"Does that bother you?"

"Being small?" Sid shook his head. "Not usually. For one thing, I'm not that small, except where it supposedly counts, and fortunately, I had already proven my manhood conclusively before I found out that size was supposed to make a difference."

"I seem to be missing something."

Sid kissed the side of my head. "Don't worry about it. You will never know the difference."

"About what?"

He suddenly laughed. "I had to bring it up. Oh, well. Remember back in May, and you first got your hands—"

"Yeah. Okay, I was surprised it got that big." I felt my face flushing even as the wind cooled it.

"That was the nicest thing you could have said to me."

"Why?"

"Because compared to most other men, my equipment is considered undersized."

"So what? Like you said, I'll never know the difference. And, Sid, you are so sexy and, given your reputation, how could you have gotten it if size made a difference? I know people make jokes about it, but I never understood why."

"And you're absolutely right." He laughed and squeezed me even tighter. "It doesn't make any difference. But unfortunately, there are a lot of people who think that a man's virility is determined by the size that he comes with."

"That's silly."

"True. But I couldn't help being a little worried that you'd fall into that trap. You have no idea how tired I got of hearing, 'That's all?' Every time it happened, I had to prove myself and that always takes work. I didn't think that would happen with you, but it was there in the back of my mind. I have enough trouble living up to the legend."

"You do quite nicely." I nudged him playfully, then grew serious. "And, really, Sid. I don't want a legend. I want you."

"Thank you for that." His hand cupped my face, and he kissed me. As he pulled away, he leaned his forehead on mine. "My dear sweet Lisa, you are so loving and kind and generous and intelligent."

"All the things I love about you, Sid. I just wish I'd said it first."

"And I wish that you could see just how wonderful you really are. No matter what you believe about yourself, you have incredible grace and style. Even I couldn't tell how bugged you were last September. In fact, I didn't know how much you hate those kinds of parties until you told me just now." He smiled and shrugged. "Although, I suppose I could have figured it out. I just forget a lot of the time how shy you really are."

"Does this mean we can skip tomorrow?"

He winced. "We already said we'd go, so unless we get an emergency, I'm afraid we should."

It was too bad that an emergency was exactly what we got.

It was sometime between midnight and one a.m. when we got back to the condo. We woke Nick up just long enough to get him and Motley upstairs. Sid helped our boy get ready for bed while I washed my face and got out of my clothes. I was asleep by the time Sid got into bed.

Urgent beeping woke me up. I couldn't tell what time it was, but I had not been asleep that long. Sid was already out of bed and had the gun he kept in his nightstand in his hands. Motley growled from Nick's room, where he was sleeping

"Intruder," Sid whispered.

I looked up at the box above the bedroom door. A small light glowed red. I shook the sleep from my head. I grabbed my robe from the hook in the closet and pulled my snubbed-nose revolver from my nightstand. Sid was wearing his jeans, as always. We flanked the bedroom door, listening.

Someone was in the condo. We heard him bump into something and softly curse. I stood on the side of the door that opened and Sid, on the other side, had his hand on the knob. I go through first because I'm the better shot. I tightened the robe around me and nodded. Sid slowly opened the door. I rolled silently into the living room. Light from the street leaked in through the drawn blinds, but it was still very hard to see. The dark form bent over the dining room table.

I just barely heard Sid hiss under Motley's whining. I braced for a shot and shut my eyes. The intruder groaned as the light made him recoil. I opened my eyes. The man in the knit mask tried to aim his good-sized automatic at us but realized that no matter which of us he shot, the other of us would shoot him.

"Drop the gun," Sid snarled, slowly advancing on him. "On your knees, hands on your head."

The intruder complied, but then another man, also masked, burst through the open front door into the condo. He drew back as he saw me draw a bead on him. His partner dove for the gun he'd dropped, but Sid let off a round into the floor.

"Drop the gun, now." I snarled.

The second man pulled back but didn't drop his gun. I shot the wall next to him.

"The next one goes into your kneecap," I told him. "Drop the gun."

He did and a second later, a smallish white form dodged all four of us, scooped up the two guns and disappeared into the back of the condo. Motley remained in Nick's room but barked loudly.

"Face down," Sid barked. "Both of you. Hands out in front of you."

The two men complied. Sid shot me a glance, and I went over to the desk, my snub-nose still at the ready. Kathy and Jesse appeared in the doorway, both carrying Model Thirteen revolvers.

"Hey, we've got the cavalry here," Sid said, his tone almost jovial.

I picked up the phone and dialed quickly.

"Code nine," I told the person who had answered and gave her the address.

Code nine meant there was an arrest to be made, and since we were undercover operatives, we couldn't do it. We do, technically, have the power to arrest, and I don't mean a citizen's arrest. We just don't use it because we're undercover.

I tossed a roll of strapping tape from my desk at Kathy, then pulled a roll of duct tape out as well. With Jesse and Sid covering us, we bound the intruders' hands behind their backs with the tape. When we heard the elevator ping, all of us hid in Sid's and my bedroom. The Feds made short work of the intruders as Motley whined and barked some more.

As soon as the special agents had taken the intruders away, Sid tried to close the front door to the condo. It didn't really work. The intruders had drilled around the dead bolt lock and gotten it open that way.

"Nick!" Sid called. "Please bring those guns out here."

Nick showed up, wearing a robe, at least. I knew vaguely that he'd taken on his father's habit of sleeping in the raw. Okay, my recently adopted habit, too. It was more than a little ironic that Sid was the only one in our little family who wore clothes to bed, and he only wore a pair of jeans to protect me from his bodily fluids. Except for the saliva, and by the time we realized he may have been exposed to the AIDS virus, it had been way too late to protect me from that. [That's right. They didn't prove that saliva didn't transmit the disease for another year, right? - SEH]

"The cats are out," Nick said as I blinked.

All four of the kittens had escaped, but fortunately, hadn't gotten into the elevator with the Feds and the prisoners, which surprised me a little since Fritz had been known to slide into an open elevator when he could. We got the kittens rounded up and Kathy and Jesse put all four in their guest room. Long John stayed shut in Nick's room with Motley.

"So, what happened at your place?" Sid asked Jesse and Kathy once I'd put Nick back to bed.

"They drilled our door the same way they did yours," Jesse said.

"The weird thing is," Kathy said. "As soon as the guy saw us, he bolted. We didn't even get to draw our guns. Jesse and I weren't sure what to do. Then we heard the commotion at your place and came over. He obviously came here."

Sid frowned, thinking. "So, the guy didn't give a damn about you."

"Not as far as we could tell," said Jesse.

"Interesting." Sid glanced my way, but I was either too tired or I really didn't get what that meant.

Sid may be hard to wake up out of a sound sleep, but he wakes up fast, especially compared to me.

"Can we think about this in the morning?" I asked, then realized we were pretty close to that already. I yawned. "Okay, maybe later this morning?"

"That would not be a bad idea," Sid said. He looked at Kathy and Jesse. "Would breakfast at ten work?"

Kathy yawned. "Ten? Okay. It should. Maybe."

Jesse laughed. "Come on, lover. We'd better try and get some sleep."

Sid tossed him the roll of duct tape, but Jesse tossed it back.

"I got some," Jesse said with a grin.

Sid duct taped our door closed and reset the alarm wiring while I staggered back to bed. I was just upset enough that I didn't fall back to sleep until Sid slid under the covers next to me.

"Any good landing?" I whispered. His response was filthy.

He was awake at some obscenely early hour, as usual. [I slept in until seven-thirty, which I get is still obscenely early to you. - SEH] I was almost alert by ten when Henry arrived, along with Kathy and Jesse. We sent Nick over to Kathy and Jesse's condo to watch TV, although that really did not help. Nick knew we were in trouble. He'd helped by retrieving the guns the intruders had dropped. I tried to reassure him that we grownups needed to talk things over so that we could protect him better, but part of the problem was that he wasn't worried about his own safety. He was worried about Sid and me.

"We'll be alright, son," Sid told the boy. "But we need to have our conference so that we can make that happen, and it's hard for us to concentrate when you're worrying about us. I understand why you do, and that's fair. But for us to make sure you're okay and that we're okay, we need you to do something else. I'm sorry about that."

Nick looked at me, blinking his eyes. It took everything I had to hold firm.

"Your father's right," I said. "We'll let you know what's happening just as soon as we can. I promise."

Nick slunk off to Kathy and Jesse's condo and turned up MTV really loudly.

"You can't make that promise," Sid growled.

"Yes, I can."

Sid backed off. [Hell, yes. You went all mama bear on me. Okay, you were also right. - SEH]

None of us was in a good mood, but it really did not help when Sid said that we were leaving the area.

"You can't do that," Henry growled.

"We can't stay here," Sid shot back. "They know where we live."

"How the hell did that happen?" Henry all but yelled.

"I have no idea."

Kathy, Jesse, and I watched the two of them as if we were watching a tennis match.

Sid continued. "And we have a lead in Carla Caponetti."

"She's clean," Henry groaned.

"On paper," Sid countered. "That doesn't mean squat, and we both know it. Look, Henry, they tried both condos, so they must not have known which one was ours.

When the guy found Kathy and Jesse, he ran. That's got to tell us something."

"And what about Kathy and Jesse?" Henry jerked his thumb. "They're still green."

"We're up for it," Jesse said.

Kathy did not look at all certain that she was.

"It doesn't matter," said Sid. "They've got all the basic stuff down. That's all they need right now. Lisa and I need to find out who's coming after us. It's not going to help them improve their skills if Lisa and I are dead."

Henry groaned. Unfortunately, Sid was right. I did not want to think about that. Kathy looked worried, but Jesse held her tight.

"Where are you going?" Henry asked.

"South Florida," said Sid. "About the last place you'd expect to look for me."

"Sid," I said. "There's no reason I wouldn't be there. I have relatives, remember?"

"And when, besides that joke of a wedding, was the last time you visited them?"

I had to give him points on that one.

"It's our best lead," Sid said, glaring at Henry.

"You know, I could send a couple of special agents out to question her," Henry said.

Sid glared at him. "And we both know it wouldn't turn up anything useful. Lisa and I are hip deep in this. We know the subtleties. We're the ones who stand the best chance of turning this around, and you know it."

Sadly, Henry did.

Our biggest problem at that point was Nick. We couldn't avoid that someone was out to get us, not after the attack on the condo and the fact that Sid and I were vacating the three of us to a hotel until we could get a flight to Miami. The problem was how much to tell our boy. I talked it over with Sid before we let Nick back into the condo and volunteered to take the lead on that conversation. It wasn't one either of us wanted to have with him, but it was unavoidable.

We called him in after Henry had left. Kathy and Jesse each gave him a hug, then went back to their place. I settled Nick onto the couch at our place and held him close to me. The kittens were still at Kathy and Jesse's, but Long John came over and curled up in Nick's lap.

"Sweetheart, you've figured out that things are getting scary for your dad and me," I told him.

"What's going on?" he asked.

"There is someone who wants to hurt your dad and probably me, as well," I told him. "We don't know who. That's the problem. It's hard for us, Nick. We don't want you worrying, especially when it's not that serious. On the other hand, we don't want to fib and keep you out of things."

He closed his eyes and gasped a few times. "I'd rather know what's going on."

"Even if it makes you worry more than you should?"

"I always— worry." His voice broke, and he flushed a little.

"Oh, my sweet guy. I know you do. Your dad and I, we just don't want to make it worse." I sighed. "Only now, it's kinda worse. The good news is that we're taking you with us."

"Really?"

"Yeah. We're going to see my parents."

His eyes lit up. "Grandma and Grandpa?"

"Yeah." I wasn't entirely enthused, but Sid had made a good argument that the two guys who had come after us in the condo hadn't been in the least interested in Kathy and Jesse. "We're hoping that the bad guys aren't interested in them and will leave us alone long enough to investigate the one lead we have."

Nick sighed. "It's not for sure."

"No, but it's better than sitting around here volunteering for target practice."

Nick shuddered and, truth be told, so did I.

November 17 – 20, 1985

We spent the night at a hotel in Los Angeles, with Kathy and Jesse offering to take care of our animals yet again. Early that Sunday morning, Sid, Nick, and I sat at LAX waiting for a flight to Miami. That we were coming in to spend some time with Mama and Daddy had Mama waxing ecstatic.

"You sure your mother's not going to wonder about us taking Nick out of school to visit?" Sid asked as we sat near the gate. "I mean, why wouldn't she?"

I shook my head. "They always took Mae and me out of school for vacations. They work in the tourist industry. The only time we could get away was the off-season, which usually meant when school was in session. Now, can we work on the wording for the invitations?"

"Sure. Why not?"

We came up with something that we thought Mama would go for, which I wrote down and stuck with the sample invitations I brought with us.

I hadn't told Mama exactly when we would land so that Sid could get away with renting a car for us. If I had, Mama and Daddy would have been at the airport with their car and that would have made getting around awkward.

Thanks to the time change, we showed up at their motel near the edge of Everglades National Park late that afternoon. Mama and Daddy have a little apartment behind the main desk, although they have employees to watch the desk during the busy afternoon and overnight times. Truth be told, the motel pretty much runs itself, which is how my parents set it up. Daddy had, however, taken over one of the barbeques in the motel's courtyard that day. The scent of smoking pork meat made me happy as Mama led us to the two connected rooms on the bottom floor of the motel where we would be staying.

"Ribs?" I asked her.

"Shoulder," she said. "And your daddy has made his extra spicy sauce.

I sighed. "This is going to be good."

Sid looked at me curiously, but declined to say anything, for which I was grateful. Sid does not eat red meat, and given how tetchy his system can be, I'm willing to give him points on that. But Daddy's pulled pork, smoked all night and day, with the extra spicy sauce. It wasn't as good as Sid usually made me feel, but it was getting there.

We got settled in, then went to my parents' apartment for dinner. Sid tried the pork and agreed with me that it was pretty amazing. He loved the sauce, too. Sid, Daddy, and I really love anything that will sear our nose hairs. Nick and Mama were less enthused, but there was a milder sauce as well to accommodate them.

We spent the rest of the evening kicking back around the motel's pool, chatting and otherwise relaxing. Nick was excited because Daddy was taking us ocean fishing the next day. Sid confessed that he wasn't interested. Mama reached over to Sid.

"You and I will find a perfectly lovely way to spend our day," she told Sid.

I grimaced. I had a bad feeling that perfectly lovely way would involve Sid's and my wedding and probably a concession or two that Sid and I didn't really want to make, but there was no help for it. It wasn't like Sid didn't know what Mama could do. [For once, she was fine. - SEH]

The ocean fishing trip, however, was a monumental success. Nick even won the fisherman's pool when he reeled in a monster bass. I was so proud of him. The only downside was that the prize was a case of beer. Nick hated beer. Daddy proudly took custody of the case, and I took custody of the cleaned fish. Thank God, Mama figured we'd have something for the grill that night. [Bullshit. She had a bunch of chicken thighs in the fridge, just in case. - SEH]

I was ecstatic when, back in our room, I told Sid about Nick's prize.

"Oh, the poor kid," Sid said.

"You want to hear how he caught it?"

Sid smiled. "Not really. I'm sure Nick will want to tell me himself, and I really don't need to hear it twice."

"Sid." I sighed. "Why is it that all the things I like you don't?"

"That's not true."

"You hate backpacking, horse riding. You don't like fishing."

Sid shrugged. "You don't like opera, cooking, or antiques. We're even. Besides, there are a lot of things we do like together. We love theatre."

"True."

"We like ballet, fine food, movies, long romantic walks, and certain sexual activities." He grinned lecherously at me.

I giggled. "And there's also Bach and Shakespeare and our kitties and our dog."

"Good wine and sitting in front of a fireplace." He held me close.

"And necking and breaking into buildings."

He laughed. "That is kind of fun, isn't it?" He looked at me. "You really like our side business, don't you?"

"Yes." I shrugged. "It definitely has its unpleasant side, but then, so do most things. It certainly makes life more interesting."

"It does at that."

"Do you like it?"

Sid looked pensive. "I don't know. Liking it or not never really made a difference. I had no choice, so I did it. If I were given the opportunity to get out of it, I'd seriously consider it." He looked at me. "On the other hand, last summer, when you suggested we go on Code Five status for Nick's sake, I hated that idea." He shrugged. "I guess what I always resented was that I was given no choice. Now, it's such a part of me, I can't imagine life without it."

"I can." I snuggled up close to him. "It would be boring." I made a face. "It's no fun having someone after us. But it's better than being in boring jobs."

"You're probably right, sweetheart."

We went to the courtyard arm in arm. Daddy had the grill ready to go, with bass fillets seasoned and at the ready.

"Well, Sid," Daddy called as he saw us. "You showed up just in time. Need someone to help me drink up all this beer your son won for us."

"Too bad it's not Champagne," Nick complained, never mind that there was an open bottle of beer in front of him at the picnic table next to the grill.

"Don't mind if I do," Sid said, grabbing a bottle from the cooler full of ice that Daddy had set up.

I took a bottle, as well, and twisted the cap off. I'm not overly fond of beer, but every now and then it tastes okay. Even Mama was drinking from a bottle.

It turned into one rowdy night. Daddy, who is a really large man, had to dare Sid to match him on the beer. Sid pointed out that his heavy drinking days were long past him, and that he did not have Daddy's larger size to help sustain him. Daddy just laughed.

We all enjoyed the grilled bass with Mama's insanely delicious cole slaw and pan-fried potatoes. Nick conked out in the middle of his second beer.

"It's too bad Malcolm O'Malley ain't here," Daddy chortled shortly after Nick passed out. "He's Neil's daddy, Sid."

"I have heard the name," Sid replied.

"We both went to Columbia University, up in New York City." Daddy settled back into story-telling mode. "That there Irish lush could out drink the entire pledge class of Nineteen Forty-Nine. Hell, he out drank all the other classes, too. Malcolm and me, we used to take the subway to lower Manhattan, find all the gin joints, and make bets that Malcolm could drink three boilermakers in a row and still stay standing. And Malcolm would be half-crocked to begin with. We damned near paid our school fees on those bets."

I could tell Daddy'd had a few. He's usually pretty quiet. But then Daddy told the story about the time he and Malcolm had gotten tanked and put a No Parking sign in Mama's dorm room. I still don't know why the sign wouldn't fit through the room door, and apparently, Daddy and Malcolm didn't know, either. By the time they sobered up, neither of them could remember how they'd gotten it in there in the first place. Which meant they had no idea how to get it out.

Sid was a touch lubricated, himself, and launched into a tale about his more infamous high school days, namely the speech he gave as class valedictorian. Um. Let's just say that Sid's talent for double entendre was already well-developed at that point in his life. He apparently began the speech, exhorting his fellow students to begin the rest of their lives with a bang, and then finished with something so filthy Daddy choked on his beer, he was laughing so hard.

"I don't understand," Mama said. "That was a perfectly lovely allusion."

Sid laughed really hard.

"Althea, honey," Daddy said, wiping his eyes. "He weren't talking getting up at dawn with the roosters."

Mama thought about it, then suddenly gasped and swatted Sid. "That was disgusting, young man. How in Heaven's name did you get away with it?"

"My English teacher, Mrs. Gridley, vetted the speech and didn't get it, either," Sid said, chuckling.

"I'm surprised they let you give the speech," Daddy said.

Sid shook his head. "Well, that was kind of the problem the school had. Me and my friends, we were all the best and the brightest. There were only three people who had a higher GPA than I did. Loser Renfrew had the highest."

"Loser?" Mama asked. "What a horrible nickname."

"It was better than his real name." Sid frowned, trying to remember. "It was Louis. Even his mother called him Loser. Anyway, the administration didn't want him doing the speech because they couldn't count on him not to make trouble. The same with Liz Warner, who had the next highest grade average. She was always mouthing off and becoming a radical feminist, too. Plus, she was easy with the boys. Tom Freeman was next and was an All-American. Football, basketball. But they couldn't count on him to be sober. So, that left me next in line, with Wallace Merton, Stan Ford, and Bob Kinney after me. Stan and Bob were both jocks." Sid took a pull on his beer. "All six of us guys totally looked establishment, but just radical enough to be with it. I was the most sober of the group, and that isn't saying much. The rest of them were the biggest boozers and potheads I have ever met in my life." Sid chuckled and shook his head. "This one Saturday afternoon, Loser tells us he's got a case of whiskey in the trunk of his mom's car. I'm almost positive he stole it somehow. But it was something else. A whole case of Wild Turkey bourbon whiskey. Well, that settled it. We had to have a party. Bob's dad and his wife were out of town, so we went to his place. Stan and Wallace somehow contrived to get six absolutely huge pizzas, and Tom came up with a butt load of roaches. I'm not talking the bugs. I confess, I do not remember how many he had, but it was a lot of grass. There was only one thing missing. Girls. Naturally, they looked to me, and I admit I had a certain prowess in procuring females. But I ask you, where does one go to get six to however many girls to spend the night with six tanked up, stoned, horny guys for a party in fifteen minutes?"

"I have no idea where," said Mama.

"Everywhere," Sid said, laughing. "I pulled strings I didn't even know I had. But we had plenty of girls. I think the ratio was something like four to one. I made it at least six times that I remember, and with a different girl each time."

"Six times?" Daddy stared in amazement. "How the hell did you do that?"

Sid shrugged. "I was sixteen." He paused. "And the party lasted until Monday evening. It must have been a holiday weekend. Or was it during the summer? I think we emptied the Kinney's fridge, too. I know I also drank and smoked myself into oblivion at least twice."

"That must have been some hangover," Mama said.

Sid winced. "I was sick for a week after, and I think the other guys were, too."

We didn't finish the case of beer, but we put a good dent in it. Nick was the only one feeling perfectly well that next morning. Daddy was in the worst shape, with both his head banging and his stomach queasy. Mama was better. Sid had a nasty headache. He was mildly perturbed that I had escaped with only some gas and mild nausea. The funny thing was, I'd ended up drinking more beer than he had.

"What did you guys do all last night?" Nick asked over breakfast in my parents' apartment.

"Told stories," Mama said.

"And I missed them?" Nick pouted.

"Son," Daddy said, wincing. "Maybe when you're older. Stories about the dumb things you did when you were young and stupid are only funny when you're no longer young and stupid."

Nick frowned. "I'm not stupid."

"No, you're not," I said. "Just inexperienced, and that's what Grandpa means."

Mama and Daddy had work to do that day, which was just as well. On the pretext of seeing some of the sights, Sid and I took Nick with us. We all three were wired. Not that it did much good. Carla Caponetti didn't leave her house in Coral Gables. It was a huge pink stucco house, with white columns in front, and a perfectly manicured lawn surrounding it. The neighborhood was full of big, fancy houses and manicured lawns, so we'd had to be careful, shifting where we parked every so often, so the neighbors didn't call the police on us.

"Think it'd be worth bugging her place?" Sid asked as we drove back to the motel.

"How are we going to monitor it?" I asked.

Sid glanced at Nick in the rearview mirror. "We might be able to get some support on that. I'll have to make a call."

"Why don't we wait?"

Sid nodded.

The next day, Nick got a workout. Carla, a tallish woman with some decided rolls around her middle, went all over the Coral Gables area. As I watched, I wondered if she could have been the woman on the roof top a couple weeks before. We followed as she got her blond hair re-poufed and re-glued at a beauty salon, then did some shopping. Around three, she met my Aunt Amanda at a local restaurant, which put a fast end to our tailing operation. Sid waited until we'd gotten back to the motel.

"Odds on how Caponetti got our personal information?" Sid asked me as he soaped up for his second shave.

We were alone in our room. Nick and Daddy were off doing something or other.

"I'd say better than good." I frowned and leaned against the door to the tiny bathroom. "It would explain those two guys breaking into both condos, looking for us. Mama's been there. She may not know the address, but I bet she remembered the cross street and what floor we're on. And there are only two condos per floor in that building."

"That would make a lot of sense." Sid paused to shave his under his nose. "Your mother would have no reason not to share the information with your aunt."

I sighed. "I'd better give Mama one. The last thing we need is that kind of leak." Something else occurred to me. "Sid, remember that conversation I overheard at Maggie's wedding that I wanted to check out, only Nick got sick?"

"What was that about?" Sid rinsed his razor and started in on his right cheek.

"That's just it. They didn't name names. But Aunt Marie and Aunt Amanda were going on about Nick and about how much you and he looked like this somebody. I'm wondering if that was Mama's old boyfriend. Amanda also said that 'she' looked like this person and his father, and that somebody else, a woman, was not going to be happy about it."

Sid raised an eyebrow. "If that's how Caponetti is connected to me, it would be one of the most bizarre coincidences ever recorded."

"But things like that do happen. Look at how Mama and Daddy met."

"True." He paused to shave the cleft in his chin.

"And Mama was so startled when she first saw you. Remember?"

Sid thought about it. "I guess. Come to think of it, I remember her asking me if we'd met before."

"Do you have any idea what your mother's real name was?"

Sid sighed. "Absolutely none." He rinsed and scraped away at his left cheek.

"Well, I'd better go talk to Mama about spreading around our personal information."

"Yeah, you'd better. Listen, you okay with us taking your folks to dinner tonight?"

"Sure. That sounds like fun."

I found Mama in the motel office.

"Oh, Lisle, honey, I'm so glad you're here. We need to get you registered for your wedding presents."

"We're not registering, Mama." I folded my arms across my chest. "I agreed we won't say no gifts on the invitations. But we don't need gifts and don't really want them, okay?"

"But, Lisle, everybody's already asking."

"If they ask, you can tell them we don't want anything. If I read it right, presuming people will bring things is the part that's rude."

"Still, do you really want to let the relatives come up with their idea of a good present?"

"We'll just have to risk it." I winced because she had a point. "I'm sure we can find somebody who wants a stuffed and mounted baby gator."

Sid walked into the office at that point and blanched. "A what?"

"One of Mae's wedding presents." I turned on Mama. "And Mae was registered for gifts."

"Landsakes. Why do you have to be so difficult?"

"Because you're being difficult."

She looked at the two of us. "Both of you say no?"

"Both of us," said Sid.

She sighed deeply.

"One other thing, Mama." I took a deep breath and hoped Sid would get what I was going for. "Um. Has Aunt Amanda been asking you for information about Sid and me?"

"Well, she did ask me for your house address, not the mailbox, right after Maggie's wedding, so I gave it to her. You know. For the thank you note." Mama shrugged, then cocked her head. "Come to think of it, a week or so back, Amanda wanted to know where you two were staying since you weren't living in your house yet. I told her I didn't know the address but told her what corner your building was on and what floor. Hm." Mama paused and thought it over. "I don't think I ever told Amanda you two had moved out of your house 'cause of the remodeling. I wonder how she knew that."

"Carla Caponetti, perhaps?" I asked. "We almost ran into Aunt Amanda today and she met with a woman Amanda called Carla. And there's been a Carla Caponetti who's been trying to get a hold of us, only she refuses to leave a message."

"Why would Amanda tell Carla—" Mama looked at Sid and put her hand to her mouth. "Oh, dear!"

"What's the matter, Mama?" I asked.

Mama shook her head. "It's a really long story and I gotta get dinner made."

"We'll take you and Bill out, Althea," Sid said, watching her carefully. I strongly suspected he was feeling as flustered as Mama was acting. [More than. - SEH]

"Th-that would be very nice, Sid." Mama swallowed. "But we are not going to talk about this until Nick has gone to bed. 'Tisn't a nice story at all."

I do not know how we got through dinner and a trip to the beach for Nick's sake without bringing up Carla Caponetti, but we did. Mama and I put Nick to bed in his motel room. Nick could tell something was up, but the look I gave him reminded him not to say anything.

Mama and I went back to the apartment living room, where Sid and Daddy were waiting for us. Mama got us all settled in, with Sid and me on the couch and her sitting in the chair closest to Sid. Daddy had gotten some more of Nick's beer out, although there were four shot glasses and a jug of Grandma Caulfield's corn liquor on the coffee table, as well. He settled into a chair across from us.

Mama took a deep breath. "Sid, honey, you said your mama's name was Sheila, right?"

"Yes." Sid seemed to be holding his breath.

"Then I think I know who your mama really was."

"Sheila Caponetti," Sid said softly.

Daddy leaned over and poured out corn liquor into the shot glasses.

"I'm afraid so, honey." Mama looked away. "It's not a very nice story at all. I had a boyfriend my senior year of high school who looked very much like you. John Caponetti."

"Yes. Lisa's told me." Sid accepted a shot from Daddy.

Mama shot me a glare - I wasn't supposed to have told him - then turned back to Sid. "He had two sisters. One older, I don't remember her name. She was off at that fancy music school in New York when John and I were dating."

Sid sipped and nodded. "Stella went to Juilliard."

"And he had a younger sister named Sheila. She was two years behind me, and I didn't know her. The Caponetti family was one of the richest in the area. John's father, Salvatore was his name, he owned a fish processing plant, the only one for miles, plus a lot of real estate, as I recall. He was not a very nice man, and he had a way of, well, getting under other men's blankets, if you know what I mean. There was all kinds of cleft-chinned babies in this town what had no right to have 'em. I broke up with John right before I graduated from high school. He was in college, and it was fun dating an older boy. But then John got nasty one night. He'd wanted me to marry him and not go to college, and I told him I most certainly was going to college. He blew up and shoved me, and that scared me. Then he got very mean about me breaking up with him. Fortunately, my brothers, Steven and Leonard, made sure he didn't give me any more trouble." She smiled at Daddy. "Well, you know what happened when I went to New York. I met Bill, and we fell in love. We got married right after I graduated. We wanted to stay in New York but had to come back here to run his daddy's hotel for a while. Which is neither here nor there." She took a swig off her beer bottle. "I later found out that John's younger sister had gotten into trouble and that their father had kicked her out. Or that she'd run away. It doesn't make no difference. No one knew where she'd gone. Well, then Salvatore died in..."

"Nineteen seventy-two?" Sid asked. I knew that's when he'd inherited his money from a then nameless relative.

"No. I think it was the end of seventy-one. Mae was in her second year at Sacramento State and Lisle was in eighth grade. And Mae and Neil were engaged, but not married yet. There was quite a big fuss about the will, though. The estate had been split three ways, with one part going to John, another to his older sister, and another to Sheila's son."

"I knew that it had been split up," Sid said. "I wasn't supposed to know the name of the relative, though. Stella was supposed to tell me, only we were estranged by that point."

"Well, I only heard about all this from my mama since we'd already moved to Tahoe by then." Mama rolled her eyes. "She was still mad at me for breaking up with John. She wanted that money bad. Well, anyway. About four years ago, John Caponetti died. Now, I only know the rest of this from Amanda and Marie, so make of it what you will, but John's will stipulated that a pension be set up for his widow, Carla Caponetti, with the rest of the fortune and the family business going to his lone nephew. The only problem is that they didn't know your name. Carla had to make a good faith effort to find you within five years and if she couldn't, then she'd get everything. John and Carla never had any children, and it may have been John because he was just as loose as his daddy. Well, Amanda told me that the lawyers had decided that Carla wasn't making enough of an effort to find you. Then you and your son showed up at Maggie's wedding, of all things."

"So, that was what Marie and Amanda were talking about in the ladies' room that day." I sat up and looked at Sid. "I knew I should have tracked that conversation down."

Sid looked at me, then Mama. "And Amanda wanted our address right after the wedding."

"Yes, she did."

"Well," said Sid. He took a long sip of the corn liquor. "That's very interesting. Quite a coincidence."

Mama laughed. "Well, honey, this is South Florida. Wouldn't be the strangest thing to have happened."

November 21, 1985

"Nick?" Sid knocked on the connecting door between our rooms the next morning. "Can we come in, please?"

"Sure." Nick wore jeans and a t-shirt. A worried frown creased his face when he saw his father and me.

"It's good news," I told him. "We think we know who is trying to hurt us."

"Really?" Nick's mouth opened. "Like that Caponetti lady?"

"Exactly," said Sid. "So, we've got a really important job for you. We need you to distract your grandma and grandpa so your mother and I can check things out. Now, Grandma didn't want to talk about things last night in front of you for whatever reason, but we told her we saw no reason not to tell you. It appears, however, that you and I are probably related to the Caponetti family, which is why we got so many strange looks at that wedding last month."

"Wo—" Nick's voice both cracked and squeaked.

"Pretty strange, huh?" I said. "The problem is, there's a connection to our side business, which is why it's really important that you keep Mama and Daddy busy."

"When are you coming back?" Nick looked a little anxious.

"We don't know, but sometime tonight," Sid said with a smile. "We'll call as we can."

Nick nodded and hugged us, then hurried out to the apartment behind the office. We followed. Sid told Mama that given the revelations from the night before, he just wanted some time alone with me to think things through.

"I understand completely, honey. You take as much time as you two need." Mama smiled at Nick. "I'm sure Bill and I will have a perfectly lovely day with our little man."

As soon as we hit the parking lot of the motel, Sid tossed me the keys to the rental car. I headed for Coral Gables. We were both dressed casually in jeans and nice shirts. I had a vest over mine. Sid was wearing a white sport shirt but had a light blue Italian-cut blazer over it. We both had our transmitters on under our clothes.

"Okay," I said, pulling onto the highway. "So, how much of what you told Mama was cover versus what you're feeling about now?"

Sid smiled and sighed at the same time. "A most excellent question. It's pretty amazing, but it does explain a lot of things. Just not the most important one - who's coming after us?"

Daddy had also told us the night before that the Caponetti thing was probably why my Grandma Wycherly had refused to speak to Sid. She hadn't mentioned any names but had told him she did not want to see me marry into "that" family. Daddy just told her that Sid didn't have any relatives in the area, but that apparently hadn't mollified her. Sid and I had talked in our room for some time the night before and had reached no conclusions about Carla Caponetti or anything else.

We found a coffee shop close to the highway. Sid made a couple phone calls while I waited, then we got a booth and ordered breakfast.

"Well?" I asked.

"The Dragon agrees that Carla has one hell of a motive, but has no idea how she could be connected to our business. Systems said that there was an old code that came through right around the fifth of October, maybe after, but it looked legit, and she had been updating the caller, per the usual protocols. That, of course, is no longer happening. But there's also no way to tell who was using the old code. Both the Systems woman and the Dragon are doing some digging and not finding much. All they know is that the caller is female. Henry's thinking that if it is Carla, she must have some help somewhere. That would account for her being clean and having no connection to the business."

Sid pulled back as the waitress came by with fruit salad and whole wheat toast for him, pancakes, eggs, bacon, sausage, and hashed browns for me. I also had a cup of tea. Sid had his usual prune juice and stirred some Metamucil into his water glass and knocked it back.

"You doing okay, system-wise?" I asked, digging into my breakfast.

"Well enough." Sid borrowed my water glass to rinse his and drank again. "Just trying to avoid problems."

"So, do we confront Carla or not?"

Sid winced. "I have no idea. That whole business part of it makes things really tricky." His eyebrows rose. "I think

I've got an idea. What are the odds she knew we were tailing her yesterday?"

"She didn't act like it." I thought. "On the one hand, Nick is really good, so if she made one of us, I'm willing to bet she didn't make Nick. On the other hand, she could have made all three of us and didn't react because that would have given herself away."

"Why don't we tail her today? Depending on what happens, we'll see about planting a bug at her house."

"Sounds good."

Which is how Sid and I ended up spending all that morning and a good chunk of the afternoon, shifting positions around Carla's house. Around two, Carla's garage door opened, and she backed her Jaguar out onto the driveway and then the street. We waited just long enough for her to get around the corner of the housing tract where her place was located. Sid was taking his turn at driving.

The reality is, if a subject is looking for or expecting a tail, the odds are good the tail is going to be spotted. Even Nick, who is the best tail I know, gets made. That's why you need a full team changing clothes and their appearances to tail somebody effectively. On the other hand, if the subject is not expecting a tail or doesn't know what to look for, it's not hard at all to follow that person. Carla didn't seem to spot us. In fact, she wasn't even looking around. She drove to the downtown section of Coral Gables and found parking in a municipal lot, and left the car. Sid nodded toward a restaurant and bar near the lot.

"Catch you there if we need to split up?" I asked, getting out of the car.

"Around five?"

"Sure. I'll page you if it doesn't work."

"And I'll page you if anything changes." He winked at me.

I blew him a kiss.

Carla ambled down the street. I followed her from the other side. She didn't seem all that interested in the storefronts, and, in truth, the stores were pretty utilitarian, and the neighborhood was a bit run down, although it wasn't seedy. Sid stayed where he'd parked about a block down. We did a quick check to be sure we were broadcasting. Carla stopped in front of a store and glared at the window.

"Sylvester Music School," proclaimed the gold lettering on the window. "Piano - Strings."

Carla went inside the store, and I quickly crossed the street. In spite of Carla's height, she was not at all imposing. As I walked past the window, I noticed that the woman that Carla was talking to inside was very imposing. The second woman was on the short side with dark gray wavy hair cut just above her shoulders. The face looked vaguely familiar.

"You got something?" Sid's voice asked in my ear.

My heart stopped. "Uh, yeah. I'm going to go inside. If Caponetti comes out, can you take her?"

"Sure."

"See you at the restaurant at five-thirty. I'm tuning out." I switched off the transmitter before Sid could object.

I desperately hoped Sid would trust me, and as it turned out, he did. Taking a deep breath, I went inside the store.

"You sure you don't want his address?" Carla was telling the other woman.

"I don't need it," the woman said. Bright blue eyes flicked my way, and I smiled.

"But—"

"Carla, you have been in here at least once a week for the past month or so, and I have not changed my mind."

Carla sighed and flounced out of the shop. The space was crowded with four baby grand pianos and music stands next to pairs of chairs. Several bins of sheet music lined a side wall. There was an office in the back corner, which you could tell was an office because the bottom half of the wall was dry wall, and the top was glass windows. The other woman looked at me.

"How can I help you today?" she asked, her imposing nature not diminished a bit.

I swallowed. "Ms. Hackbirn?"

Her eyebrows rose. "Now, there's a name I haven't used in a long while."

"I need to talk to you."

"Why?" Her eyes turned on me, fierce and bright.

I almost fled. "I need to know why Ms. Caponetti is looking for your nephew."

She stiffened. "Why doesn't he ask her?"

"There are extenuating circumstances."

"Well, that's his problem. We haven't had a thing to do with each other since he was nineteen and I don't plan on changing that."

That got me angry. "Ms. Hackbirn, your nephew's life is in danger."

"Let him worry about it, then. He survived Vietnam without a scratch."

"Maybe not a physical one." I blinked and took a deep breath. "Don't you care at all?"

She winced. "He doesn't care about me."

"How do you know?"

"Young woman, you are obviously assuming a great deal. I do not wish to discuss this. Will you kindly leave?"

"No!" I'll concede it had taken every last bit of nerve I had.

She stepped back, then swallowed. "Why are you pressing this?"

"Sid's life is in danger. Carla Caponetti has something to do with it. I need to know why she was talking to you."

She looked me over. "I'll wager it doesn't have anything to do with what you're talking about."

"Then tell me what it was."

"I don't care to."

That did it.

"Stella Hackbirn, there is someone out there trying to kill your nephew, the boy you raised. Don't you care about that? My god, he's your only living relative. Doesn't that mean anything to you?"

"No."

"What do you mean, no? For Heaven's sakes, he's for all practical purposes your son!"

She became very cold. "He was never *my* son."

"Of course he was. Is. You raised him. Just because you didn't give birth to him doesn't mean a thing."

"Oh, but it does." She turned away from me, her voice going a little flat. "You don't know what you're talking about. You don't know what it is to raise another woman's child."

"But I do know." I closed my eyes, then opened them again. "I'm doing it right now. Worse yet, he remembers his mother. She only died last summer. And you want to know something else? I'm raising that boy knowing darned well I can't have one of my own."

The downward shift of her shoulders was subtle but clear. "Maybe you would understand." She looked at me, Sid's brilliant blue eyes piercing me to the core. She pointed to a nearby chair. "Sit down." I sat, and she sat in the chair next to me, her face almost twitching. "You see, I wanted a child. I had a lover, a young man who was everything to me. We wanted to prove to the world that relationships were better without contracts and priests. So, we decided to have a child together." She blinked but kept her voice even. "Nothing happened. Finally, we lied about being married to the Free Clinic. The doctor there told me I was sterile. I couldn't have children. My lover said it was just as well. But it wasn't for me. We were both at Juilliard then. He got a chance to study in Vienna. I wanted to finish my degree. So, he left without me. Then, after I was out of school and was teaching, Sheila turned up."

"Your sister."

"Yes. She was pregnant and wanted an abortion. I couldn't let her do it." She gazed off into space. "I wanted a baby so badly and here was my chance. It wasn't mine, but close enough. When Sid was born, Sheila wouldn't nurse him, wouldn't even name him. The nurse ended up naming him. Never could stand that name, but Sheila insisted. I guess she wanted revenge on him. Poor little thing. It wasn't his fault. Sheila didn't want anything to do with him. I did everything. The first thing that boy did was crawl out of my lap." She put up her hand. "I know now that toddlers do that, and Sid was the most curious boy, into everything." Her face softened, then she winced. "I still felt rejected. The only way I could reach that boy was through music. Finally, even that wasn't enough. I laid down the law, and he rejected it."

I sighed. "All those wasted years."

"Well, I did my best. I still failed him somehow."

"You were a raving success. Even he admits that." I bit my lip, afraid I'd given too much away.

"Don't worry." Stella chuckled bitterly. "You obviously know him and care about him."

"I love him."

She smiled. "They all do."

"Yeah. They did." I looked at her. "It's a lot different with him and me."

She looked away. "How is he?"

"Apart from our current problem, he's doing very well. We live in Los Angeles."

"I know that. Well, I didn't know you were there."

"I am." I debated explaining the situation but decided against it. "We're out here checking out this problem and visiting my folks."

"And the boy you're raising?"

"He's Sid's, but I'm adopting him."

"Sid get married?"

"No." I chuckled. "It was his usual brief affair. There was just a bad box of condoms involved." I shrugged. "Sid had no idea Nick existed until Nick was eleven."

"Why are you raising him?"

I flushed. "Things are different with Sid and me. We're committed to each other." I ducked my head. "We're getting married in March."

"I see." Her voice went flat again.

"We really love each other."

She nodded. "Love."

"It's not a lie. At least, it isn't for us."

"I guess not."

I closed my eyes, then looked at her. "Would you like to see him?"

"I don't know." She blinked again, but her voice remained flat. "I don't think I could take it again."

"He's been thinking about you a lot lately, and I know he regrets hanging up on you that time you called. He's told me that several times. It won't be easy for either of you. There's a lot of hurt on both sides. But I do think the time is ripe."

Stella squeezed her eyes shut, then relaxed them and nodded.

When we arrived at the restaurant, I realized we had a tactical problem almost immediately. Neither Sid nor I like sitting with our backs to the room, or especially, a door. So, I was not surprised to see Sid sitting in the restaurant bar with one eye on the foyer of the restaurant. The good news was that there was a second entrance on the restaurant's patio, so that's where I led Stella. We wove our way around the tables to where Sid was sitting, watching the front, a glass of what I had to guess was bourbon and water in front of him.

"Hey, lover," I said as I slid around to where he could see me.

"There you are," he replied with a happy grin.

He got up and gave me an all too brief kiss.

"I have someone with me," I said.

I gently turned him in Stella's direction. Honestly, I was not sure who was going to run first. I held my breath, and they both stayed put, although the look of shock on Sid's face was impressive.

"Hello, Stella," he managed to get out.

"Hello, Sid," she said, her voice also tight.

He looked at me frantically. "We're waiting for a table for two."

I put my hand on his arm. "We'll fix it when they call us."

"Uh, yeah. Right." He looked at her. "Stella, have a seat."

I pulled a chair over from another table as Sid seated his aunt.

"What would you like to drink?" Sid asked her awkwardly.

"Given the occasion, what's the highest alcohol content we can count on?" Stella replied.

"Vodka," Sid said and waved at the waitress.

He ordered three rounds of Stolichnaya vodka. Stella lifted her eyebrow.

"May as well go for the good stuff," Sid muttered.

Stella shrugged.

"How are you?" Sid asked.

"Well enough. You?"

"Reasonably well."

I almost started cursing. The hostess called us at that moment. I got up and dealt with the change to the table setting, then waved Sid and Stella over. Sid reached me first and took my arm.

"What the hell have you done?" he hissed through his teeth.

"Sid, she's just as scared as you are. But she came because she wanted to."

Sid sort of nodded, then we all followed the hostess into the restaurant. We got settled into the booth, but neither Sid nor Stella knew what to say to each other. So, we spent a lot of time talking about the weather. Finally, I brought up the subject of Nick.

"What's he look like?" Stella asked.

"Well, he's definitely mine," Sid said, a hint of a smile on his lips.

"Imagine Sid about this tall," I said, gesturing. "And he wears glasses."

"I've been wondering about that," Stella said, looking at Sid. "What happened to yours?"

"Contact lenses," Sid said.

"Still vain." Stella shook her head.

"True," said Sid. "But they have helped my vision and I get a better correction."

We went back to talking about the weather.

When the waiter came to ask us about dessert, I did order something exceptionally large and fattening. Stella just asked for a cup of coffee, then lifted an eyebrow when Sid declined as he usually did.

"No coffee?" she asked when the waiter had left.

"No," Sid said. "I swore off all that stuff a few years ago. I don't eat red meat, no salt, no refined sugars, caffeine, preservatives, artificial stuff. And I eat lots of whole grains, vegetables, and fruit. It does wonders."

"I can see no sweets," Stella said. "You never did like them that much. Never thought you'd give up your coffee habit, though."

"If I can find a good de-caf, I'll indulge." Sid shifted uncomfortably. "But I don't miss it."

The silence that followed was at least as awkward as the conversation about the weather.

"You know," I said, getting up. "I get the feeling I'm in the way. Why don't I call a taxi and get on back to my folks' place?"

"No!" both almost yelped.

They looked at each other and sat back nervously. Stella was the one to break the silence, however.

"Sid, you and I have got a lot to work through. On both sides."

Sid nodded. "You're right, Stella." He swallowed. "And I do want to work through it." He looked at me, then handed me the ticket for the valet. "Honey, take the car. I'd rather call the taxi."

I shrugged. "If you insist."

"I do." He looked at Stella. "Would you mind if I walked Lisa out?"

"By all means."

As the valet fetched the rental car, Sid pulled me into his arms. He was just barely trembling.

"I am scared to death," he whispered into my ear. "And I do not know how this is going to go. But thank you, Lisa. I don't know how you did it. I don't want to know. But I'm glad you did. I love you so much."

"I love you, too, darling."

He kissed me hard. Then the valet pulled up the rental car. He helped me into the driver's seat. I smiled at him.

"And you wonder why I believe."

He rolled his eyes, but kissed me again and went back inside the restaurant.

It was incredibly hard, but I didn't say anything about what had happened when I got back to my folks' place. Nick, fortunately, was focused on how Mama and Daddy had bought him a new train set and he couldn't wait to set it up in his new bedroom. Once Nick was in bed, I tried watching TV, but it was so inane I couldn't deal with it. Even the cable re-runs of the shows I'd loved when I was a teen annoyed me. I tried reading, but that didn't help either. Finally, around eleven, Sid slid into our room.

"Still awake?" he asked.

"What the heck did you think I'd be?"

He sighed and sank down onto the edge of the bed.

I slid up next to him. "You want a back rub?"

"I don't know. Not really. Oh, hell. I need something."

"You poor baby." I helped him out of his sport coat.

"Don't you want to know how it went?"

"I'm dying to, but I'm more worried about you at the moment."

Sid let out a very soft snort. "I have to say it went pretty well. She drove me here." He sighed and closed his eyes. "We're both still hurting. I mean, there's no way we could make up for all those years in one night. But there's something there." He winced. "I wish you hadn't told her we're getting married."

"Why not?" I started in the middle of his back, rubbing in a circular pattern.

"She's not happy about it."

"She didn't seem to mind when I told her."

"I get that." He looked, unseeing, at the wall in front of us. "She told me she was surprised I hadn't done it earlier."

"You're not that conventional."

"But I am that indifferent."

"And we both know that's not true."

"Yes." Sid frowned. "But not from Stella's perspective. She always saw me as having a strong need to be accepted, especially when I was in high school. She figures you're the first woman to insist on being quote, unquote, respectable. Then she said I ought to have the decency to quit leading you down the garden path." He looked at me. "She really likes you."

"And thinks I'm a sucker."

"She does, but you have to understand, Stella really believes that marriage and love are lies."

"And we know they're not."

"Well, yeah." He winced. "Lisapet, I believe that I am about to be repaid for every snide comment I have ever made about your difficulties standing up to your mother. I don't know that I was all that convincing. It wasn't you. It's just that, well, as a kid, I could back talk Stella with no problem. But I could never stand up to her convictions. That may be why she thought I was spineless. I've just now discovered that I still can't. I do believe that you and I are doing the right thing, but I found it really hard to say that to Stella. All I could say is that while marriage might be a lie for some, I believe in our marriage. I conceded that I was doing it for your sake, but that I believe it's the right thing to do."

"And what did she say?"

He rolled his eyes. "That it was about time that I developed some convictions." He sighed again. "That was the one thing that galled her more than anything else. My indifference."

I smiled. "And we both know that's when you care the most."

"I know." He shrugged. "I don't know if I was able to explain that to her. Maybe it got through anyway. She didn't seem unhappy."

"So, what's next? Are you two going to see each other again?"

"Tomorrow. She wants you to come, and she wants to meet Nick."

"That's a good sign."

"Yeah." He sighed. "I do want a continuing relationship with her. For some reason, it seems important right now. But why does she make me feel so damned nervous? I am a fully grown man. I have been on my own for over sixteen years and successful by almost any standard you choose. So, why do I feel like I don't measure up around her?"

"Possibly because your values have changed?" I pulled him close to me. "I can't explain it either, Sid. But I feel the same way around my mother, and I get the impression she feels the same way around hers."

"Perpetual childhood," he grumbled. "I hated being a kid."

I laughed. "I'm guessing you were never a kid. You were just a child-sized adult."

Sid snuggled closer. "At least you have faith in me."

November 22, 1985

S id had set up an early lunch meeting with Stella, so we had a little time after breakfast for Sid to almost completely lose it. I told Mama and Daddy right before breakfast what had happened the day before. Mama thought it was hysterical and pointed out again that we were in South Florida.

Sid was trying to help Nick get dressed for our lunch date. Nick is picking up his father's fussiness about his personal appearance, albeit in a different way. He was not happy with how Sid had trimmed the boy's hair that morning.

"You want a neat appearance," Sid growled at him.

"But I like my hair longer," Nick answered. "Why are you so weird this morning?"

"I'm fine. I just want you to make a good impression, is all."

Nick sighed deeply.

Then there was the tie. Nick didn't object to wearing it, just how Sid tied it on him.

"I can't breathe, Dad. It's too tight."

"Don't loosen it. You'll look slovenly."

That's when I stepped in.

"Sid, honey, come into our room, please."

Sid flashed me an angry glare but did as I asked. I shut the door between the rooms.

He began pacing. "What is wrong with me wanting my son to make a good impression?"

"You're overdoing it. You're such a nervous wreck—"

"I am not a nervous wreck!"

I rolled my eyes. "You cut yourself shaving this morning. You almost dropped your pocket watch. It took you two tries to get your tie even."

"Okay. I'm a little tense."

"You're five seconds short of a nervous breakdown."

He rolled his eyes. "Lisa, do you always have to exaggerate?"

I just looked at him. "You're going overboard and making Nick even more nervous in the process. My god, he thinks he's meeting a cross between Attila the Hun and the Wicked Witch of the West. It's a little ridiculous. First off, he's essentially Stella's grandchild, which means he's perfect right there. And it's Nick, only the most charming kid in the world."

"You're biased."

"Okay, but how many women do you know that aren't wowed by him?"

Sid sighed. "Not too many."

"Now, you've got to find a way to relax a little or he'll get so nervous, he'll mess up in spite of himself." I touched Sid's face. "I know this is important to you, honey. Nick does, too. He'll be fine. Now, I'm going to help him finish dressing. He's not going to wear the tie." I stopped Sid's objection by putting my finger on his lips. "We're going to lunch, not a funeral, and he's only twelve. He's got a nice sport shirt he can wear and some good jeans. He'll be more comfortable that way."

Sid sighed. "I suppose."

I was wearing a chambray skirt with a lacy top and sandals. Sid was, of course, decked out in one of his beloved three-piece suits.

In the other room, I told Nick to take off the tie and got out his other clothes.

"Relax, sweetie," I said after he changed. "She's really quite nice. All you have to do is be your own lovable self and you'll charm the pants off her."

"But Dad..." He made a face.

"Yes, I know. It's the shock of running into her after all these years. They never had that good a relationship and your dad is trying to build one. Besides, he wants her to be proud of him, like you want me to be proud of you. Now, try not to be too rambunctious. If Stella asks you something, be honest and straightforward, but polite. Okay? You'll be fine. I'm already proud of you and I'll bet your father is, too."

We met Stella at the music school. She seemed just a touch startled when she saw Nick, but recovered with a very familiar grace.

"Good morning, Stella," Sid said, gently pushing the boy forward. "I'd like you to meet my son, Nick."

"Pleased to meet you, Ma'am." Nick stepped forward and firmly shook Stella's hand.

"Pleased to meet you." Stella was all smiles. Everything about her had softened.

Sid began breathing more easily.

"What do I call you?" Nick asked.

Sid looked a little panicked, but Stella nodded.

"That's a fair question," she said. "I think Stella will do. That's what everyone else calls me."

"Okay."

Stella led Nick to a nearby piano bench and had him sit next to her. "Why don't you tell me about yourself?"

"Well, my official name right now is Nicholas Flaherty. Flaherty is my first mom's name, and I don't have a middle name yet. But my second mom..." He pointed at me. "She's adopting me and after that goes through, I'll have two middle names. Wycherly Hackbirn. So, I'll have everybody's name. And I'm keeping my last name the same because it's my first mom's, and she's important." Nick suddenly sniffled. "I'm sorry. She died just last summer, and I miss her a lot."

"I'm sure you do. It's not easy losing your mother."

"My second mom really understands. It's nice having two moms." He took a deep breath. "Anyway, I'm twelve years old. I'll be thirteen in February. I'm in the seventh grade. My favorite subjects are math and science. English is okay, but history and spelling are boring, and I hate geography."

"So, did I." Stella nodded. "What are your friends like?"

Nick primped. "I only hang around with the best." He laughed. "That's what my best friend, Josh Sandoval, says."

"Well," said Sid. "I think it's time to head out for lunch."

In the car, Stella chose to sit in the back seat with Nick, and Nick chattered away happily about his life. It didn't take long to get to the restaurant, and we were seated right away. We talked about food for a few minutes, then the waitress took our order.

"Do you have a girlfriend?" Stella asked Nick.

"Girls. Yuck!" Nick made quite the face. "I mean, I know I'm not gay, but I don't like girls. They're always shrieking and giggling and start every sentence with, 'Gee, Nick.' They're stupid. What's so funny?"

Stella was laughing. "I'm sorry, Nick, I can't help it. Your father felt exactly the same way when he was your age."

"Dad didn't like girls?" Nick looked at Sid in amazement.

Sid shifted uncomfortably. "There was a time, yes. But that changed, as I told you."

Nick whispered to Stella, "Dad used to sleep around. A lot."

"I know about that. He started when he was living with me."

"I don't anymore though," Sid said firmly.

"Oh, Sid, don't be so proper." Stella chuckled. "It wasn't what you did that I objected to. It was your utter lack of discrimination."

"You can't complain about that now."

"I wasn't recommending the other extreme."

Sid took it with grace. "In any case, there are good reasons why I don't want Nick emulating me that way that have nothing to do with being proper."

"AIDS," Nick told Stella.

"That is something to worry about," Stella said. "It wasn't when your father was a boy, though. Why don't I tell you about the day your father lost his virginity?"

"What do you know about that?" Sid asked with a smug smile.

"It was one of the few times in your life when you were utterly transparent." Stella chuckled.

We paused just long enough for the waitress to serve us our food. Then Stella started right in.

"It was just after Sid's thirteenth birthday. I was home with a cold. I was reading when I heard whistling in the hallway. It sounded like a Beethoven sonata, and the only reason I thought it might be Sid was that he was working through them at the time. I'd never heard him whistle before. Well, sure enough, he swaggered in, put his arm around my shoulder and said, 'Ain't it a great life, Stella?' Then he plopped down on the bed and began to read some book."

"Plato's Republic," Sid said with a chagrined sigh.

"That's right." Stella laughed. "I knew it was something inappropriate for the occasion. Anyway, I thought about it and realized that there was only one thing that could have happened to cause all that. He had gotten laid." Her face grew wistful. "My little man child was growing up. His body and mind were finally catching up to his heart. That's why I always called him my man child." She looked at Sid. "He was never a boy. Just a little adult who needed some physical and intellectual growth."

"Man child, huh?" Nick grinned, but then caught Sid's warning glare.

It wouldn't be the last one. Stella was obviously besotted with Nick. Nick loved hearing about his dad as a boy, and I must confess, I enjoyed it, too. Sid was so embarrassed, but took it well considering, only snipping back at Stella when he couldn't take it anymore. Stella treated me with an odd mix of kindness and condescension. I finally confronted her about it when we'd gone to the ladies' room.

"Stella, I'm getting some funny signals from you." I looked at her reflection in the mirror. "Sid told me you're not too thrilled about us getting married."

"I think you deserve what you get." She stopped and sighed. "I don't know. You two seem sincere about this, and I've always had a weak spot for idealists. If anything, young lady, you are that."

"Is that why it seems like you're thinking if I'm crazy enough to want to spend my life with Sid, I need sympathy?"

She laughed. "That about says it. I am also a realist and I know what a pain in the butt Sid can be."

"I do, too. And I still want to be with him." I shrugged. "I love him."

"Idealism." Stella turned thoughtful. "I have always thought that marriage was a lie."

"Sid did, too. He may even still feel that way about some marriages."

"I had a feeling you'd pushed him into marrying you. Funny thing is, he's happy to be pushed." She gazed oddly at the door. "When you first went up to him in that restaurant yesterday. I don't think I've seen him that happy before. Later, he told me was going to be faithful to you. He hedged, as usual. He never could stand up to me. But ultimately, he did this time, and he not only meant it, he wanted to be."

"I know. That was kind of my fault. He wanted to be faithful because he knew it was important to me, but didn't think he could. Then we both got a nasty shock, and he realized that he wasn't interested in fooling around anymore. That's when we made our commitment to each other."

"You make him happy. That's the important thing."

I smiled. "Stella, may I hug you?"

"What?"

"Come here. I want to give you a hug."

She received it a little awkwardly, but smiled.

I laughed. "You are so much like Sid, I can't help but love you."

She chuckled ruefully. "I think I'm beginning to see what happened to Sid. Poor thing. He didn't stand a chance."

"Neither did I." I paused. "Can you ease up on him a little, please? He's really trying, and your opinion means a lot to him."

She nodded.

Later, as we walked to the car, I checked to see that Stella and Nick were absorbed with each other.

"I talked to her," I said softly.

"I figured." Sid looked back at his aunt and son. "Now, what do I do? How do I reach her?"

"What was the one thing you two shared?"

Sid smiled and nodded. At the music school, Sid went to the bins of sheet music and started going through them while I heard Stella talking to Nick about playing the drums. I was trying to figure out a way to put a stop to that one when Stella looked up as Sid walked over.

"Are you still playing?" she asked him.

"Yeah. In fact, I'm taking lessons again," Sid said.

"I don't know why," said Nick. "He's really good."

"What's that you got?" Stella nodded at the flat book covered in yellow paper in Sid's hand.

"Something you always wished we'd had two pianos for."

Stella nodded. "Brahms, Sixteen Waltzes, Opus Thirty-Nine. We have two pianos, and I've got something better than that book. Are you sure you're up for this?"

"Yeah."

Stella pulled a small stack of folded sheet music from a piano bench. "Alright. Let's try one. You take the walnut and I'll take the ebony. You're piano two."

It was as if all the tension between them melted as they sat down, facing each other over the pianos, and unfolded the sheets of music across the pianos' music stands. This was clearly a challenge, but not to outdo each other. This was a cooperative effort. Their eyes shone, and they smiled at each other as Stella gave the count.

When Sid is working on his playing and really concentrating, he gets almost solemn, but with a faint hint of a smile. That day, I saw that same smile on Stella's face as they played. I sat back and prayed it meant a breakthrough.

Nick and I clapped when they finished. I, because I'd been so enthralled by the music, Nick, because he was glad it was over. He'd gotten kind of bored even though the waltz was pretty short.

"Very good," said Stella, and Sid grinned. "Not perfect. We'll have to go over it again."

"No!" Nick groaned.

Stella laughed. "I didn't mean now."

Nick heaved a sigh and plopped down next to Sid's left side.

"Do you play, Nick?" Stella asked.

"Mostly guitar. But Dad showed me how to do this. Can we, Dad?"

"Peanuts? Sure."

Nick began playing the rolling left-hand part of the Peanuts theme, then Sid began playing the treble. Stella watched them, utterly bemused. Sid laughed as they finished.

"Hey, Dad, can we sing Piano Man?"

Sid launched into the piano part. His eyes caught Nicks' and they both sang, "It's nine o'clock on a Saturday..."

That shocked Stella. "He's singing."

"Yeah. Nick talked him into it last September."

"He only did that when he was really happy."

"Or he got laid."

"That's generally when he was happiest."

Sid pulled me over after the last chorus and we sang Two Sleepy People together.

"They're getting goopy-eyed." Nick told Stella, disgusted as only a twelve-year-old can be.

"They are, indeed."

As the song ended, Stella shook her head. "Sid, if you had learned to be that sentimental about all your music, you might have been a concert pianist."

"That's okay." Sid grinned. "I don't care to be one. I'll stick to writing, thank you."

He ran his fingers up and down the keys in a defiant jazz lick.

Later, as we got into bed, he noticed me watching him.

"Everything okay?" he asked.

"Oh. Fine."

"Uh-huh. I know that look."

I sighed. "No. It's me being silly."

"Did Stella say something?"

I made a face. "Actually, sort of. She was surprised to hear you singing. She said you only did that when you were really happy."

Sid shrugged. "Well, I told you I don't think I'm that good a singer. We knew some pretty good ones, too."

"I sort of remembered when you used to come home after a particularly well mis-spent evening, you'd be humming a certain little folk ditty."

"Oh, crud." [I didn't say crud. - SEH] He rolled onto his back. "I was wondering when you were going to ask me about that."

I moved onto my side and looked at him. "I know you keep saying it's been really good and all, and I believe you. But I just now realized you haven't been singing afterward."

"I've been singing. It's only that I don't want you to hear me."

"Why?" It suddenly occurred to me that every so often I had heard snatches of some tune or other coming from the shower. It hadn't registered because it wasn't All Day, All Night, Maryann.

He rolled to face me. "Lisa, you once told me that what hurt about me sleeping around was that you had no way of knowing that what I said to you I wasn't saying to someone else."

"That was a nasty fight." I sighed.

"It was. And you definitely had a point." He reached over and touched my face. "So, I made up my mind that when the time came for us, I would never give you reason to believe that what I said to you, how I touched you, any of that, bore even the least resemblance to anything I'd done before."

I smiled. "Obviously, there's plenty that resembles former activity."

"Maybe in the actual mechanics of it."

"I wasn't complaining about that part. As Angelique once said, I'm reaping the benefits of your prior antics."

He chuckled. "Maybe. But what I do with you is so utterly different. Which is why, if I'm not singing afterward, it's not because I don't want to. It's because that song, in particular, belongs to a past that neither of us can erase and that I do not want in our bed. I do not ever want to give you the least reason to distrust me."

"You haven't. I wouldn't be lying here next to you if you had."

He smiled softly.

"Not to bring up another downer, but..." I rolled onto my back and looked up at the ceiling. "What do we do about Carla Caponetti?"

Sid sighed. "It's probably time to confront her. I'd rather Nick wasn't around for that. I don't want the distraction."

"I don't know. It might be useful if we have to plant a bug."

"Might be." Sid frowned. "I don't know. That's something else that's been eating at the edge of my brain these past couple days. We haven't been touched, not even a hint of trouble. If Carla Caponetti is behind these attacks, what are the odds that she knows we're right in her backyard?"

"Given Aunt Amanda, pretty decent."

"Then why haven't we had any trouble? It doesn't make sense. Why go all the way to California when we're right here?"

"You're right. But I just thought of something. Carla wanted to give Stella your address. That's why she was at the music school."

"You don't think Stella...?"

"No. Stella said she didn't need it, which could mean a lot of things. The thing is, Carla's passing our address around. What if she gave it to someone else?"

"Now that makes sense. So, confrontation it is. Think your folks would mind having Nick around tomorrow?"

I snorted. "Are you kidding? They're spoiling him rotten and having a blast doing it."

Sid grimaced. "We shouldn't be encouraging that."

"You want to tell them not to?"

"Point taken." He shook his head. "Stella has her day off on Sunday. She wants to spend it with Nick."

"Another grandma."

"I am afraid so."

I sighed. "As long as it doesn't involve a drum set. They were talking about playing drums today."

Sid cursed.

"One other thing. I told Mama this morning that we'd rather she didn't give the relatives any information about us without talking to us first. Given the blow up about your mother the other night, she agreed it was better that way."

"That's all to the good." Sid smiled at me and soundly kissed me. "Goodnight, Lisa. I love you."

"I love you, Sid. Goodnight."

November 23, 1985

Mama and Daddy decided to take Nick out on the Everglades that next morning, which left Sid and me free to go out for breakfast again. Sid was again wearing a three-piece suit, and I had on my chambray skirt with a nice knit top. Realizing that I hadn't picked up our phone messages in a few days, I called the answering machine and got them. Fortunately, there weren't that many.

"Well?" Sid asked as I slid into the booth across from him.

I glared down at the place setting in front of me. There was a bowl of fruit salad set neatly in the middle. I shook my head.

"I'm not ordering that crap," Sid said.

I signaled the waitress. "Fair enough."

When the waitress arrived, I ordered French toast, scrambled eggs, bacon, and ham. Sid rolled his eyes.

I started in on the fruit salad. "No writing work in the messages."

"It's that time of year," Sid said.

"Mae called. I'm going to have to call her. Mama already told her where we are."

"Terrific."

I sighed. "Mae sounded pretty miffed, too. Also, Maria Campos called yesterday. She knows we're still out of town, but wants to know if we'll be back before Thanksgiving. The newsletter is due."

Sid cursed. "Already?"

"I'll call Kathy and have her pick up the paperwork from Maria, then have Kathy send it overnight to Mama and Daddy. It's not like Kathy doesn't know we're here. I'll get it written so you don't have to. There's got to be a typewriter around that we can use."

"I'll do it. You do enough for those people and Nick is my kid, too."

The waitress arrived with my breakfast, and I dug in. I even finished eating before Sid, even though we were debating about whether to call Carla Caponetti before visiting her. We finally decided to go without calling and see just how surprised she was to find us on her doorstep.

She was utterly shocked when she opened her front door. No, she was more than that, but I couldn't quite put my finger on it. There was something that didn't add up about the house, either.

"John," Carla whispered, suddenly backing up.

"No," said Sid. "I'm Sid Hackbirn. I understand you've been looking for me."

She gasped. "Oh, dear!"

"I'd like to have a little chat with you." Sid folded his arms. "We could come in or we could talk right out here on the doorstep."

"No. No." She swallowed and opened the door wider. "Please come in."

We followed her into the house, through a wood-floored entry way featuring a sweeping staircase upstairs, into a carpeted living room that smelled almost like a furniture store. Everything gleamed and looked brand new.

"Can I get you some sweet tea? Water?"

"We're fine," I said.

"Please sit down." Carla indicated the light green and yellow-striped couch. She was wearing a pink velour running suit that did not favor her. Sid and I sat on the couch, with Sid waiting for Carla to sit in a coordinating wing-back chair before sitting down. "Well. How did you find me?"

Sid smiled at her. "Mrs. Caponetti, when some stranger starts calling my house and refuses to leave a message, I start checking around."

"Oh, well, I suppose so." She smiled shakily, then looked at me. "And if you're Sid, then you must be Amanda Caulfield's little niece. Lisa, isn't it?"

"Yes," I smiled back.

"Quite a coincidence, isn't it?" Sid still looked pretty annoyed.

"Well, Sid, honey, we're in South Florida. What do you expect?" She smiled. "It is a pleasure to finally meet my husband's nephew. In fact, Sid, why don't you call me Aunt Carla?"

"Mrs. Caponetti, you are a total stranger to me." Sid growled.

She swallowed. "Did Stella teach you to hate us?"

Sid's voice took on that cool edge it got when he was angry. "Stella didn't tell me anything. I didn't know your family existed until a few days ago."

Fear flickered in Carla's eyes. Suddenly, I understood at least part of what was going on. My foot gently pressed Sid's.

"This is a lovely place," I said. "Have you been here long?"

She smiled, but there was no joy in it. "No, I'm afraid I had to move out of the family home last summer. My husband's lawyers finally prevailed. They said my pension was not enough to keep up the place, and that if I wanted to keep my pension, I'd better start looking for the heir." She blinked, then recovered herself. "But you know how it is, honey. My father-in-law wanted the business to stay in the family and my John insisted on abiding by that. I'm just a silly woman, you know. It wouldn't be right to entrust a business to me. And not having any children, well, that did make things difficult."

I looked at her softly. "I'm so sorry. I get the feeling he wasn't very nice to you sometimes."

She glanced at Sid and laughed sadly. "Well, you know how men are. It's just a woman's burden, isn't it?"

I nudged Sid with my foot and glanced at the front door. He glanced at Carla, then rose.

"Mrs. Caponetti, if you'll excuse me, I've got to go check something in the car."

I smiled at Sid, and waited until he left, then scooted over on the couch to where I could pat Carla's knee, surreptitiously turning on the transmitter under my top.

"Thank you for getting rid of him," she said, softly weeping. "I didn't think I'd be able to take much more."

Sid coughed quietly in my ear.

I patted Carla's knee again. "I know. It seems awfully unfair after what you dealt with for your husband to leave you like this."

"Well, you know. The business was supposed to stay in the family, and your Sid was John's only relative, except for his sister." She shook her head.

"I think you deserved better than this."

She started crying. "What I put up with for that money, only to have him give it away to a total stranger."

"I'm so sorry, Carla."

"At least, you understand."

"Of course. I'm a woman."

"I suppose I'd better contact the lawyers."

"We'll need the information, too."

A brief flash of deceit crossed her face. "Oh. Of course, you will." She took a deep breath and got a tissue from the pocket in her top.

"Carla, I know Aunt Amanda gave you my address. Did you give it to anybody else?"

She looked up and blinked. "Well, yes, as a matter of fact. John and I had some friends. He had a restaurant supply business, and that's how Art and John knew each other. The Beldons, Art and Carol. Very nice couple."

"Like hell they were!" Sid gasped into my ear.

I, personally, was working incredibly hard not to let my consternation show.

"Well, Art passed on a couple years ago. Carol and I've stayed in touch. Then some time after Art died, Carol told me she'd met someone who was the spit and image of John and wasn't it interesting? I told her that I was looking for John's nephew. John had been dead a couple years by then, and she told me the fellow's name was Ed Donaldson, although she wasn't sure that was his real name for some reason. I looked for Ed Donaldson and didn't find anybody by that name."

There was a very good reason for that. Ed Donaldson had been Sid's alias when we were posing as other than ourselves.

"Anyway, last October, when Amanda met your Sid, I happened to tell Carol that we thought we'd found my nephew and he looked just like John, and she asked for his name and address, and I thought why not? So, I gave it to her. Did she get a hold of you?"

"We think she did."

"Oh, good."

It took everything I had not to choke. "Um. Thank you, Carla, for talking to us. Can you get me that lawyer's information, please?"

"Oh, yes."

I followed her as she scuttled into the back of the house to a kitchen counter that had a phone and a small bulletin board next to it. She wrote the information down, I put it in my purse, and she walked me to the door of the house, thanking me profusely for being so kind and listening to her babble and so on. I thanked her, patted her hand, then left the house, all but running to the rental car.

I was barely inside it when Sid pulled out with a roar.

"Beldon's supposed to be dead," Sid growled. "What the hell happened?"

"But she fits perfectly."

"Except that she's supposedly dead! And how the hell is it that she knew the Caponettis?"

"We're in South Florida? Actually, it's not that much of a stretch. Isn't the Yellow Line based in Miami?"

"That's right. It is."

"And Art was in restaurant supplies. The Caponetti business was a fish packing plant."

"They told us they were in ladies' fashions."

"And we told them we were in office supplies."

Sid cursed.

"We'd better call the Dragon," I said.

Sid cursed again.

We stopped at a diner near the highway, and I went in to make the call.

The Dragon answered the page right away and cursed when I told her my news.

"She's dead," the Dragon said.

"Apparently not."

"If she isn't, then there are two CID agents who have some explaining to do. Very well. I'll get right on it. We'd better do a face-to-face meeting. Let's set it up for… Wait. You're traveling as yourselves, right?" I heard a keyboard clicking in the background. "Okay. I've got you scheduled for a flight out of Miami to DC at six a.m. on Monday."

"I didn't know you were a travel agent."

"I'm not. I just sometimes need to book people quickly." She gave me the flight information. "We'll see you at the music store by eleven. Page me when you land."

"I will."

I also called Kathy and left a message asking her to pick up the school information from the office and send it overnight to my parents' place. When we got back to my parents' motel, my parents and Nick were still out on the Everglades. There was a message from Stella that she'd be done with her students at one and inviting us to join her for lunch.

"Are you up for that?" I asked him. "It's been a pretty stressful morning."

Sid sighed. "You know what? She called. Let's do it."

"Okay."

Sid decided to change clothes for lunch and put on a pair of jeans, sport shirt and his light blue blazer. While he did that, I called the music school and left a message for Stella that we'd meet her where she suggested at one-thirty. We had some time, so Sid called the law office for the Caponetti lawyers and found one of them in that day, which wasn't entirely surprising even though it was Saturday. They'd heard that Sid had been located, and obviously, wanted to be sure Sid was who he claimed to be.

"I'll have to get a blood test," he told me as we drove to the restaurant. "And there's paperwork. The advantage I have is that I did get Salvatore's bequest. Knowing where it came from and where it ended up should help."

"Do you know how much?"

"One-point-seven million or so in cash and real estate." Sid shrugged. "The processing plant has gone under, so that's less of an issue."

"That doesn't sound like very much, although it's a lot of money for around here."

"My original inheritance was just under two million, and that was only one-third of the total."

"But you're worth— I mean, we're worth a lot more than that."

Sid laughed. "Damn well better be." He sighed. "Alright. Like I told you, when I first got the money, I didn't spend much at first. I got my surgery." We both winced a little. "I got contact lenses. Then one weekend, I blew through a hundred and fifty thousand dollars."

"I remember you told me about that."

He shook his head with an odd smile on his face. "We had a good time." He glanced at me. "That trust fund girl at Stanford I thought I was in love with. The good thing was that I realized if I kept that up, I was not going to have my money for very long, and I was pretty tired of the whole being poor thing. So, I changed from majoring in journalism to business and took journalism as a minor. I still had to have an excuse for my intelligence work. From there, I worked on building my investments. By the time I was transferred to Los Angeles, I had a nice enough pile to qualify for the loan on what is now our house and paid it off in about five years."

"Pretty impressive."

"Like I used to say, just enough work to keep a comfortably high standard of living." He chuckled. "It was more work than you might think, though."

"I'm glad you did it. I mean, I'd still be in love with you if we didn't have a dime, but it's nice not having to think about how much I'm spending."

He laughed out loud. "You're still cheap."

"Well, yeah. But you have spoiled me. I spent ninety bucks on a pair of heels last September. I've worn them all of three times and the strap's already broken. What a waste."

Stella was waiting for us when we got to the restaurant. She smiled when she saw us walking up, hand in hand.

"Hey, Stella." Sid bent down and gave her a kiss on the cheek. It was the first time I'd seen him share any affection with her.

I gave her a hug. "It's good to see you."

"Nice to see you, too."

We were seated in the open-air part of the restaurant. The menu featured all sorts of wonderful seafood. Sid likes things with tentacles more than I do, but we both adore shellfish of all kinds and they had conch. We had to try that. Stella watched us go over what we wanted to eat with a bemused look on her face. I could tell she still didn't get what was going on with Sid and me, but she seemed to like it.

As soon as our food arrived, Stella looked at Sid.

"I've been meaning to tell you," she said slowly. "I'm still in touch with Tom Freeman."

Sid looked up with a happy grin. "Really? We lost touch after I moved to L.A."

"I know. He gave me your address in Beverly Hills." There was just a touch of disdain in Stella's voice. Apparently, she associated Beverly Hills with the bourgeoisie.

"It was the first place I found that looked livable." Sid pasted a smile on his face. "So, how's Tom? Last I heard, he was teaching at the high school."

"He still is. He got sober about six years ago."

"No kidding." Sid put his fork down. "Tom? That's saying something. How's Beth doing?"

Beth was Tom's wife. Or had been.

Stella rolled her eyes. "She divorced him five months after he got sober."

Sid shook his head and sighed.

"He took it pretty philosophically," Stella said. "Said it probably reflected what their relationship was really based on."

"Actually, I can believe that." Sid glanced at me.

"He said that after you came home from Vietnam, you had gotten hard."

Sid pressed his lips together. He'd been drafted and had gone into the Army rather than go to Canada or find some other alternative. It had been what estranged him from

Stella. Surviving the war had also caused him to hang up on Stella the one time she'd tried to call him after he got back.

"I had," Sid said quietly. "Two of the worst years of my life, and let's leave it at that."

There was an awkward pause. I wondered if Stella had brought it up on purpose and strongly suspected she may have. Neither of them appeared to be ready to discuss it, however.

"Lisa and I talked to Carla Caponetti this morning," Sid finally said.

"So, is it safe to say you've heard about my brother's will?" Stella asked.

"We have, indeed." Sid looked at her. "I even talked to the lawyers today. One of them was in the office when I called to leave a message. Needless to say, they're pretty anxious to prove I'm who I say I am."

"Well, I suppose that makes sense." Stella shrugged.

"We could do some forensic accounting, look at the birth certificate, and I can get a blood test. But the easiest thing to do would be to have you sign an affidavit that I'm me." Sid lifted an eyebrow.

Stella sighed. "What a nuisance. Another damned mess that I have to clean up."

She completely missed it. But the hurt flitted across Sid's face. He recovered almost immediately.

"There are other ways of doing this if you don't want to."

"There's no point," Stella grumbled. "If you don't deserve the money, who does? Not Carla, that's for sure."

"Lisa and I will have to talk it over first, but I was thinking about putting it into a trust for Nick."

"Now, that's a nice idea." She looked over at me. "But why do you two have to talk about it first?"

I smiled weakly. "All our assets are tied up in a business partnership we have. We did it last year."

"Given that we do work as a team most of the time, it made more sense," Sid said.

"Oh."

"It has been really interesting finding out so much about Sid's background, though," I said with a touch of desperation.

"Yeah." Sid nodded. "Why did you keep so much of it back?"

"Well, if you met Carla, you know." Stella sighed. "Honestly, Sid. Most of it isn't that pleasant. Take your mother, for example. When she got pregnant, our father demanded that she tell him who the father was. It never occurred to him or anyone else that Sheila didn't know."

"She didn't?"

"She hadn't the faintest idea." Stella sighed. "When we counted back, the best we could figure was a series of three frat parties over the course of a week at which she was the object of a series of gang bangs."

Sid laughed. "How appropriate. I am the son of all men."

Stella glared at him. "She wasn't at those parties for the fun of it."

Sid looked a little chagrined. "A situation like that could only be fun for the guys."

"She was paid, Sid."

"Paid?"

Stella sighed. "She may have been our father's favorite, but he kept her awful short of cash. She ran up some gambling debts and resorted to selling herself to pay them off. After that, she decided she liked the extra money and went into business with the college boys. She was even able to leave our parents' house and moved to Miami. After you were born, that's how she supported us. She was a call girl. Worked in a real fancy house not far from Wall Street. The rich guys liked her because she had a lot more class than the other girls. She also liked her work most of the time. At least, that's what she said. Until one of her johns bashed her head in."

"She was murdered," Sid said softly.

"Yes. Part of why I didn't tell you what had happened to her or what she did for a living. I didn't want to see you caught in that trap. Your mother was an extremely intelligent woman. But it all went to waste. And after she started hustling, she became very hard. I didn't want that for you."

"I'm grateful I didn't have to." Sid frowned. "Okay. I wasn't above trading for favors every now and then. But hustling was never my favorite way to go. Did they ever find out who killed her?"

"I seriously doubt it. They probably didn't look that hard. Her johns were wealthy, powerful men, and she was just a hooker. Whose life was more important, do you think?"

My heart broke for Stella's bitterness. Later, back at the motel, Sid looked at me.

"Are you alright?" he asked.

"Why wouldn't I be?"

He sighed. "Finding out that my mother was a prostitute and that I'm the result of a paid orgy."

I laughed a little. "It's a terribly sad story. But what difference does it make to us? How are you feeling about it?"

"I'm not sure. It's interesting." He looked thoughtful. "I guess I just don't understand why Stella felt she had to keep all that from me."

There was a loud knocking on our door.

"Sid? Lisa?" called Mama's voice. "Can we talk for a minute, please?"

Sid opened the door. "Sure, Althea. What's up?"

"When are you two going home? We'd love to have you stay through Thanksgiving this coming Thursday. But I just don't know where I'm going to put you. We have every single room booked starting Monday night. Now, Nick can stay with us. He'll be happy on our couch. But there is no room in that apartment, even for sleeping bags on the floor."

"We'll find something," I said. "And Monday, we've got to take a little side trip. A writing thing came up. We'll probably have to stay overnight, anyway."

"Are you going to take Nick with you?"

"No, Mama. We can't."

"Oh." She smiled. "That'll be nice. Sid, do you think your aunt might be able to put you up starting Tuesday?"

Sid got the strangest look on his face. "Um. We'll see."

November 25 – 26, 1985

O h, Sid was grumpy that Monday morning as we waited for our flight to Washington, DC.

"It's only for three nights," I told him.

The night before, when Stella had brought Nick back to the motel after her day with him, Mama insisted that she come in and have dinner with us. Now, I did get a chance to let Mama know that Stella was feeling pretty ambivalent about the whole wedding thing, and Mama completely backed off on the wedding talk. I forgot about the room situation. Stella was perfectly happy to take Sid and me in. She even had an extra bedroom. Sid accepted, but he was not happy.

"You don't get it, sweetheart. We are not getting any while we're there." Sid shook his head.

"It's only three nights. We've lasted longer before."

Sid snorted and I rolled my eyes.

"You know," I said. "You're acting just like you used to when you couldn't get any."

"It's worse now, believe it or not." Sid crossed his arms across his chest and looked at me with an odd mixture of lust and annoyance. "Even with the limitations, I am getting the best sex of my life with you."

"Oh, come on."

"I mean it. Lisa, whatever you insist on believing about yourself, you are an incredibly sexy, sensual, passionate woman." Sid smiled softly at me. "And, yeah, being in love with you helps. I'm surprised at how much of a difference it makes. But even if we weren't, you'd still be damn good in bed."

"I'm glad you think so." I shifted as I thought briefly about really good sex. "But you're getting petulant, which leads me to think that this isn't about us having to hold off messing around and more about you and Stella."

"Possibly." He sighed deeply. "Probably. But you don't get it, honey. We're not getting privacy of any kind. Stella literally does not understand the concept of a closed door. She'll walk in on you while you're using the toilet."

"So she spied on you when you were a kid."

"She wasn't spying on me." Sid shook his head and shuddered. "The best I can figure is that she associates closed doors with being ashamed of sex. At least, that's what she said when I or anyone else tried to hide it from her. Just normal, natural behavior. And it's not only the sex. She doesn't like wearing clothes, so decent odds, she won't. And you'd better hope like hell she doesn't try to cook us anything."

"But we don't have any other option besides going home. Everywhere in the area is booked. It's Thanksgiving week."

At least Sid went to sleep as soon as the plane left the gate. Once we landed in Washington, Sid got a rental car and we drove to a music store just inside the city limits.

The Dragon was waiting for us, a nine by twelve manila envelope in her hands. She was a tall matronly woman with light-colored hair that had gray liberally spread throughout.

"Well?" Sid asked.

She shook her head. "We have no idea what happened. Our British friends were, in fact, handing Beldon over to us. They were quite perturbed to find out she'd gotten away. We have a dossier on her. She was doing some pretty amazing work for a while there and was definitely the brains of that team."

"Any guesses as to why they leaked?" I asked.

"Money." The Dragon shook her head. "We later figured out that she had connections with the KGB and several other agencies as well. Her first job was to cripple our courier network. It might sound like a soft target, but information isn't any good if it doesn't get into the right hands. Apparently, she had quite a few deals set up when you two scuttled everything."

"You were in on that," I said.

"Which probably means I'm next on her list. And she has my real name and address." The Dragon paused. "Floaters do for a variety of reasons, including quick access. Now, her real name is Catherine Bolinaro. Her brother has a chain of meat-packing plants around the country. He also has significant connections within organized crime."

Sid nodded. "That accounts for the way she likes to use paid help."

It was not unheard of for operatives to pay local criminals to do some of the dirty work. Most of us didn't like to because it got expensive very quickly, and paid help was notoriously unreliable.

"Possibly." The Dragon looked at the manila envelope in her hands. "Bolinaro took a job at her brother's plant in downtown Los Angeles shortly after the beginning of October. She may have had to. Marissa, in Systems, got a good look at her financials. Bolinaro sent almost a hundred thousand dollars to her brother in the middle of October, and I'm guessing that was to pay for the help she was using. But there isn't much left in her accounts. If she has funds elsewhere, she has done a masterful job of covering it up or can't get to them that easily."

"Thus making her that much more desperate," said Sid.

"And more dangerous."

I looked at Sid. "We'll have to find a way to do some surveillance."

"You have a team," the Dragon said. "Why don't you use them?"

Sid looked at me and back at her. "You're right. Why don't we? I'll call as soon as we're done here."

"Oh, and speaking of." The Dragon handed Sid the envelope she'd been holding. "Red Sky called Henry Saturday afternoon. Said you wanted a package sent to you. It came in this morning." She smiled. "School stuff?"

Sid snarled.

I sighed. "I told her to send it overnight to my parents' place."

The Dragon chuckled. "Henry decided not to take the chance and was able to get it attached to another Priority One coming through. Believe me, it wouldn't be the first time personal materials came through the lines. You'd be surprised what our people are doing with their pagers, which are supposedly for official use only."

Sid and I did not look at each other, especially since we were, in fact, using our pagers to keep tabs on each other whether or not on Quickline business. I wasn't sure if the Dragon knew that we were for certain or just had a good idea that it was going on. We didn't question it.

We went over a series of options for what to do about Bolinaro/Carol Beldon. None of them looked terribly attractive. We couldn't have a team just sweep in and arrest her because we had no evidence that she'd done anything wrong. Okay, the CIA sometimes does, but they're not supposed to. In addition, because we work under the auspices of the FBI, which is part of the Department of Justice, it's a lot harder for us to get away with that kind of thing. Then there's the problem that the type of evidence Sid and I usually turn up is seldom admissible in court. Finally, for whatever reason, the Dragon wanted Bolinaro alive, if at all possible, which was fine with Sid and me. We don't like killing people.

The Dragon took us out to lunch near the Mall. It was an interesting meal. The Dragon told us to call her Lillian, and we got friendly, talking about music, and art, and bashing the Company. She took the Metro back to her store. Sid called Kathy and Jesse and got them started on a surveillance plan. We'd check in with them the next day. Then Sid and I went to see the Lincoln Memorial. It was my idea. I'd missed it the last time I'd been to the capital. We had decided to spend the night in the area and fly back to Miami in the morning. I'd even convinced Sid to take a somewhat later flight so that we didn't have to be up before dawn.

I really enjoyed looking at the gigantic statue of Abraham Lincoln and the building around it. But I had no idea what trouble I'd gotten us into until we came down the steps. Sid saw it first. His breath caught, and he trembled slightly. I looked at him, then where his eyes had landed. The Vietnam Veterans Memorial was directly ahead. It was only about three years old, but was incredibly popular.

"I'm sorry," I gasped. "I didn't know it was this close."

"It's okay, honey." Sid closed his eyes and took a deep breath. "It's time I looked at it."

Sid was hardly the only veteran there, let alone the only one having a hard time with it. As we approached, he stopped suddenly and just looked at the enormity of the black wall with all the names. A little apart was the newest addition to the wall, the Three Servicemen, who looked as though they were reading the names.

"Wow," he whispered. We started at the one end and realized there was a directory available. It listed the servicemen who had died on the wall in order of the date of their deaths. The directory had the names listed alphabetically to make it easier to find a specific person. Sid took a deep breath as he opened the directory to the R section.

"Do you want me to look up some names?" I asked.

He chuckled ruefully. "Honey, if I tried to look up everybody I knew who didn't come back, we'd be here a week. I just want two names."

The first one didn't surprise me in the least. Kevin Robinson. It was the name Sid called in his sleep when he was having his nightmare. The second name surprised me, Louis Renfrew.

"Your friend from high school?" I asked.

"Yeah. We got called up at roughly the same time, although we were in different units. Tom didn't tell me until I'd gotten home that Loser had been killed about four months into his tour."

Sid was solemn as he put his hand on Kevin Robinson's name. He still felt guilty about Robinson's death, even though it had been a sniper that had caused it. The sniper had also been the first man Sid had killed. I laid my head against his and held him.

Then, with our arms still around our shoulders, we found his friend. Sid looked at it for a long time. Finally, he shook his head, and we started back to the car. He stopped for a moment, then turned and looked back again.

"I can't help but wonder how it is that I came back, and they didn't," Sid said softly.

I just shrugged. My faith gave me a straightforward idea, but I seriously doubted it would answer Sid's question. He was still quiet as we ate dinner in one of the suburbs around DC. Then we drove toward Dulles to find someplace to stay. But pretty much every place was full. I finally spotted a nice little motel that advertised water beds. Sid looked at the sign, then looked at me.

"Are you sure you want to stay here?" he asked me, a slightly incredulous look on his face.

"Why not?" I asked. "Besides, it's not like we have that many options."

He glanced up at the sign, then sighed. "You've got a point there. Come on."

We registered as a married couple and paid cash. The clerk seemed a little surprised that we paid for the whole night, which I did not get. The room was nicely furnished and smelled perfectly clean. The waterbed was as advertised. Sid checked the sheets for some reason, though.

I got the toiletries bag out of my carryon. "Listen, I'm going to go wash up."

"Okay. I'll be there in a minute." He was taking off his suit coat and vest.

I stopped when I saw the bathroom. "Oh, my god! Honey, you gotta see this. They've got a heart-shaped tub in here."

"That's no surprise." He, nonetheless, came over and looked at it. "If it weren't for avoiding bodily fluids, we could have a lot of fun in that thing."

I shivered. "That does sound like fun, but I am exhausted. I just want to get some sleep."

"I don't think sleep is the idea here."

I turned to him. He grinned lecherously and finished unbuttoning his shirt.

"So, how do you want to start our evening?" he asked. "That ever-popular classic Deep Throat is playing on the room TV."

"Euw!" I made a face. "Why would I want to watch that?"

"I thought you were curious."

"Not about porn. Yuck. What else is on?" I looked at the list on top of the TV. "Um, these are all porn flicks."

"Yeah. What did you expect?" He slid out of his undershirt and got out a pair of jeans from the suitcase.

"Not this."

"It's an adult motel."

"So, they don't want kids."

He squeezed his eyes shut and started shaking. "They're advertising room rates by the hour, and you thought they didn't want kids?"

My face flushed. "Oh, my god. What did I do?"

One thing I had done was make Sid laugh really long and hard. He sank onto the bed and literally rolled, he was laughing so much.

"Honey!" I groaned. "Why didn't you say anything?"

"I thought you were curious. You've been getting that way." Sid still couldn't stop laughing. "I keep forgetting how naïve you are."

"I'm sorry." Blushing, I sat down on the side of the bed.

"Don't be, angel." He pulled me down next to him and kissed me hard. "I needed that laugh. I really did. Oh, my darling, I love you so much."

"I love you, too." I still felt silly.

"Let's have some fun," he whispered, his voice a little husky.

"Sure."

A minute later, a low thrum rippled through the bed and the water vibrated. How Sid had gotten out of his suit pants and into a pair of jeans so quickly, I have no idea. But he was already pulling off my shoes and nylons, and another minute later, the rest of my clothes were gone.

Let's just say that things got incredibly intense after that. More than that. It was wonderful and good and all that. But it was also bizarre. When we talked about it later that next morning, Sid figured that what happened the afternoon before had probably played into it. He found our encounter very life affirming. Better yet, he'd slept through the night without dreaming anything, let alone about patrols in the jungle and blood on his hands.

"I'm also hoping our little motel adventure will keep us sated for the next few days," he said, as we waited for the flight to Miami.

"I hope so, too." I smiled, in spite of myself. "But we usually find a way."

"If you're okay with being walked in on."

I ignored him. I wasn't okay with being walked in on, but figured we'd find a way to get cozy without having to worry about it. Or at least, I was trying to believe that we'd find a way to get cozy. Truth be told, I was getting nervous. I know Sid was still feeling pretty raw about his relationship with Stella, as was she. But I think Sid was also getting a little worried for my sake. [No, I was a lot worried and you had no idea what you were getting into. - SEH]

I knew there was a reason Sid was perfectly comfortable being naked no matter who was around, and that reason was Stella. Me? Honestly, I'd been surprised how easily I'd adjusted to being in my natural state around Sid. I was even getting used to occasionally catching Nick in the raw. But Nick had only seen me naked once, and it had been embarrassing for both of us. I had no idea how I was going to react if Stella walked around naked, or what I'd do if she expected me to strip. [The nudity was the least of my worries. You had forgotten another habit I'd picked up from living with her. My tendency to keep going no matter who else wanders in, although back then, that was usually Stella. - SEH]

We got to Stella's music school late that afternoon. I'd called Kathy and Jesse from the Miami airport. They outlined what they were doing, and I double-checked with Sid and okayed it. There hadn't been much to report yet.

Stella was finishing up with a student, a young girl about ten years old. I was impressed by Stella's patience and how she pushed, corrected, and encouraged all at the same time. I suddenly realized that Sid did the same with my nephew Darby. Darby was principally a violinist, but Sid had pointed out that Darby would be expected to be proficient on keyboards as well. Darby's last piano teacher had turned out to be an idiot, so Sid had taken over and usually gave Darby a lesson once a month, sometimes twice, and made sure the boy practiced.

Stella's student left with her mother and a boy the same age arrived with his mother. Stella asked them to wait, but didn't say why, then beckoned Sid and me upstairs. She had a two-bedroom shotgun apartment above the school. We went in at the back of the building and into a large living room area. The hall to the back led to a bedroom, the lone bathroom, another bedroom, and the kitchen, which featured a decent-sized eating area.

"You two get settled in the front bedroom," Stella said. "Today's my long day. I've got students until seven."

"Why don't I cook dinner?" Sid offered.

Stella paused. "Yes. That would be nice. Thank you, Sid." There was a slightly awkward pause. "I've got to get back to my student."

"I'll go pick up some groceries," Sid said.

"Good." Stella left the apartment as Sid stared after her.

"Are you okay?" I asked once Stella had gone.

Sid frowned. "The thank you for dinner? Definitely not her usual modus operandi."

"Maybe she's mellowed."

He shook his head. "She has, but that wasn't it." He blinked, then got a hold of himself. "We'd better check the kitchen out."

Sid was more preoccupied with whatever was, or actually wasn't, in the cupboards and refrigerator. I noticed a washer/dryer unit in the corner beyond the eating area. It was a stacking unit, and there was plenty of laundry detergent nearby. A hose led from the unit to the window behind it.

"Oh, we need this," I sighed.

"What?"

"That," I said, pointing to the washer/dryer. "You've messed up a couple pairs of jeans, lover. We need to do laundry."

"We probably do."

Sid put together an extended list of both groceries and things with which to prepare and cook said groceries. We got back to the apartment sometime after six, and put away the food and the new pots, pans, and utensils. Then we went back to our room. Sid wanted to do his second shave, and I wanted to get out of my business wear. I got into my sleep t-shirt and shorts as it was rather warm in the apartment. Sid had shed his suit, shirt, and boxer shorts and was happily nuzzling me when Stella walked into the room.

"I'm done for the day," she said, undoing the buttons on her shirtwaist dress.

"Stella," Sid groaned, facing her buck naked. "The door was closed."

"Why?" Stella asked, completely not understanding.

"Privacy!" Sid snarled.

"Sid Edward, I do not understand how you became so ashamed of your natural state. There is nothing you are doing that is not natural or normal."

"I agree. But maybe we don't want you to be part of it!"

"I was never into group sex, as well you know." Stella sighed happily as she dropped her dress. She had no bra on and no underpants. "That was your thing."

Sid gasped, blinked, look back at me, then faced Stella again. "Okay. Maybe. But not anymore. What Lisa and I have is something we'd really rather keep between ourselves."

"Not according to what your son says."

"We're trying." Sid's voice got really tight.

Stella sighed and picked up her dress. "Whatever."

She left the room. Sid looked at me.

"I told you so," he grumbled.

I smiled weakly. "You did."

Sid rolled his eyes and got into his last clean pair of jeans. He went ahead and made dinner wearing them, which I understood. I was pretty invested in keeping his family jewels unharmed, such as it is. I think Stella got that, too. She was perfectly happy to let me use the washer/dryer, too. After dinner, I did the load of dark clothes first and Sid slid out of his jeans and tossed them at me so they could be washed at the same time. While those went through the wash cycle, Sid asked Stella to let him use her typewriter. There was that parent newsletter to get out. Stella said yes but didn't ask why Sid needed it.

"Did you get the liner paper out?" I asked as Sid rolled the first sheet of mimeograph paper into the typewriter, which sat on Stella's coffee table in front of the couch.

Sid groaned, pulled the mimeograph paper out, and pulled the liner sheet out from between the main page and the inked page. "Yes."

"What the hell?" Stella asked.

Sid rolled his eyes. "I have a son. He goes to school. The school requires that parents put in a certain number of volunteer hours every year."

Stella couldn't help laughing. Sid cursed.

"I know," I said. "But the condom broke, dear."

He cursed again and Stella lifted her eyebrow, then nodded. As Sid typed the newsletter, he cursed repeatedly, using every one of the seven words you can't say on television. He used them all multiple times.

"He's not really your conventional parent," I told Stella, watching Sid on the couch, buck naked, typing away, and cursing.

"Is that why he volunteered to do this newsletter?"

I nodded. "Oh, yeah. We try to keep him as far away from the other parents as we can."

Stella smiled. "He is my boy."

I got the load of dark clothes into the dryer and went to put the light-colored clothes in, then realized that I wanted to wash my sleep t-shirt and shorts, too. I couldn't believe it. I sighed and went ahead and stripped. As I came into the living room, Sid stopped typing and cursing long enough to look at me and softly laugh. Well, it was kind of awkward being the only person in the apartment wearing clothes.

November 27 – 28, 1985

S id and I did find a time to make each other happy, as it were. The only problem was that he woke me up a half-hour early to do it. Stella was asleep and apparently does not share his affinity for the pre-dawn any more than I do. If I hadn't been so horny, I might have passed. Then Sid pulled me out of bed to go running, as usual. At least, we'd been able to stay in bed a little longer than normal. I was also able to drop off the dry cleaning and Sid's dress shirts at a shop across the street. As we returned to the apartment, the acrid smell of smoke hung heavy in the air.

"Oh, no!" I gasped and tried to get up the stairs before Sid.

Sid held me back. He was utterly indifferent, and I winced. Once in Stella's apartment, Sid went straight back to the kitchen. The smell of smoke was almost overpowering, but that had nothing to do with anything catastrophic. Stella sat at the table, buck naked, reading the newspaper. Two black squares sat before her on a plate, one of which had a couple bites taken out of it.

"Is this what you call breakfast?" Sid picked up the plate.

"I like my toast dark." Stella did not look up from her newspaper.

"This is white bread! You are eating cancer-laden cardboard."

"It's what I like."

"We have only our health to depend on." Sid gestured with the plate. "Seriously, Stella. Why are you eating this crap? I have a perfectly good fruit salad in the refrigerator and delicious whole wheat bread on the counter next to the toaster. And you resort to this stuff?"

[I did not say stuff. - SEH]

"Sid, I am sixty-one years old. I have managed quite nicely eating this way so far."

"I'd like some orange juice," I said, perhaps vainly hoping to disrupt the argument.

"'Fraid not," said Stella, holding up the glass filled with the dark purple of prune juice. "We drink this, instead. It's the family complaint."

"The one thing she told me about my ancestry," Sid grumbled, tossing the two charred pieces of bread into the waste can under the sink. "We were all plugged." He turned on Stella. "I'll bet you're treating it with chemicals, too."

"Whatever works." She glared at him. "Are you fixing something else for breakfast?"

"Yes." Sid slammed a griddle onto the stove, then pulled a bag of whole wheat flour from a cupboard. "Will pancakes do?"

"They'll do enough."

It didn't get any better. The tension began to get to me. Sid was insanely grumpy. Stella wasn't in a much better mood. We finished breakfast, but the bickering went on until I was ready to scream. Okay. I did. We were in the living room, with Sid and me still in our running suits.

"What?" Stella asked.

"I've had enough!" I yelled. "You two have been at each other's throats since we got here. This is ridiculous!"

"What do you mean?" Stella demanded.

Sid rolled his eyes. He, at least, knew what was coming.

"All you do is put each other down." I folded my arms across my chest.

"We don't," said Sid, who, frankly, should have known better.

"Bull-puckey!" I snarled at him. "You had to go after her on the whole health food thing and believe me, I know how annoying that is."

Stella let out a satisfied snort.

"And you." I turned on her. "You haven't had one nice thing to say to him. He's only trying to show that he cares about you. Why can't you see that he's not some mess that you have to clean up?"

Stella's eyes got wide with shock.

"Lisa," Sid said, his voice thick with warning and fear.

"I don't care." I turned on him. "That's what the problem is. If you two don't start facing it, it's never going to get better!"

"He's not some mess," Stella said softly.

"That's what you called him last Saturday." I glared at her. "I saw you do it. He asked about that affidavit, and you said it was another mess that you had to clean up."

She looked at Sid desperately. "That is not what I meant."

"I know." Sid looked away, blinking. "But I gotta say, that's what I heard."

"I never said you were a mess that I had to clean up!"

"Maybe not directly. But every time you said it, it was about something I'd done or was involved in."

Stella stepped back and gasped. "Is that what you heard? That you were a mess for me to clean up?"

Sid closed his eyes. "Yeah. I'm afraid so."

Stella cursed, repeatedly using the f-word.

"It's alright, Stella." He reached out to her. "I understand."

"It is not alright. In no way is it alright." She backed away, glanced at me, then looked at Sid. "I didn't mean that. I know that doesn't mean much now. But..." She closed her eyes and swallowed, then cursed again. "I tried so hard to keep that part of my family from you. That's the reason why I never told you about them. Only now to find that I gave it to you after all."

"I don't understand," Sid said. "Please tell me."

Stella's eyes shut, and she took a deep breath. "If you were something I needed to clean up after, to fix, it is only because that is what I was to my father." She looked at Sid, the blue eyes the two shared blazing. "My father was an evil man, truly evil. He cheated our fishermen out of their catch. He cheated on our mother, sleeping wherever he decided he wanted to, whether the woman wanted it or not. He beat my mother. He beat my brother. He seldom hit me. Or Sheila. She was his favorite. But what a curse that was. I remember when she was twelve, he pulled her onto his lap and grabbed her chest and asked, 'How are those boobies coming along?' Sheila said he never did anything more than grope, but it was enough. Me? I wasn't the son he wanted. I was useless." She sniffed and held herself. "When Sheila came to me, I thought here was a chance to have someone to love me, and I didn't mean my sister. I meant a baby. The problem was, I knew love was a lie. The people who were supposed to love me didn't. My mother had completely shut down. She barely knew I existed. My brother saw me as a problem to hide. Sheila just saw me as someone to use. Sid, I know you didn't mean to reject me when you left. I was probably pushing you away, too. When you yelled at me that you were going into the army, I just couldn't take the hurt anymore."

It was Sid's turn to use the f-word, and he did. Repeatedly.

"I didn't want to hurt you, Stella."

"Then why did you go?"

Sid closed his eyes. "I didn't know what else to do."

"You could have gone to Canada. Hell, with my politics, we could have gotten you conscientious objector status."

"No. It wasn't that." Sid glanced at me. "I didn't know what to do with my life. All my friends, all they'd heard from when they were kids was, 'What do you want to be when you grow up?' I never got that." He put up his hand. "It was not a bad thing. But after high school, I had that scholarship and no idea what to do with it. I didn't want to be a musician. It was too hard to make a living. I was kind of thinking about the restaurant business, but you don't need to go to college for that and I didn't want to wait tables for the rest of my life. Beyond that, I had no idea. When I got the letter, I was terrified, but... It was something to do."

"Why didn't you say so?"

He glared at her. "Probably the same reason you never told me about your father. Or my mother, for that matter."

He shook his head. "And, hell, I was nineteen. Maybe I wasn't that on top of it."

"But then you hung up on me when I called right after you got back." Stella looked away as the room grew thick with the silence.

"I know," Sid said finally. "That was my fault." He swallowed and blinked his eyes. "The problem was that I couldn't talk to you just then. It wasn't about you kicking me out. Or maybe it was a little. I mean, that did hurt a lot." He shook his head. "It was what Tom said. I'd gotten hard, but mostly I was angry. At everything. When I was first discharged, I went on a bender and a half. Those three days, when I wasn't passed out, I was drinking. Then my former C.O. found me, got me dried out and pushed me into enrolling at Stanford. It turned out to be what I'd needed, but I was feeling so lost. I had spent two years in hell, only to come home just as lost as I'd been when I'd left. The worst of it was, I really, really wanted to talk to you. I'd missed you, believe it or not."

"You did?" Stella sniffed. "I missed you, too."

"Yeah. But I was so angry when that call came. There were so many things I was pissed at besides you, and I didn't want to unload on you. That wouldn't have been fair, and I guess I was afraid you'd reject me again. But I couldn't tell you what I'd seen and done." Sid winced. "I still have trouble talking about it and even have nightmares occasionally. I wish I had found a way to talk to you, and I hope you can forgive me."

"I hope you can forgive me." Stella hung her head. "I shouldn't have kicked you out. You didn't need that, not going where you were headed. I was just so afraid that I wouldn't get to talk to you again. That you were coming home in a box." She looked at him. "That's what hurt the worst, that I might not see you again."

"Well, I'm here now." He took a deep breath. "Stella, I forgive you and I do love you. I'm pretty sure I did then."

"I forgive you." Stella smiled at him, but then her voice went flat. "But love... I don't even know what that is."

"I didn't either for a very long time." He looked over at me and reached out his hand. I took it. "But then I tried to pick up a certain woman in a bar who had ditched her blind date, and ended up buying her dinner, and sending her home untouched."

Stella looked at me. I smiled and shrugged.

"Look, Stella," Sid said softly. "I know you did the best you could. If I didn't get that then, I certainly do now. It's amazing how having a kid of your own puts a whole different perspective on that."

"He is a sweet boy," Stella said, smiling softly.

"Probably due to his first mom." Sid looked over at me. "And a great deal to his second mom." He sighed. "I haven't exactly been the greatest father, either. If Lisa hadn't been around when Rachel, his first mom, dropped him on my doorstep, I would not now have the relationship I have with him. I did not care what he looked like. I did not want to acknowledge him." He sighed again. "Stella, I can't fix what happened with your father."

"I don't expect you to, Sid." She gazed at him fondly. "I do want to try and get over it, though. My little man child. You were always so dear to me."

Sid went over and pulled her into his arms and just held her.

"This is not going to be an easy relationship," he said to her.

"It never was, my boy." She pulled away and smiled at him. "But it has been worth it."

His cheeks were wet. Her cheeks were wet. Yeah, I was crying, too.

Stella had a few students that afternoon, which is when I took the newsletter to the overnight shipping office and got it sent to Nick's school, then picked up the dry cleaning and shirts. I called Mae from Stella's apartment, using our calling card so as not to rack up long distance charges. Mae wanted to know when we were coming home and wanted us to stay at their place for the rest of the weekend. Sid and I wanted to stay with her and the family, so we agreed and told her that we'd call when we got back into L.A. and got our own car. Mae wanted to know when, exactly, we were coming in. I waffled and tried to distract her. It only marginally worked.

Sid made dinner again, lovely pan-grilled chicken breasts with a lemony sauce, and Stella had the grace to not only thank him for it but say how impressed she was at how good it tasted. We continued sitting at the table and talking long after we'd finished eating. That was when my religious beliefs came up.

"Catholic?" Stella asked, one eyebrow lifted. "You understand that I have no respect for the Catholic Church. There was a time when my mother tried to escape my father, only to be told that she would go to hell if she did. I was told I was going to hell for questioning my father. He was a pillar of the parish as far as the priests were concerned and could do no wrong."

I nodded. "I've heard those stories, and I know they happened. But my experience has been very different. If anything, the Church helped teach me how to love. I mean, I know that some people in the Church are narrow-minded and hurtful. And, if I'm being honest, I get judgmental about them and think they have no business calling themselves Christians. But it's the people, not the Church, that are the problem."

"Stella, I have to agree with Lisa." Sid made a face. "I know your experience was terrible, and, sadly, not that unusual. I'm not saying otherwise. My only experience, though, was just hearing about it, and most of what I heard supported what you'd always told me. Then I met Lisa and her friends, who became my friends, and there is a different part of the religion thing. I don't believe and they respect that, and I respect that they do believe."

Stella looked at me. "Is that why you demanded that Sid be faithful?"

"Stella, she didn't demand," Sid said firmly. "She could have, but she didn't."

"Oh, my god, no." I shuddered. "That would have been a disaster."

Sid cocked his head and looked at his aunt. "You're still thinking Lisa pushed me into this, aren't you?"

"Didn't she?"

"I hope not!" I gasped.

Sid chuckled warmly. "No, Stella. Lisa did not push me into anything. In fact, she turned me down a couple times when I tried to force myself to be what she needed, just like I turned her down when she tried to force herself my way. We got to where we are because we both want it. Believe it or not, I was getting tired of the whole sleeping around scene. I just didn't know what else to do and didn't want to promise that I wouldn't go back to it if Lisa wasn't around." He looked at me and smiled. "Although, even if you aren't around, I don't think I will."

"Well." Stella looked up at me, then fidgeted with her wineglass. "Actually, Sid. I'm not surprised. Maybe that it took so long. But I figured there'd be somebody who'd catch your heart, and you'd settle down and start having babies."

Sid laughed. "Kind of did it in reverse order, though, didn't I?"

"And we won't be having babies," I said, suddenly sad.

Sid reached over and held my hand, then glanced at Stella. "I had surgery to prevent that. The first thing I paid for after I got my money. I had no idea that I'd ever want to have children."

"What did you do after you got your money?" Stella asked.

"Stayed in school, then moved to Los Angeles and tried to make sure I kept my money. You?"

"I was pretty disillusioned after you left." She sighed. "Some of my friends had heard and invited me to come up to their commune in Mendocino." She shook her head. "That was a mess. I went back down to San Francisco and did some private teaching, cash only, of course, and was doing fairly well when the lawyers caught up with me." She snorted. "That was almost as big a burden as it was a blessing. The Internal Revenue Service found me, and I had to take my original name back. Of course, with you gone and my father dead, it didn't matter about staying in hiding."

"You were in hiding?" Sid asked.

"We both were." Stella's eyebrows rose. "Your grandfather tried to take you away from me when you were three.

That's why we moved to San Francisco. To get away from him. He was desperate to take you back to Florida and raise you there."

"Why?" Sid asked, then suddenly frowned and swallowed. "I, uh, know what you said about the frat parties and that my mother said he never did more than grope. But it's still possible..."

Stella shook her head. "There's a good reason why I know that my father is not also yours."

Sid winced. "Oh?"

"Your mother and I had a cousin. Mina." Stella blinked her eyes. "She died last year, and her father, Uncle Pasquale, is long gone. When I left to go to Juilliard, Uncle Pasquale paid for it. He was a musician, too, and wanted me to develop my talent so that I could come back here and teach. Father was furious, but was willing to let me go because he assumed that I would do what Pasquale wanted. Only I didn't, at least not then. I got my master's degree, then got a job in the public school system in New York. Pasquale didn't blame me. He knew what kind of man his brother was." Stella winced. "Father tried to pressure me into coming home a couple times. But I eventually realized that he was perfectly happy having me gone. He knew he couldn't control me, which infuriated him. So, if he couldn't control me, then he didn't want me around. Well, Mina, on behalf of her father, did stay in contact with me. She also stayed friends with Sheila, even hid Sheila the first time she ran away from home. When Sheila moved to Miami to get away from Father, it was Mina who told me where she was. Father tried to get me to tell him, but I kept saying I didn't know. Which is how I know that Father hadn't been near Sheila in over six months when he finally tracked her down. And by then she was pregnant." Stella shuddered.

"With me, I presume," Sid said.

Stella nodded. "However, there is more to it. When your mother came to me for help, it wasn't just that she figured I could get her an abortion. She was also looking for the last place anyone would think to look for her. The two of us were not friends by any stretch of the imagination, but I was all she had. That's when she changed her name to Hackbirn. She was determined never to see Father again."

"She changed her name?" Sid almost gaped. "I always thought you had when you broke with your family while you were at Juilliard."

"You did?" Both of Stella's eyebrows rose. "I don't think I ever said that." She stopped and thought about it. "Although I'm not surprised you thought that. But no. It was Sheila who changed her name, and I eventually went along with it. Once you were born, she went back to hustling and I quit my job to take care of you. Lord knows, she wasn't going to. I told you the nurse had to name you, right?"

"Yeah." Sid frowned. "But if she wanted nothing to do with me, or even you, why did she support us?"

Stella's eyebrows knitted together. "I did something that I am not proud of. I told her that I would tell Father how to find her if she didn't. Believe it or not, I had no idea she'd gone back to hustling. She told me she'd gotten a secretarial job for an import company and had to work nights to answer the phones from other places. I believed her for some stupid reason. I didn't find out what she was really doing until the police came to tell me she'd been killed."

Sid swore. "I'm so sorry, Stella."

"Oh, for Heaven's sakes, Sid, there's no reason to get all sentimental about it. It's just a fact of our lives." Stella shut her eyes for a moment, though. "I told Mina what had happened to Sheila. I had to, both for hers and Pasquale's sakes. I assume that's how Father eventually found out. Mina had told me several times that Father was still looking for Sheila, and I think that's how he eventually found you and me." Stella sighed. "I gave him the slip, and that's when we moved to San Francisco. That's also when I changed my last name to Hackbirn. But it meant only taking cash jobs. I didn't have the right identification, and I did not want Father finding us. I was going to change our names to something else, but your kindergarten insisted that you use the name that was on your birth certificate, so that was the name we ended up using most of the time. I kept loosely in touch with Mina, and she eventually told Father your name. However, we lived with all those bohemians and hippies, and I worked at all those different schools partly because I had an affinity for that kind of thinking, but also because it would make it harder for my father to find you. Only taking cash, though. That was why we were so poor."

Sid frowned. "I thought it was because you were a communist."

Stella laughed. "Sid, we lived in San Francisco. Nobody gave a damn about my politics. I know you didn't like not having any money, but I was perfectly happy that way." She made a face. "Then there was the inheritance, and I couldn't justify turning it down, not when I thought I'd finally be able to do some real good with the money my father had gotten off the backs of the people. But that meant back to paying taxes and I haven't been Stella Hackbirn since then. Well, technically, I never was Stella

Hackbirn. I never officially changed my name, which is why I never had the I.D. I just started using the name. But once I had to start paying taxes, I would have had to do all the paperwork, and it simply wasn't worth it. So, I'm back to Stella Caponetti."

"Why did you move here?" Sid asked. "Given how you feel about your family, I'd think this would be the last place you would want to be."

"It was." She fidgeted again. "After the money was settled, I did go back to New York for about four years, trying to make a go of it. Then Mina told me that my Uncle Pasquale had died. That had been his dream, that I'd come here and teach. I decided that was the least I could do, so I came down in seventy-seven and started the school. My brother John would come sniffing around. He said he wanted to make peace, but he only wanted to control me and my money." She smiled bitterly. "I didn't let him and got the satisfaction of rubbing his nose in the fact that he couldn't." Her smile went from bitter to happy. "And now you're back and you have a boy of your own. I'd say it's working out rather well, all things considered."

Sid grinned and shook his head, but then looked at me. "You okay?"

I guess I looked a little sad. "Yeah. I'm just looking at the two of you and thinking about my boy is all."

I got to see him the next day. It was Thanksgiving Day, and Sid and I were to meet my parents and Nick over at my Grandma Caulfield's place. I could have skipped it, frankly. Part of the problem was that I was Grandma's new Golden Girl. Not only had I snagged a rich husband, well, fiancé, we had finally gotten our hands on the Caponetti money that we were due when John Caponetti had been dating my mother. I'm not entirely sure my grandma had ever forgiven Mama for dumping John, although the Wycherly money hadn't been bad, either. Worse yet, my darling son had done his work well. Grandma Caulfield was besotted with him.

"We had a great time," Nick told me. "Granny let me lick both the beaters and the bowl when we made dessert last night. She gave me a bottle of holy water and a new baseball mitt."

"Really?" I asked.

Sid sighed. "The idea is not to shake everybody down, son."

"I'm not!" Nick grinned. "It was Stella's idea to give me the electric guitar and amp. And Grandma only bought me a new sweater and taught me how to knit socks. She bought me a bunch of yarn, too."

"And a new train set," said Sid.

"Isn't it cool?" Nick grinned, completely unrepentant.

The kid had made out like a total bandit and didn't care. And, I had to concede, he was such a sweetheart, I could hardly blame him for cashing in. Then Grandma Caulfield waddled up. She was short, like Mama, but very round and rocked back and forth as she walked.

Her eyes lit up when she saw Sid. "I must say, young man, that boy of yours is a caution."

Sid smiled. "We enjoy him, too."

"How would you like to see the still?"

Sid grinned. "I'd be very interested."

"I want to see that, too!" yelped Nick, and he followed Grandma and Sid out to the back yard.

Mama showed up at my side, shaking her head. "I do not know why I am surprised, but I swear, Nick has had her eating out of his hand since we came by yesterday. And now, look at her, taking Sid out to the still."

I shook my head. "Those Hackbirn men. You have to watch out for them."

Mama gave me a solid squeeze. "How are you doing, darling?"

"Pretty well, Mama. How about you?"

"We have had the loveliest time with Nick. He is such a sweetheart."

Alas, Uncle Steven and Aunt Marie, and Uncle Leonard and Aunt Amanda all arrived at the same time, with Maggie and Jed in tow. Maggie and Jed did not look happy. We womenfolk went into the kitchen and began setting up the buffet on the dining room table. Grandma Caulfield's place is so small, there's no way we could eat around the same table, which was just as well, since I really did not want to talk to either of my aunts or Maggie. Some of the other cousins showed and Sid kept an eagle eye on them and warned Nick not to touch anything they gave him. Nick had no problem doing that. After we ate, the crowd did thin a bit. The cousins went out back. The older adults settled in the living room, including Sid and me. Nick wandered in and sat down on the floor at my feet. Then Uncle Steven got a jug from the bookshelf and several shot glasses from the china cabinet. Both Mama and I stiffened because we knew what was coming. It was time to test Sid's manhood with Grandma's corn liquor.

Thank God, Sid figured out what was up almost immediately and that he was also familiar with Grandma's famous blend. It's good stuff. Uncle Steven was so friendly-like as he poured a shot for himself and Sid. Sid sipped the shot delicately, savoring the taste.

He nodded. "Very good. Nice and smooth. It's got a good kick, too." Without batting an eye, he knocked the rest back and set down the glass. "But I wouldn't recommend lighting any matches around it."

Steven sat back and looked at Uncle Leonard. Neither of them could knock that corn liquor back without gasping, which isn't saying much because it's a darned potent brew. Daddy laughed loudly.

"And y'all called him a sissy," Daddy chortled. "I think you boys owe me some money!"

Chagrined, both Steven and Leonard reached for their wallets.

"Daddy!" I snapped. "You were betting on Sid?"

"Hell, yes." He reached out to Steven and Leonard. "Teach you two to make snide comments about my little girl and her choices."

"You give that money back!" I demanded.

"Absolutely not," Sid said. "I'm getting a forty-percent cut."

I rolled my eyes as the rest of the room burst into laughter. Daddy grinned. Sid winked at me. That darling fink. His smooth urban sophistication had out-macho'd every man in that room, except possibly Daddy.

"It's in the blood, I dare say," Aunt Amanda said with a smug grin.

"Amanda," Grandma growled. "'Tisn't nice."

"Oh, please, Granny," Amanda went on. "It's only obvious where he comes from."

"Is it?" Sid asked, smiling. "Then where?"

"From right here."

Sid shrugged. "Odd. I was born in New York City and raised in San Francisco."

"But your seed was sprung here." Amanda nodded triumphantly.

"I will not have such filthy talk." Grandma sent Amanda the sort of look that should have scared the pee out of Amanda.

Amanda glared at Grandma. "You said yourself that he was one of them. Who was your mama, sweetheart?"

"Her name was Sheila Hackbirn." Sid smiled, knowing full well what Amanda was getting at.

"Sheila?" Marie gaped happily. "For real?"

"Yes, Sheila Caponetti," Amanda said. "She changed her name when she went to New York. Remember when Sheila got in trouble?" She pointed at Sid. "That's the trouble."

Sid laughed loudly.

"Aunt Amanda," I groaned. "You don't know anything about it."

"I know Carla Caponetti was stuck finding him." Amanda glared at both of us. "And now she's been cheated out of John Caponetti's money after he beat the tar out of her for all those years."

"I am aware of that," Sid said quietly. "That doesn't mean I don't have the option to do the right thing. So, while I am accepting the bequest on behalf of my son, I will do right by Carla. She didn't deserve what she got."

That pretty much took the air out of Amanda.

"Is there any more of that corn liquor?" Sid asked, lifting his shot glass.

Sid wasn't in the best of shape by the time it came to drive all three of us back to Stella's. So, I did the driving. I wasn't sure if I was peeved that Sid was tipsy or proud that he'd drunk both Steven and Leonard under Grandma's coffee table. That latter was no mean feat.

We said goodbye to Mama and Daddy around eight because we were taking yet another ridiculously early flight out of Miami in the morning, which was why we had Nick and his luggage with us. Including the electric guitar and amplifier. The only reason I wasn't ready to pound Stella for that one was that it wasn't a drum set. Stella was waiting up for us and wearing clothes, for which I was thankful.

"Did you have a nice day?" she asked.

Nick gaped sleepily.

"Nice enough," Sid said. I think he didn't want to admit that we also had a nice, full jug of Grandma's corn liquor to hide in our luggage somehow. "How about you?"

"Sometimes it's just lovely having a day entirely to yourself," Stella said.

Sid and I put Nick to bed on the living room couch, then went to our room. We decided to just get undressed and go to bed, which was just as well because Stella walked into the room about ten minutes later, wanting to know what time we needed to get up.

November 29 – December 3, 1985

"**M**om?" Nick asked, looking over me at his father, who was across the aisle of the plane and asleep, as usual. "Does Dad always pick such early flights because he knows he's going to sleep through them?"

I leaned back in my seat and blinked. "It's entirely possible, son." I tried closing my eyes, but they wouldn't stay closed, no matter how tired I was. "Maybe next time we should try ganging up on him."

We were on a flight to Burbank rather than Los Angeles International Airport. That Saturday before we'd left for Florida, besides moving us to a hotel, Sid had gotten the Beemer and had it stowed at the same garage in the San Fernando Valley where both my Datsun pickup and his Mercedes 450SL were stored. Burbank was a lot closer to the garage than LAX was, so Sid had decided to fly there. Okay, I wasn't unhappy about which airport we were flying to. Just the miserably early hour we'd had to leave. Yes, I was truly a partner, not just an employee. Somehow, that had to mean I could convince him that we didn't have to be up all the time before most normal people engaged in conscious thought.

We got into Burbank airport around ten-thirty, had the Beemer before noon, and were in Pasadena a little over a half an hour later. As soon as the Beemer pulled into the narrow driveway, the kids came streaming out of the house, Mae and Neil following them. I couldn't help noticing Mae inspecting my neckline, but I happened to have on the necklace Sid had bought me the month before in New York. I was also wearing a sweater, shirt, and my jeans. Sid looked particularly stylish in his light blue blazer, snowy white sport shirt, and tight jeans. Neil had on an old t-shirt and worn, baggy Levi's. Nick grabbed his suitcase, showed Darby the boxes for the electric guitar and the amplifier, then the two of them ran inside and upstairs to Darby's room.

Sid was occupied with distributing hugs and kisses to the younger children.

"I'll put you in with Janey and Ellen," Mae told me. "Sid can have the downstairs guest room."

I pulled my suitcase from the trunk of the Beemer. "Okay."

I tried to remember if Sid and I had stayed over at Mae's since we'd started sharing a bed and didn't think we had.

"It's for the kids' sakes," Mae told me sternly.

I sighed. Mama obviously had told her that Sid and I were sharing the same room and Mae obviously did not approve. It was probably just as well, given the tendency Sid and I had to get noisy, no matter our best efforts not to. I looked over at him and wondered how I was going to tell him about it. Mae took care of that part of it, and Sid took it philosophically.

Besides, Sid and I were quickly pulled into the big family debate - how to set up the Christmas lights on the house that year. It hadn't been an issue in the past. But this was the first holiday season in this house for the O'Malleys. Neil had inspected the eaves of the two-story place and had found some hooks in place. The other issue was that the front yard was rather small and overgrown with two really old, and consequently tall, trees and lots of huge yucca plants and some other bushes that had probably been there since the house had been built in the early aughts of the Twentieth Century. Neil pulled out the boxes that held the Christmas lights from their previous home in Orange County, and we measured the lengths, then got out a ladder and measured the eaves of their current house. Then there was the problem that a lot of the vegetation in front of the house obscured the house from the street, so even if the strings they had would fit (which, it turned out, they did), who would see them for all the trees and yucca?

Mae was completely against spending more money on new lights and extension cords. I was thrilled that Sid didn't offer to cover it. Neil, being the generally unflappable person he was, just shrugged and told Mae they could squeeze it. The subsequent trip to the local hardware store was a little scary, what with Marty and Mitch running all over the place, Ellen and Nick checking out various chemicals, and Janey hanging onto Sid and showing him paint chips for the bedroom she shared with Ellen.

The actual installation would take place the next day and I was really looking forward to it. Or I tried to. Neil offered to take us all out to dinner, and Sid graciously accepted. However, as I was getting ready to go, I was in the upstairs bathroom and couldn't miss the fight that was going on in the master bedroom.

"Why didn't you say anything?" Mae yelled.

I shuddered. I lived with Mae and Neil when I was in college, starting in 1976. They'd only been married for four years and had Darby and a new-born Janey. At the time, Neil had the terrible habit of not saying anything when he was annoyed or mad, then blowing up when he couldn't take it anymore. [Which explains why you were so adamant about trying to settle things when we had our first fight. – SEH] Fortunately, Neil and Mae got into Marriage Encounter and that gave both of them a safe way to talk things over that needed it. But every now and then, Neil would backslide.

"Because you've been feeling crappy enough!" Neil shouted back. He was seriously mad if he was yelling. "I didn't want to make it worse. I'm trying to be sensitive here."

"All I did was ask you to dress up a little."

"And we both know that has nothing to do with why you asked. Mae, I am fed up to my sinuses with how competitive you are with your sister."

"This has nothing to do with Sid."

"Bull!" Okay, he may have used the naughtier version. "It has everything to do with him and with Lisa. What is your problem with her?"

"She gets everything she wants!"

"No, she doesn't. You know that. You just don't..."

I didn't hear the rest. I fled downstairs and out of the house. Sid caught me at the end of the drive.

"They're fighting," I sobbed as he held me.

"I know. We've all been staying downstairs."

"But they're fighting over us."

"Lisa, you're not responsible for that."

"We're just making things worse."

"Do you really want to cut us off from the children?"

"No." I buried my head in his neck.

"I know, Lisapet. It sucks. But I'll bet they resolve it. They usually do."

I sniffed. "I know."

They did, and within time for us to go out to eat at our favorite seafood restaurant. Neil wore a sport coat and followed through on picking up the tab. Mae wasn't entirely thrilled, but she did smile at me. Ellen whispered something to Nick, who checked his watch.

"No, we've got time," Nick said. "We don't have to check it until later."

"Check what?" asked Mae.

"We did a chemistry experiment," Ellen said. "It's in the refrigerator. What time does it come out, Nick?"

"Nine o'clock." Nick grinned. "It's really small, Aunt Mae. But it'll be really cool. Man, if I don't decide to be a rock star, I'm going to become a chemist."

"I want to be a surgeon," Ellen said. "That way, you get rich."

Nick shrugged. "But I'm already rich. I can do what I want."

"I do that anyway," said Janey. "Personally, I think having money is okay. But I know a lot of people who have it and are unhappy, and a lot of people who are happy and don't have it."

"That's very wise, Janey," said Mae thoughtfully.

It turned out to be a rather nice evening, after all. However, some time well after midnight, my stomach burned, and my throat tightened. Another minute later, I groaned loudly and went running to the bathroom in the hall. How or why I was sick, I had no idea, but I emptied my guts into the toilet. Sid was, miraculously, there a minute later.

"I heard you crying," he whispered.

"How?" I asked, using my hand to cup some water from the sink and rinse my mouth out.

"Have no idea." He pulled me close and kissed my forehead. "You've got a fever. What have you eaten in the past twelve hours?"

"Nothing you or anyone else hasn't, I don't think."

Sid mused. "Probably not. And you seem to be the only one who's sick. Come on. I'm going to take you downstairs."

"Mae..."

"Will have to get over it. The bathroom down there is closer to my room, and do you really want to give Janey and Ellen whatever you've got?"

It was a rough night. Every thirty minutes, I was in the bathroom downstairs. Sid stayed with me the whole time.

Sometime around six-thirty, I woke up to see Mae standing over me.

"What are you doing in here?"

"I'm sick." I looked up at the ceiling, praying that my stomach was sending me a false alarm. "I've been throwing up."

"So have I every morning for the past two months. Don't be such a baby. Why are you in here with Sid?"

"It's where he put me. He didn't want me giving this to Janey and Ellen." It wasn't a false alarm. "Oh, no!"

Sid groaned and followed as I ran to the bathroom. It was especially rough. I was at that point where there was nothing to bring up, let alone how much my guts wanted to. Sid held my forehead and tummy as I retched, then helped me back into bed.

"Lisa!" Mae groaned.

Sid pulled her outside the room.

"Sid, she doesn't need to be babied like this."

"Nor do I when I get sick, but that's how we take care of each other."

"She's just a spoiled brat and always has been."

"Mae, I don't know how, but I heard Neil asking you if you needed any help this morning. You were not very nice about telling him no."

Mae let out a little sob. "You're right. I probably shouldn't be so rough on her. It just seems like she gets everything."

"Well, right now, she has the stomach flu. And there are a lot of things she doesn't have. You might want to think about that tomorrow morning."

"That's no help."

I heard the stairs creak and assumed Mae had gone back upstairs. Sid came back into the room, and I looked away.

"Let me guess," he said. "You heard us."

"Kind of hard not to. She doesn't want that baby, you know."

Sid slid into bed next to me. "I'm told she didn't want the twins, either, at first."

I sniffed. He gathered me into his arms and kissed my forehead.

"Honey, you're the one who believes in miracles." He sighed. "However, we're not officially married yet. You're not even thirty. Why don't we table this discussion for a year or two? We've got plenty to deal with right now."

"You're right." I swallowed.

Eventually, I drifted off and spent the rest of the day dozing on and off. I could hear Neil, Sid, and the kids going back and forth about the lights. The good news was that I was able to get on my feet long enough that evening to go outside and see what they'd done.

"It looks gorgeous!" I crowed.

The eaves were lined with lights, and the yucca plants and bushes had lights threaded throughout them, as well.

It was a good thing that I was pretty much over my bug by Sunday. Sid moved the three of us to a three-room suite at a hotel in Los Angeles to make it easier for Nick to get to school. That night, Sid ran for the bathroom, and I held him. He only barfed three times, but it was still bad. Nick was perfectly fine the next day, so I took him to school while Sid rested. When I brought Nick back later that afternoon, Sid was up and moving, though slowly. Nick was not in a good mood, although that had more to do with the pile of make-up work and homework that he had. Jesse had come by with our mail and some of the stuff from the condo so neither Sid nor I would have to go back there.

"She's been watching the condo off and on," Jesse told us. "And watching your house the rest of the time. It's looking like it's getting close to done."

"I know. I talked to Mary Smith today." Sid looked at me. Mary was the interior designer on the project, and, yes, another previous girlfriend. But she'd done Sid's house a couple times before I got there. I liked her. "We'll have to get out there sometime this week to finalize where everything's going and what we want from the condo."

Jesse sighed. "If you're going either of those places, do it between nine and noon. That's when she's at work. Kathy just called me that she'd ducked out at three today and went straight to the house."

Sid looked over at me.

"We should be functional tomorrow," I said. "Why don't we have a conference over at the condo in the morning? That way, we can take care of both things."

"Sounds good," said Sid. He looked at Jesse. "Does that work for you?"

"It does."

I went to call Mary Smith to set up a conference at the condo for that Friday morning. Fortunately, Sid had gotten bored just resting and had gotten the phone messages in order and had started on going over the writing work, which had, fortunately, slowed down. That made getting the mail taken care of rather easy, which was good because I was barely recovered, myself. At least, I was on solid foods again and Sid was eating toast.

That night, we both listened for Nick, but he slept through the night and was fine the next morning. I decided I was grateful for that.

Kathy and Jesse didn't have anything different to share the next morning. Henry joined us, as well, adding that he'd gotten both Beldon/Bolinaro's home and work phone lines tapped.

"It seems like she's working alone," Henry said. "I'm not sure why."

"Well, we've shut her down on the Quickline side of things," I said. "And based on her financials, she is running very low on cash."

Kathy smiled. "That's a relief. She won't be able to do that much."

"Which will also make her more desperate," Sid said grimly. "And that makes her more dangerous."

"Any reason we shouldn't bug her place?" Jesse asked.

Henry smiled. "Absolutely none. I can even arrange for a team to swap out the transmitter boxes and transcribe the tapes for you. It won't help with a court case, but it could help us set something up. You guys will have to get the bugs in place, though. It is pushing it on the legal side of things. Although it's not like we haven't done that before." He shrugged. "And I think we can make a good case that she can be considered an enemy agent."

So, the five of us went into planning mode. Sid and Jesse would break into Bolinaro's apartment the next day. Kathy, who was nervous about a break-in, would go with me that night to plant a bug in Bolinaro's office at the meat packing plant. Henry sent over some blueprints of the plant late that afternoon. I'm still not sure how he'd gotten them, but they made it easier to plot out our entrance and some alternative ways out of there should they be needed.

"I thought you said we wouldn't be doing anything il-legal," Kathy said as she drove us over to the plant shortly after midnight.

I shrugged. "Henry's blocked any police response tonight. Would he do that if it weren't legal?"

"I don't know."

"You'd just better be glad that Jesse didn't get into The Company." I shook my head. "Those guys don't give spit about legal, and you don't even want to know about some of the crud they're up to."

"I'm already finding out."

I looked at her. "Are you okay?"

"I'm just getting used to it."

"Yeah. I know. It took me a while, too. In some ways, I still am." I looked out the window. "Let's park it over here. It's a little chilly out, so I think we should put our sweatshirts on, but don't zip it up yet. Keep the mask and gloves in your pocket. We'll zip up and put the rest on right after we get to the target."

Kathy nodded, and we did exactly that. I double checked for signs of video surveillance but didn't see any. The blueprints didn't show any, but that didn't mean the plant wasn't wired. In fact, I was pretty sure it was, or if not that, then there had to be some sort of security, although not necessarily the legal kind.

I let Kathy pick the lock on the back door next to the receiving dock. The offices were all upstairs, and there was a staircase next to the back door. I kept a good eye on the surrounding area. The last thing we needed was someone to see us and there was a light on over the door. Kathy got the door open. I pulled my snub-nosed revolver out of my back holster and rolled into the plant first. Kathy slid in after me. As my eyes adjusted to the darkness, I saw that there was a wall with another door in it next to us. Somewhere deeper toward the front, a door shut. I saw the bobbing light of a flashlight on the balcony above us, where the offices were. It stopped for a moment. The guard tried an office door, then moved on to the next one.

I didn't curse, but I wanted to.

Softly, I opened the door next to us. A blast of cold air whipped out as Kathy and I scrambled inside. We got the door shut silently, then crept along the wall deeper into the pitch-black refrigerated room. I turned on a pen light, then moved into the middle, turned out the light and slammed into something cold, slimy, and greasy. Yelping, I almost dropped my gun.

I swallowed down the bile. It was just a side of beef. Still, I have this little phobia of corpses.

"You okay?" Kathy whispered, the low thrum of the refrigerator covering her voice somewhat.

"Fine. These things are just easier to deal with on little Styrofoam trays."

"What are we going to do about that guard?"

"Nothing, if we can help it."

The door at the front of the room opened. We froze in place. The beam from the flashlight bobbed around a little, but came nowhere near us. The door shut.

"Now, what?" Kathy asked.

"Start praying he's just doing his rounds." Flashing my light a couple times, I headed back to the side of the room, and we crept along the wall back toward the door.

I slowly and softly opened the latch and peeked my head out. There was a light on at the end of the hallway toward the front of the plant and the blue glow of a video. I listened and could only hear some very unconvincing moans and a bad soundtrack.

The stairs, thank Heaven, were metal, which meant we didn't have to worry about any surprise squeaking. However, it meant we'd have to step very carefully to avoid clunking noises. Kathy stumbled near the top and we froze. The sound of coarse laughter came from the office in the front. The moans and bad music also continued. We walked softly along the balcony, flicking the penlight on and off at each door until we found one that said C.

Bolinaro, Accounting. Kathy picked the lock while I stood guard.

Inside, I sent Kathy to set up the bug under the desk while I took a quick peek through the files, my penlight in my mouth. It was taking a chance, but somehow, I figured the guard was more interested in his porn flick. There was only one file that interested me, and it included several surveillance photos, including one of Sid and me at the house talking with Meilin Chu. Nothing with Kathy and Jesse, though, and I breathed a sigh of relief.

"It's in and on," Kathy breathed in my ear.

"Let's go."

My heart beating out of my chest, we slipped carefully down the staircase. The porn flick was still running.

We slid out of the door, got our masks and gloves off, and our sweatshirts open, and just in time. As we started for the car, another guard appeared around the side of the building.

"Evening, Ladies," he said to us. "What brings you out here in the middle of the night?"

"Working late," I said. "We decided to stick together. You know, just in case."

"Sure. Can I walk you to your car?"

"Thanks," I said.

"Thanks," Kathy said, forcing herself to smile.

The guard waited while we got in the car and drove off. I burst into laughter.

"Whew! You pulled it off!" I told Kathy.

"Can I breathe now?" Kathy asked. "I think I should pull over, I'm shaking so bad."

"You did a great job. Just go around the block. We have to check the receiver."

We went around, then pulled over next to a utility box across the street from the packing plant and I checked the box inside. A small red light glowed from a small box in the back corner. It had been installed earlier that day by someone on Henry's team.

"Looks like we're good," I told Kathy, getting back in the car. "Let's go home."

"I really did okay, huh?" Kathy smiled as we got onto the freeway.

"You did great." I grinned. "We didn't even have to pretend to be necking."

"Huh?"

"Things don't always go that smoothly. Sometimes we get chased, and Sid and I get just far enough ahead, pull off our sweatshirts and start necking to hide ourselves." I sighed. "It was fun those first few times. That was when we were trying not to touch each other."

Kathy just shook her head.

"Are you going to be okay?" I asked, watching her.

"Yeah. I think I am."

December 8 – 10, 1985

S id and Jesse planted their bug the next day without trouble, and we soon had transcripts coming in. Life was almost normal. We got into the condo in the mornings when we knew Bolinaro was at work and were able to not only get some writing done, we got some packing done, too. The house was ready, but Sid and I were debating whether we wanted to let anybody know. Bolinaro seemed to be watching for that kind of activity, and we weren't sure what to do about it.

The transcripts we got over the next few days helped a lot. There wasn't much, but she did make a couple calls, pleading for some help. According to the phone tap, the person on the other end of the line said he was only going to send her some equipment. He couldn't spare the extra men, given how many she'd lost already. She complained that she couldn't take us on all by herself, which, frankly, Sid and I doubted.

That Sunday, Sid surprised me by driving both Nick and me to Mass.

"I've got to bring communion to my shut-ins," I told him.

"I'll go with you," Sid said.

He'd been talking to Frank Lonnergan the night before and I'd gotten a bad feeling then that something was up.

"Do I want to know what's going on?" I asked.

Sid shrugged. "You'll find out soon enough."

In the sacristy, Father John Reynolds held me back just before Mass started.

"Can you be at a meeting, say, around two o'clock at the rectory?"

"I think I can do my shut-ins by then. What's up?"

"We have the planning meeting for the Christmas Midnight Mass."

"Okay. Can't Lety Sandoval be there to represent the Eucharistic Ministers?"

"She'll be there. I just think it might go more smoothly if you're there, as well."

"Why?"

John looked guilty. "We have a new organist."

My jaw dropped. "How...?"

"I do not know. Frank twisted his arm somehow."

"But the traditional choir sings Midnight, don't they?"

"Not this year." John shook his head in wonder. "I have no idea how he did it, but Frank convinced Mrs. Koch that it would be more restful for her crew to only do nine a.m., as usual. She's not that fond of the late services, anyway."

Nick was seated with Kathy and Jesse in the front of the church. As a minister, I walk in with the other ministers and the lectors. I was in the back of the church when the organ began the first soft notes of the opening hymn. Nick jumped and squirmed around, looking at the choir loft. Kathy and Jesse looked at each other and started sniggering.

I gave Kathy and Jesse the stink-eye when I slid into the pew and sat next to Nick.

"Is that...?" Nick hissed at me.

"I do believe so."

"How...?"

"I do not know, but somebody has some explaining to do."

Nick couldn't help laughing. At least, he did it softly.

After I and the other ministers processed out after mass, I scurried up to the choir loft. Sid was still playing the organ. I plopped down next to him on the bench. He concentrated on the closing hymn. But then it was over. Sid sat back and looked at me with a rueful smile.

"Let's just say I have cider in my ear," he said, anticipating my question. I frowned. "Guys and Dolls."

I gasped. It was a reference to the line about how you don't want to take an impossible bet because whoever wanted to make it had probably found a way to make it happen, as in make a card jump out of a deck and squirt cider in your ear. I looked over at Frank, who grinned, completely unrepentant.

"Rest assured, darling," Sid said. "I will never make another bet with him again."

"Dad!" Nick came running. "How did Frank sucker you into playing?"

"It's a long story, Nick." Sid gathered some sheet music together, then raised his eyebrow at me. "You have some errands to run?"

I drove to see my shut-ins. Sid mostly let me go in on my own, but I insisted he come in and say hello to Mrs. Salcido. Sid had only met her one time before, but she was a big fan of his and of Nick's. She was ecstatic when she saw both of them. Sid flirted with her and made her year.

"You are such a rascal!" she crowed. "Now, you be good to that woman of yours. She deserves the best, you know."

"I agree," said Sid.

We made it out of there in time to get a quick lunch, then back to the rectory for the meeting. Esther met us outside and offered to take Nick for the afternoon. Sid's mood had gotten tense. I saw why when the two of us went into the conference room. Frank and John were there. Marisol Torres and Julia Beckwith were there, representing the lectors. Tess Forsythe and Juanita Llanez were there as heads of the environment committee. Lety Sandoval had, indeed, shown up and looked at me with some relief. Maryann and Michael Dreyer were there, as well, although I wasn't sure which ministry they represented.

"Good," said John. "We're all here. Why don't you two have a seat?"

Sid sat down next to Frank, and I next to Sid. The Dreyers sat across the table from us. Maryann's perfectly poufed and glued hair almost trembled, as did Michael's jowls.

"Sid, you're not here to drop Lisa off?" Maryann asked, attempting to sound sweet.

"Sid's part of the committee," John said firmly.

Michael gaped. "He is? How?"

"I asked him to be here," said Frank. "He's accompanying the choir and in charge of the instruments, in general. I've chosen most of the music, but if there are to be any changes, he's got to know and okay them."

Maryann glared at John. "How could you? He's an atheist and..."

She didn't finish it, but we all knew she meant sinner.

John just looked at her. "I do not expect Sid to advise us on theology. However, he is an accomplished musician and, more to the point, willing to serve, which is more than I can say for over two-thirds of this parish."

"This is ridiculous," Michael said, getting his pudgy form up out of his chair.

"You're free to leave," said John, looking him straight in the eye.

Maryann got up as well. "We will. In fact, we are leaving this parish and going someplace else. Someplace that is more interested in the faith of its members than how good a show it can put on. That isn't going to risk the well-being of its parishioners by allowing diseased people into the school and the church. One that is more concerned about what kind of people are leading its youth." She glared at both Frank and me. "And what kind of people are Ministers of the Sacrament!"

Sid stood as well and glared at her. "If you believe your precious Scriptures, why don't you try re-reading Matthew, chapter seven, verses one through five. Or would you like me to quote? 'If you want to avoid judgment, stop passing judgment. Your verdict on others—'"

Michael pulled himself up with a sniff. "We know what it says."

"Then take the damned plank out your eyes!" Sid's voice had that really angry edge to it that should have scared the snot out of the Dreyers. "There is one Minister of the Sacrament who is beyond reproach and she sure as hell isn't you!"

I will give Sid credit. He didn't use worse language.

"We are leaving," Michael said, glaring at John. "And we are taking our money with us."

He and Maryann swept from the room. I got up and followed.

"Maryann. Michael." I said when we hit the front office. "If any of what you said about diseased people gets back to my son, you will regret it."

Michael sneered. "I do not respond to threats."

"Fine. I'm not making one. I don't have to."

They glanced at each other and swallowed, then left. I took a couple of deep breaths and went back to the conference room.

"I'm sorry," I said quietly. "I'm afraid I have just been dreadfully un-Christian."

Sid smiled at me as John cleared his throat.

Marisol Torres laughed. "You looked like you were going to kick their butts, Lisa."

"I almost wish you could have," Frank grumbled.

I caught both Sid and John trying not to laugh. They both knew I could. Probably without breathing heavily.

"John, how much is this going to cost the parish?" I asked, worried.

John chuckled. "Not nearly as much as they would like us to believe."

"Somehow, I'm not surprised," said Sid.

"But what if they go to the Cardinal?" Frank groaned. "You'll be in hot water."

John grinned. "Sorry, Frank. Nick Flaherty beat you to it. He punched Jason Dreyer out early last month."

"Oh, no!" I blinked.

"I heard about that," Julia gasped. "That Dreyer kid has been asking for it and then some."

"You can say that again," said Lety. "Josh told me that Nick had even been standing up to a couple of eighth graders who were pushing Jason around, only to have Jason unleash his nastiness on Nick."

"And Sister Maria let Nick off with only one day of suspension and Jason got detention for a week," John said. "Maria told me about it that afternoon, and I completely approved. So, the Dreyers went to the Cardinal's office. Last week, Monsignor Reed came down to check it out. He met with the Dreyers, then the two of us talked. He laughed and took me out to dinner and drinks. He's pegged them for who they are, narrow-minded, holier than thou busybodies. He heard about your plan for your new organist, Frank, and approved whole-heartedly. Now, does anyone else have any problems with an atheist playing at mass?"

Juanita looked at Sid and grinned. "Why? He obviously knows the Scriptures better than they do."

Lety, Tess, and Julia all agreed, and Sid seemed to relax a touch. Well, Tess and Juanita were big fans of his when he'd practice on Monday mornings and flirt with them. He was still feeling awkward about the whole religion thing, but at the same time, I got the impression that he didn't mind playing for the choir nearly as much as I would have thought. I debated asking him about it, but let it go. He was there. That was enough.

To Breanna, 11/14/00

Today's Topic: Describe a time when your parents made you feel safe. (cont.)

The weird thing is, if I may go off on a tangent, was that I still feel really bad for Jason, and to a lesser degree, for Josh Sandoval, too.

Josh has had a pretty hard time, although it could have been worse. At least Josh's folks supported him when he came out. Jason Dreyer did not have that at all. I think that's what made him such a little prick. I had a really hard time understanding why Josh was so in love with him. But I think it was that Josh was about the only kid in both junior high and high school who knew what Jason was and what Jason was going through. Jason's parents were not sympathetic. It really tore Josh up when Jason hung himself right before we went to college. His parents tried to cover it up. Josh wasn't having any of it.

It suddenly dawned on me that we were in the height of the Christmas season, and I was way behind on getting presents for my family and getting Christmas cards out. Well, there was getting the house ready, wedding plans, training my best friends in our side business, and, oh, yeah, someone who wanted to kill Sid and me. I was a little distracted. That Monday, Mae called and the next thing I knew, we had decided to meet at a mall in Pasadena the next day. Sid didn't have any objections but was bemused that I had agreed to go shopping with Mae when things were so fraught between us.

"I have to make some gesture," I said. "And I am really behind on the Christmas shopping."

Sid sighed. "As am I. Let me know what you come up with, will you?"

"I'll do my best."

The mall was fairly small, but I found several nice things. I was a little annoyed that I hadn't been able to make more of my presents. I usually do, but bridesmaids' dresses and cramped quarters had made that impossible.

Mae's mood had improved, but mine hadn't. I was getting peeved that I couldn't find just the right gift for Mama.

"Honestly, Lisa, she'll love whatever you get her," Mae said as we walked the length of the mall.

"She'll say she loves it," I said acerbically. "That doesn't mean she will."

"Hello, Janet Donaldson," said a woman's voice behind us.

The voice oozed evil intent, which stopped Mae in her tracks. I pretended not to notice, never mind that my heart was about to beat out of my chest.

"Or should I say, Lisa Wycherly?"

Mae turned first, and I turned with her. I noticed Mae's right hand slipping into her purse, which had been slung over her right shoulder. My right hand slid into my purse as well. I was going after my Model Thirteen revolver.

The woman was about average height. Her blond hair was poufed and glued. But there was a hard, mean look about her face that chilled me to my core.

"You're lucky there are too many people around here," Catherine Bolinaro said. Or, as I'd known her, Carol Beldon. "Otherwise I'd just waste you right now."

"I have no idea what you're talking about," I said.

Bolinaro cursed. "You do, too." Her eyes flicked over to Mae. "But I suppose you want to keep your sister out of it. Just keep in mind, I have no reason to keep her or anyone else in your family out of it."

"Get the hell out of here," Mae growled.

"Are you sure you don't want to know what all your baby sister is up to?"

"Get away from us," Mae said. "Now."

Bolinaro shrugged. "Fine. I'll see you later, Janet. Oops. I mean, Lisa."

Mae and I both watched her walk away. Then Mae almost collapsed.

"Let's go get something to eat," I said in a weak voice. "The seafood place?"

"Yeah." She looked at me, hurt and fear in her eyes. "And we'll only wait 'til we get there to talk about this."

It was early yet, but that did mean happy hour. Mae and I both ordered wine and some appetizers. As soon as the waitress was gone, I looked at Mae.

"I saw your right hand go into your purse," I said, praying that I could get her distracted enough to skip questioning me and figuring I probably couldn't. "Are you carrying?"

She nodded sadly. "That year you were unemployed I got attacked. Neil bought it for me. It's why I always bring my purse up to my room as soon as I walk in the door. We have a gun safe in the closet and the twins learned early not to touch Mommy's purse. Believe me, I don't tell anybody."

"All those self-righteous types, hell no." I sighed. Sid and I had installed locks on all the doors, drawers, cabinets we could to hide our armory and other equipment even before we remodeled.

"You're carrying, too," Mae said.

"Not because I want to." I sighed. She wasn't going to skip the questions.

The waitress brought our wine and Mae waited until she was gone.

"Why are you carrying?" Mae demanded. "Does it have something to do with that crazy lady?"

"I can't say," I said weakly.

"Bull-puckey. Who is Janet Donaldson?"

My head ducked. "I have no idea."

"You're lying."

"Mae, I can't tell you." I gasped and closed my eyes. "I mean it. I can't tell you."

"Oh, come on."

"If I could, don't you think I would?" I looked at her, practically begging. "You're my sister. I love you. If I could tell you what that was all about, I'd tell you in a New York second. It's… It's the contract for a ghost-writing project. I can't say anything about it to anyone. Can't you trust me?"

The waitress came by with the appetizers and we paused until she'd left.

"A contract?" Mae snorted. "That's ridiculous. Nobody expects you to keep secrets from your family, contract or not."

I swallowed and thought fast. "In most cases. But… Um… A breach of contract is kinda, sorta the problem."

Mae saw right through it, which scared me because I'm usually better at that kind of story-telling. I have to be.

"I'm not sure I can believe that," she snapped.

"Well, it's the best I can do right now." I reached over and grasped her hand. "Seriously, Mae, it really is. I hate that there's this barrier between us. I hate that you're jealous of me."

She looked away. "I'm not jealous."

"Bull-puckey."

Mae glared at me. "Why is it you have to keep outdoing me?"

"Okay. So, I did better at skeet than you did. It was still only fourth place."

"You got the lead in the musical your senior year. I barely made chorus." Mae sat back, folding her arms across her chest.

"You were also in the Chamber Singers. I never made that. You got the solo your senior year. And I was the understudy in the play. The only reason I got to play Annie Oakley was that the girl who had the part broke her leg. I didn't even get my name in the program. Her photo was in the newspaper." I threw up my hands. "You got to go to Great-Aunt Aggie's every summer. I got stuck fighting with the cousins at Grandma Caulfield's. I don't get it, Mae. You were the golden girl. All my life, all I heard was, 'Why can't you be more like your sister?'"

Mae rolled her eyes. "Mama and Daddy never said that to either of us!"

"But Mama kept expecting me to act like you. Even last summer, with the wedding, Mama thought I'd get all excited about it like you did. I've lived my entire life in your shadow. Straight A's Mae. I never got straight A's even when I was in grad school."

"Straight A's Mae." She closed her eyes and shook her head. "You really don't get it, Lisa."

"Get what?"

"Oh, come on. You've got the gorgeous rich fiancé. The nice house in Beverly Hills. You get nice jewelry to celebrate the date you met. Neil doesn't even remember what date we met!"

"You don't, either. And he's Neil. You love him."

"Yes, I do." Mae tried to blink back her tears and failed. "And you know what? I don't really care about what you've got. It's just that you've always gotten what you've wanted."

"I'm not an English professor. That was what I wanted."

"At least you knew you wanted it!" Mae's eyes blazed. She closed them again. "All my life, all I have ever done was what was expected of me. I took care of my baby sister. I got straight A's. I went to college. I got married and had children. I did everything for those children. The last thing I did for myself was fall in love with Neil. And you know what? In a way, I was expected to do that, too. Maybe not with Neil specifically, but with somebody. I don't even know what I want. I'm not sure I ever did. I mean, I love my babies and I love Neil. But where am I in all of that?"

"You're in there," I said.

"How can you be so sure?"

I looked away. "I don't know. But you must be, Mae. Mama raised us to be independent."

"I hope so." Mae took a deep breath. "Neil keeps saying that he's worried about me. That I've lost myself."

I winced. "Maybe you have."

"How do I get myself back?"

"Maybe do something for yourself for a change?"

She looked at me. "Like you do?"

"Well, yeah. Not that I always do everything for myself. I do an awful lot for Sid and Nick, and the teens at church."

"I didn't mean it that way. Come on. You take communion to shut-ins, for crying out loud." Mae glared at her wineglass. "It's just... things like you and Sid sharing a bed already. I was a virgin when I got married and it was only because that was what I was supposed to be. Believe me, I would have loved not waiting."

"I'm sure you would have." I winced. "But I have my reasons, and they have a lot to do with who Sid is and who I am. And you did what you did because of who you and

Neil are. It's like what Sid says. We have to be who we are on our own terms."

"Neil says the same thing." She sighed. "Now what do we do?"

"I don't know." I frowned. "Just so you know, my life isn't all sunshine and roses. Yeah, Sid is wonderful, but he comes with a pretty insane past."

"How do you deal with that?"

I shrugged. "He's over it. That helps a lot. But it's still there."

"Yeah." Mae rolled her eyes. "The weird thing is, I think I know. Last summer when you were at camp and Sid had us over to that beach house? One night, I was reading in our room, and I could hear Sid and Neil laughing their backsides off downstairs. They'd only had a beer or two, so it wasn't that. I found out later, though. It's probably how I ended up pregnant again. Neil had asked Sid what the big secret to his popularity was."

My jaw dropped. "You're kidding."

"I'm not. Things were different in the bedroom after that night. I called Neil on it, and he told me that he'd asked Sid, thinking it was some little trick. Turns out it was a philosophy. Neil wouldn't say what it was, but it definitely had its impact." Mae looked at me and blushed. "Mama said you and Sid are not... You know."

"Well, not all the way." I winced. "Did she say why?"

"No." Mae blushed. "But with Neil and all, I think I know what your sex life is going to be like better than you do."

"You and at least a third of the female population of the greater Los Angeles area." I couldn't help how bitter that sounded.

"You're exaggerating."

"Not by that much. Trust me, he's gone through a lot of women."

Mae grimaced. "Aren't you worried about things like AIDS?"

I sighed. "That's why we're not doing it all the way. Last spring one of his girlfriends called. She had it. Turned out she'd been exposed after her fling with Sid, but then we found out he could have picked it up, anyway. He's tested negative so far. But they don't know for sure how long it takes the virus to show up in the bloodstream after exposure, and he's waiting until right before the wedding just to be sure."

"And now you've got a crazy woman after you." Mae shook her head. "Take the jewelry and the fancy house. I don't want to live with AIDS scares and crazy people."

"And what about what you do want? How are you going to find that?"

"I don't know. Neil wants me to find a job. He thinks it will help."

"It might. Do you know what you'd like to do?"

"No. But I heard there's a volunteer opening at the local library. That could be fun." She sighed. "And it won't matter if I'm pregnant. I might also be able to audit classes at USC. With Neil being faculty there, his family members can take classes for free."

"That means you can try a lot of different things."

"Yeah. It does." Mae looked at me. "Do you think I should?"

I shrugged. "Maybe. But I'm not the one who gets to decide that. You do."

"Oh. You're right."

Later, Sid was not happy that Bolinaro had found us. "How could she have? Our phone lines are secure."

I suddenly groaned. "Mae's aren't."

We slipped out that night and snuck into the O'Malley house. Sure enough, we found the taps and got rid of them, then got out of there with no one inside any the wiser.

December 14–20, 1985

It was really annoying having to limit ourselves to certain hours to go to the condo or the house, but we finally got everything out of the condo that we needed or wanted in the house, then got that stuff moved into the house and arranged the way we wanted. We also got my truck out of storage, which helped with moving some of the smaller items we didn't want to box up.

We took advantage of having the moving and storage people at the house to work later than we should have and there was no question that Bolinaro knew we had moved in. We saw the conversation with her brother in a transcript. She'd gotten her equipment but was still on her own as far as paid help was concerned.

Sid, however, thought of a way that we could at least celebrate the holidays in relative peace. He invited Mama and Daddy to come in early, then asked Stella to join us, as well. After all, if Bolinaro didn't want to waste us with other people around, it would be good to have them around. Sid stipulated with Stella that clothing would be required in all common areas of the house and that she would need to respect any closed doors. Stella agreed, then asked if she could bring a friend and Sid said sure.

When we got Mama and Daddy from the airport that Saturday, I was in high spirits.

"Mama, the place is gorgeous!" I crowed in the Beemer. "We're almost completely moved in. We need to put away the clothes is all."

"The breakfront and the pantry need organizing," Sid said.

I sniggered in spite of myself. Conchetta had been to the house the day before and had already started organizing the big, new pantry the way she liked it. She and Sid were still working out how they were going to share the kitchen space.

We'd kept the footprint of the house - there really was no reason to change that. The center of the house, from where our offices had been, through the former library to the rumpus room, had all been opened up. The two walls on either side of the library had been load-bearing walls, so we couldn't take those down easily. But there were wood floor hallways across both ends of what was now a huge living room and dining area. Sid's ebony baby grand piano had been moved into the middle of the living room, which also had three couches and several wing back chairs in various groupings. Our now single office was in the one corner where Sid's bedroom had been, with three bedrooms and bathrooms along that side of the house. The rumpus room may have had an open arch into it, but it was pretty similar to before, with a wet bar, and shelving holding our records, video tapes and Sid's stereo system. The television was on the opposite wall, and chairs and pillows were scattered about. On the other side of the new living room from the bedrooms was another hallway, stairs leading to the new upstairs, and Nick's bedroom, which had been the dining room. We'd expanded the kitchen into what had been the breakfast room and the new breakfast room took up what had been my bedroom and workroom. The former living room was now the library, with a fireplace, wing back chairs, a cozy window seat just perfect for reading in overlooking the front yard, and a walnut baby grand piano.

Upstairs was the loft, which led to the sundeck and hot tub. On the other side of that was our bedroom. A new semi-waveless waterbed was set up at the far end and it had bedposts. I put my rosary there with great satisfaction. The antique dresser we'd had in the condo had been set on the front wall, flanked by full-length mirrors. Across the room from that, there was another fireplace with two more wing back chairs and ottomans and a reading table between them. Near that was a door that led into the gigantic bathroom and walk-in closet. The door on the other side of that led to the work room. The upright piano, shelves for sheet music, music racks, and chairs took up half, near another door into the loft. The other half held all my sewing machines, my flat presser, a perfectly sized cutting table, and tons of storage and hanging racks.

And one other goodie that had my mother's eyes open wide with envy. It was a professional, gravity-feed iron, with a hanging tank, like the one we'd had in the laundry at the resort my parents own in South Lake Tahoe. It was how I got into sewing in batches. Both Mama and I would keep sewing on our different projects until we couldn't anymore, then take everything down to the laundry and press it with the professional iron. The problem was that when I became a junior in high school and started working his souvenir store, Daddy decided to contract out the laundry service, and the gravity-feed iron went out with it.

"How did you get that?" Mama asked me.

"Our decorator, Mary Smith, got it for me." I grinned. "I finally have room for one."

We did have quite a few blank spots on the walls that would need filling in with art as we found it, but all our other treasures were perfectly placed. Mary Smith had even put out most of the pillows and afghans I'd made for the house before we remodeled.

"Well, this is lovely!" Mama gasped and even Daddy was impressed.

"Wait 'til I show you my room," Nick said, pulling Daddy's hand.

Kathy and Jesse arrived with the cats and Motley. Motley barked and ran around everywhere, sniffing and sniffing. The cats slunk out of sight and stayed that way for almost the rest of the week. We'd put out plenty of litter boxes, but one cat, we still don't know who, expressed displeasure by leaving a pile of poop in one of Sid's dress shoes. The first thing Fritz, the gray tabby, did was run outside. It took Nick half an hour and a full can of tuna to coax him back inside before dinner that night. Fritz did take to Daddy for some reason.

"Am I correct in assuming that Sid named this one?" Daddy softly asked me as he held Fritz and scratched the cat between the ears.

I laughed. "Yes, Daddy."

"Then you heard of the film?"

"Oh, yes. Haven't seen it and don't want to."

Daddy shrugged. "It wasn't that good."

We did have one bad patch that evening, though.

It was Nick's first Christmas without his first mom and his first with Sid and me. We'd invited him the year before, but he'd had an inkling that his mom hadn't been doing as well as she'd said and had chosen to spend the holiday with her. Sid and I hadn't known then what was going on - Rachel had sworn her son to secrecy about her illness, but I was glad that Nick had taken that time with her.

After dinner, we got a call from Rachel's friend Marlou Parks, who had taken care of Rachel and Nick in the months before Rachel's death. Nick had called Marlou earlier that morning. He picked up the phone in the breakfast room. I was right there and it was a good thing I was.

"Did you find them?" he asked happily.

I didn't hear what Marlou said, but Nick's eyes filled and he blinked the tears back furiously.

"No, that's okay," he told her. "It's not your fault. Good-bye."

He slammed the phone onto the hook and burst into tears. I pulled him into my arms and held him tightly.

"What's wrong, my sweet guy?"

"My Christmas ornaments!" Nick sobbed. "We couldn't find them last summer, remember? That's why I called Marlou. I thought maybe she had. She didn't know we were looking for them."

"So, she can't find them?" I asked softly.

"No!" Nick wailed. "Mom broke them all! Marlou said she got really mad when she found out that the last round of chemo hadn't worked and took it out on the ornaments."

"Oh, Nick!" I held him even tighter.

There was nothing to be said. Mama and Sid had overheard the last part, and each took a turn holding the boy as he cried.

He cried a little again the next morning when I said I wanted to get the Christmas tree that afternoon after mass and lunch. But then he decided that he wanted to go with me to pick it out.

We got back to the house around four that afternoon and I was ecstatic.

"I did it!" I hollered into the front doorway.

Sid and Daddy came outside to the driveway to look at the Christmas tree poking out of the shell on my Datsun four-by-four pickup.

"It's absolutely perfect," I told them excitedly.

"I'm sure it is," said Sid.

"I can't believe I did it again."

"She is so picky," Nick said. "But it really is a great tree."

Sid pulled the tailgate down and tried to figure out how he was going to get in the back to get the bottom of the tree out.

"Lift it," I told him. "We don't want to break any of the branches."

Sid rolled his eyes. "I know. We've done this before. Remember?"

Daddy just laughed. Mama came outside.

"I can't believe I did it again." I hugged her. "It is the most gorgeous tree!"

There was a great deal of grunting and maneuvering, but Sid and Daddy got the tree out of the truck, and it was unscathed. It was a larger tree than Sid and I'd had in the past because we'd raised the ceiling a few feet in the living room niche at the front of the house where the offices had been. The tree absolutely had to go there, too. It was the front window. That's where a Christmas tree belongs. I opened the double front doors all the way as Daddy and Sid lugged the tree around the rose garden in the postage-stamp-sized front yard.

"Bring it in bottom first," I called.

"We know!" Sid called back.

Mama had the tree stand ready in the niche. Nick helped Daddy and Sid get the tree in the stand and then upright. It was exactly five inches too tall.

"I did it again," I sighed.

"Yeah, you did, honey," Daddy said. He looked at Sid. "Every year, the same thing."

"I know." Sid shook his head. "And always five inches. Not four, not six. Five inches." He looked at me. "Why don't you take five inches off your estimate?"

"But I do." I looked at him haplessly. "I'll go get the saw."

Nick took over helping Daddy and Sid saw the five inches off the bottom of the tree because Mama pulled me aside and handed me a medium-sized cardboard box.

"I thought it was time to give you some of these."

I opened the box. Swathed in all kinds of tissue paper were old glass balls and other ornaments that I'd grown up with.

"Oh, Mama!" I sniffed. "They're wonderful!"

I looked back over at Nick. Mama knew what I was thinking.

"It's alright." She patted my arm. "I told him I had some of yours at lunch today. We had a little cry, but he's okay."

Nick suddenly ran up. "Oh, woh." He squeaked, then took a deep breath. "Are those them?"

"Yes, Nick," Mama said. She plucked one out of the box. "This one was always your mama's favorite."

It was a blue and green glass bird with an angel hair tail, glitter falling off the sides, and a metal clip for the feet.

"I love that one." I took it from her. The paint had flaked a little here and there, but it was still very pretty.

"Alright, Nick, honey." Mama put her arms around his shoulders. "Let's go get ready. We're going to the movies in a bit."

"But we gotta decorate the tree."

Sid put his hands on Nick's shoulders. "There will be lots of things we will do together for the holidays, son. But decorating the tree is something your mom and I will save to do by ourselves." Sid looked at me and smiled. "It's something that's become pretty special for us, and I want to keep that going."

Nick looked at the two of us. "Bleah! You're going to get all goopy-eyed, aren't you?"

"Yep." I grinned at Sid.

"Let's go to the movies, Grandma."

I laughed and blinked my eyes as my boy ran off to get his coat. I was so grateful we at least had most of his baby and school pictures. So much of Nick's early childhood was lost because Rachel hadn't told Nick that much and we didn't know him until he was eleven.

The phone rang on Sid's personal line, and Daddy went and got it. The manager at the resort in South Lake Tahoe had a question. Christmas was their busiest season after summer. Mae later told me Daddy had always taken business calls while staying with them during the holidays, which I'd never noticed. Daddy's business was set up to mostly run by itself. Nonetheless, Daddy spent a lot of time talking to his managers at both the motel in South Florida and in Tahoe. Sid had told Daddy to use Sid's old personal line since no one was calling it anymore.

Daddy finished the call quickly and got Mama and Nick out to my truck. As soon as they were gone, I looked at Sid.

"Are we going to be safe?"

He sighed. "We should know in a few. Last time I checked with the surveillance team, she hadn't left her apartment."

"I wonder what she's waiting for."

"Probably for us to go off our guard." He shrugged. "We still have a tree to decorate, you know, and I really do like keeping that one for us."

"I do, too."

It was a special time for us. When I got our first tree, that first Christmas after I'd come to work for Sid, we'd had to go out and buy all new ornaments and trims. The previous three years, we'd found additional ornaments, each reflecting on the year before, not that anyone would necessarily know what each one signified. Sid grinned as he pulled out that year's addition, a glittering replica of the Gateway Arch in St. Louis, where we'd been the previous summer and discovered Nick's talent for tailing people. My offering was a trombone made of heavily starched lace, and nicely glittered.

Sid laughed. "You got that from the lace store in New Orleans, didn't you?"

We'd stopped there after St. Louis.

"Well, I did order it when I ordered the lace for my wedding dress." I grinned, my eyes getting full.

Sid chuckled. "I came close to buying it, too, but couldn't figure out how I was going to get it past you."

We had just hung the last ornament and were happily necking in the glow of the twinkling lights when Nick's disgusted groan announced that they'd come back. Sid laughed, and we all got hot chocolate, then played music and sang.

It was a nice, quiet week. No Quickline business came through at all. Bolinaro kept her distance, as we were hoping she would. We still made a point of leaving only when she was at work. Mama, Sid, and I went to the hotel where our wedding reception would be to finalize the menu and the table settings. Frank took us to audition a couple bands for the reception and we signed a contract with one then and there. The invitations arrived from the printers and Mama was thrilled, even with the non-traditional wording that left my full name intact. Jesse came over and showed Mama some of the other weddings he'd shot - he is a professional photographer, and that mollified her. And she loved the fabric Mae and I had found for the bridesmaid tops.

Thursday, Mama shooed Sid out of our bedroom.

"You can't see this," she told him, never mind that not only had Sid seen the dress, he'd helped fit it on me.

I slid into the white lace dress with the silk underlining. Mama did up the buttons in the back, then turned to look at me.

"Oh, my." Mama sniffed. "It's just beautiful, Lisle."

"I told you I'd have it done in plenty of time." I swirled and looked at myself in the two full-length mirrors on either side of the antique dresser. "In fact, it was done before Maggie's wedding."

The white dress had a Victorian collar and gathered skirt. The hem hit right at my ankles, and I was debating wearing white flats or a pair of high-heeled sandals. Sid had approved either choice, so I decided to let Mama weigh in. I put on the sandals first.

"Those are quite elegant." Mama nodded. "But are they going to be comfortable? You are going to be on your feet an awful lot that day."

"That's true." I bent and got out of the heels. "But the flats, they are a little blah."

I tried them on, and Mama sighed.

"Those heels are spectacular. On the other hand, you won't have to worry about the flats catching and ripping out the bottom of the dress."

I frowned. "There's that, too."

We remained undecided.

We also squeezed in a fair amount of Christmas shopping. Sid and I had already gotten out our Christmas cards, but kept having to send new ones out as other cards came in. The pile of presents under the Christmas tree slowly grew. Mama had brought a stack of special Christmas stockings for all of us, including Stella and her friend. Mama even had the fabric paint to put the friend's name on the stocking once we knew it. We hung the whole pile of stockings on the fireplace mantle in the library. It was a little crowded but looked very festive.

Friday, Mama and Daddy rented a car and went out to Pasadena to see how Mae and Neil's house was coming along while Sid, Nick, and I went to get Stella and her friend at the airport. Stella had told us the two of them would share a room and Sid said that was fine. I could tell he was perplexed, though. Well, Stella had been exceedingly vague about who this friend was, to the point of not even mentioning the person's gender.

As it turned out, the person who walked off the plane at Stella's side was a tallish man with a round tummy and full dark-gray beard, wearing an Alpine hat and a tweed sport coat with a dark brown wool vest underneath. He had a violin case slung over his shoulder instead of a regular carryon bag.

Sid's eyes opened wide. "I'll be damned."

"We're over here!" I hollered and waved.

A minute later, Stella and I were hugging, and the older gentleman had Sid's right hand in both of his.

"Sid, it has been too long," he said as Nick hugged Stella. "You've certainly done well for yourself. I can't tell you how good you look."

"Thank you, Sy. You're looking good, yourself. Lisa, this is Dr. Sylvester Flournoy. Sy, this is my fiancée, Lisa Wycherly."

"How do you do?" I extended my right hand.

Sy immediately took it in both of his. "Ah, my dear woman. I have long been waiting to meet the treasure that could get Sid to marry her."

"Long been waiting?" Stella snorted. "You didn't even know she existed until last month."

"I didn't have to know she existed to know that I'd want to meet her." Sy still grinned at Stella.

Stella rolled her eyes.

Sid pushed Nick forward. "And my son, Nick."

"A pleasure to meet you, young man." Sy smiled as Nick shook his hand.

"Pleased to meet you, sir. What do I call you?"

Sy grinned. "Why not Sy? That's what everyone else calls me."

"Why don't we go get the luggage?" Sid said.

We walked toward the baggage claim. Well, Nick ran ahead.

"Sy, I hope you don't mind," Sid said. "But as I explained to Stella, Lisa's parents are staying with us, and her sister's family will be joining us."

"Stella briefed me on the ground rules," Sy said. "I will do my best to keep her in line."

"I don't need keeping in line." Stella glared fondly at Sy. "It's ridiculous encouraging such shame over the human form and hiding basic, normal human acts."

"It's privacy, Stella," Sid said with a sigh. "Nobody's ashamed. They just want to keep their bodies and their love lives to themselves."

"The boy has a point," Sy said, giving Stella a squeeze around the shoulders. "I'm perfectly content keeping our love life to ourselves."

Sid stopped walking and looked at Sy and Stella. "Love life?"

"Yes. Sy and I have been lovers since before you were born." Stella apparently thought that was obvious.

Nick came up and slid his arm around my waist. I slid my arm around his shoulders.

"Lovers? I didn't know that." Sid looked away, then back at her. "You were never interested in sex."

"Bleah!" Nick dashed off again.

Stella looked at Sid strangely. "Where the hell did you get that idea?"

"You never did it."

Sy laughed hard and squeezed Stella's shoulders.

"Of course, I did." Stella rolled her eyes. "Whenever Sy was visiting or we visited Sy. You used to walk in on the two of us quite frequently when you were little. I mean, we did resort to waiting to have sex until you were asleep or otherwise not around, but that was because I didn't want to answer whatever questions you had while I was trying to concentrate on getting laid."

"Wait. There was that night I got sick when I was twelve." Sid frowned as he remembered. "Sy was there and you were sitting up in bed. You were having sex?"

"We most certainly were." Stella smiled at Sy, who smiled back. "Of course, that was before you lost your virginity."

"I knew what having sex looked like." Sid sounded remarkably like Nick at that moment.

"You were twelve?" Stella looked speculatively at him, then tapped her forehead. "Oh, that's right. That's when we realized you couldn't see past the end of your nose."

"That would explain it." Sid looked bemused. "I really thought you weren't interested. Maybe Donovan Smith."

"Donovan?" Stella let out a high-pitched snort. "Good lord, no! That stoner couldn't have gotten it up if he wanted to. And I never really liked him that much. I don't know why you did."

"He liked me."

"That he did."

Nick ran up again. "Are you guys done talking about sex?"

"For the moment, young man." Stella smiled at the boy.

When we got back to the house, I let Sid and Nick get Sy and Stella settled in their room while I called Mae's house. Mama and Daddy were still there.

"How do you spell his name?" Mama asked when I told her who Stella's friend was.

"His real name is Sylvester, but we keep calling him Sy."

"That's good enough. I'll take care of the stocking tonight. Do you know anything else about him?"

"Not yet. Just that he's Stella's lover and has been for years." I paused. "Are you okay with that?"

"Honey, we do not judge other people. You know that."

"You think Mae's going to be okay? She does get worried about the kids."

"I doubt they'll even notice. Well, Janey might, but she's the least of our worries."

"True. Just remember to lock your door. Stella's promised not to walk in without knocking, but she might forget."

Mama laughed. "So, at last, we get to see how Sid got to be who he is. This is going to be fun."

As we finished dinner, Stella left the table, then came out of her room with a box. It was made of the same cardboard as a shoe box and was about six inches tall and eighteen by eighteen inches. The white sides were in good shape, but you could tell that Stella had had it a very long time.

She sighed and pushed the box at Sid. "I thought you might like to look at these."

Sid's eye opened wide as he lifted the lid. "You had pictures?"

"Of course."

Nick jumped up from his seat and looked over Sid's shoulder. "That's you, Dad?"

"Yeah," said Sid in awe. "I've never seen these before. Crap, that's my kindergarten picture."

I looked and couldn't help saying awww. "You were adorable!"

Nick disappeared, but came back with a photo album of his own. "Hey, Dad, look! Here's my kindergarten picture."

Sid's photo was in black and white, Nick's in color, but both pictures looked like they were of the same kid. Sid passed the album to Stella.

"My goodness!" Stella laughed.

A red light popped up on the security system box near the ceiling in the front of the living room. Sid and I froze.

"Can we come in?" Mama called from the front.

We both relaxed.

"We're in the dining room, Mama," I called.

Sid got up and introduced Sy to my parents. I could tell Stella was still a little cautious around my religious parents, even after the evening she'd spent with us in Florida. Part of it was having Sy there as her lover. Neither Mama nor Daddy blinked when Stella called him her lover.

"What's this?" Mama coming around to where the photo box was. "Landsakes, Sid. Are these your baby pictures?"

Sid and I looked at each other in horror.

"Mama, no!" I put my hand over the photos. "Absolutely not! Do not even think about it."

"What on earth?" Stella asked.

Mama laughed. "It's the most adorable thing. I've seen it at several weddings. They put out a little display of the bride and groom's baby pictures."

"You're outvoted, Althea," Sid said firmly.

"They don't want to do it." Mama rolled her eyes.

"I don't see why not." Stella pawed through the photos. "Sid was a very nice-looking baby. Here. Look at this one. He was nine months old."

"Oh, wasn't he a charmer?"

Stella chuckled. "He was, indeed."

"We're still not doing it, Mama." I folded my arms across my chest. "And, Stella, you're not going to change mine or Sid's minds."

"Absolutely not," said Sid.

Mama and Stella shook their heads, and we continued poring over the photos as Mama set about finding out as much about Stella and Sy as she could. I knew what she was doing. There was going to be a shopping trip the next day.

Sy explained that he was a professor of music at Juilliard and had known Stella since the two were undergrads at the prestigious arts school. Sy's expertise was in the violin and other string instruments. He was quite interested to hear Mama bragging about Darby and his violin. Later, we retreated to the living room. Sy got out his violin and Sid offered Stella a seat at the ebony baby grand. Sid was persnickety about who touched his pianos, so that was a major concession on his part. Stella ran her fingers over the keys and smiled at Sid in approval. Sy tuned his violin, and then smiled at Stella, who nodded.

I have no idea what they played and don't really care. The music was so insanely beautiful, both Mama and I had tears in our eyes as we listened. The best part was watching Stella and Sy, completely in tune with each other, the covert glances speaking volumes about what they felt for each other. So Stella did know what love was. She just didn't know the right words for it.

December 22, 1985

S id had warned Stella that he was mixed up in parish affairs far more than she would be comfortable with. Sunday morning was a little rough for both of them. Stella was not at all excited that Sid was coming to Mass with Nick and me. But I must give Sid credit. He found the right approach for Stella. [It was Frank's idea, although he didn't know it. - SEH]

"You're not going to like this," Sid told her before dragging her and Sy along as well. "But I want you to give me a chance. You know I don't believe. That's still who I am."

Stella sighed and braced herself. Given the hurt she'd experienced, I had to give her a lot of credit for going along with Sid.

Mama and Daddy were on our heels with Nick in the car my parents had rented.

Sid, Stella, Sy, and I stopped in the church's vestibule.

Sid took a deep breath. "Yeah. I'm playing for this mass." He looked at Stella and smiled. "But come upstairs with me."

Both Sy and I followed. Sid paused right before he and Stella entered the choir loft.

"Let's just say that playing for the choir is the fee I pay," Sid told her.

Stella frowned at him. "What the hell are you talking about?"

"The fee for playing with this." Sid jerked his thumb over his shoulder, then showed Stella the organ.

Our church's organ is a magnificent example of the instrument, and Stella saw that immediately. Her jaw all but dropped. She touched the instrument with a curious mix of utter reverence and utter lust at the same time.

"Want to play a few chords?" Sid asked her, glancing at Frank, who was getting set up for directing the choir.

"Oh, yes," Stella said, mesmerized by the three keyboards and the collection of stops.

"No Toccatta and Fugue." Sid nodded at the assembly coming into the church, even as he powered the organ up. "We don't want to freak them out."

Stella sighed but went with it. She looked over the stops, selected a few, then launched into some other Bach fugue. It was so gorgeous. Sy laughed gently as he watched Stella play. I checked my watch.

"I've got to go," I told Sid and kissed him quickly.

The other choir members were drifting in and looking at the organ with bemusement. I waved at Frank, who had figured out that we'd explain later. I ran down to the sacristy.

Nick had gotten my parents to a front pew. Jesse was on the schedule as a Eucharistic Minister and Kathy was one of the lectors that day, and they were both in the sacristy when I got there.

"Sid's warming up early," Kathy muttered to me before we did our group prayer before Mass.

"It's not Sid," I whispered back. "It's his aunt."

"Really?" Kathy laughed.

"It's Bach. Written for the greater glory of God."

We had a visiting priest saying mass that morning and as he began the Mass, he remarked on the beauty of the music that had come from the choir loft before the first hymn. I don't know if that mollified Stella at all, but she'd had a lovely time. Sid also let her play after the final hymn. It was another Bach fugue. I wondered how she knew them so well that she could play them without sheet music, but didn't worry about it, either.

I took Nick and Mama with me to visit the shut-ins, and Sid rode home with Stella, Sy, and Daddy. By the time Mama, Nick, and I got back to the house, the chaos had already started. Mae, Neil, and the kids had arrived. Kathy and Jesse and Frank and Esther were also there. Kathy, Sid, and Mae were busy setting up a lunch buffet on the dining room table. Sy, Frank, and Darby had disappeared upstairs - I later found out to the music side of the workroom. The twins were all over the place. Janey had cornered Stella and the two of them were someplace in conference. Ellen left Sid's side as soon as she saw Nick and the two of them disappeared, which I had to confess had me mildly worried. Daddy, Neil, and Esther were kicking back in the library. Mama went to help with the buffet. I went upstairs to change into jeans, shirt, and a sweater.

There were sandwiches and salads for lunch, all of which could sit out without begging for food poisoning. Okay, Sid may have been taking a slight chance with the chicken salad he'd put out. It was all delicious, and I certainly made several passes at the buffet.

Around four, Sid, Kathy, Mama, and Mae pulled in the lunch buffet and started talking about dinner. That, however, got postponed when Sy came downstairs with Stella, Darby, and Frank following him.

"Mae O'Malley," Sy announced in a particularly sonorous voice.

Neil came in from the rumpus room.

"Eh, Neil, too." Sy added. "We need to have a serious discussion about your son."

"Which son?" asked Mae, in full mama bear mode.

"Darby." Sy didn't even blink, and I have to give him a lot of credit for that. "We have been playing for most of the afternoon. I am exceedingly impressed by his talent. I'm sure you, Mae and Neil, are doing everything for him you can, and that could be considered enough had Darby an ordinary talent."

"He's talented enough," Mae growled.

"Ah, but he's more," said Sy. "He's not entirely a prodigy, but he has an enormous amount of potential. His training needs to be very carefully supervised, and through no fault of your own, you are not qualified to do so."

"We're not?" Mae glared at him.

Sy didn't quail, but did realize that he'd made a gaffe. "My apologies, dear woman. You are, of course, the final judge. However, I am a Doctor of Music with a specialty in strings. I have studied in Vienna, Paris, and Israel. I am also head of the strings department at the Juilliard School of Music in New York."

Darby let out a panicked whimper. I tried not to giggle as I realized something else about Sy.

"Those are good qualifications," Neil said, putting his arm around Mae's shoulders.

"Sy will arrange for a new instructor for Darby," Stella said. "In the meantime, he will study French, Hebrew, and German. When he's old enough, he'll go to the New York High School of Performing Arts."

Mae was on her feet. "You can't come in here and tell me how I'm going to educate my son!"

"Mom!" Darby groaned.

Mae looked at him. "I'm not saying you won't. But it's not their decision."

"Mom!" Darby paled. "You can't yell at him. He's important."

"Not as important to me as you are," Mae said, glaring at Stella and Sy. "Okay. I appreciate what you're saying and I'm happy to hear your suggestions. But any decisions to be made will be made between me, my husband, and Darby. We do want to develop Darby's talent, but we have to consider other things, like finances, can Darby handle going to school that far away from home, and if he can't, is it feasible for us to move? Those are things you are not qualified to decide. Only we are."

Sy bowed slightly and held Stella back. "Of course. Pray excuse our enthusiasm. Naturally, you must consider those things. However, please do not allow money to be a barrier. A young man with Darby's potential is eligible for all manner of scholarships and grants. Stella is even considering sponsoring him as she has and does for many young musicians. There may even be money from competitions."

"We'll keep that in mind." Mae was not even close to being mollified.

"We can continue to discuss this over the next week or so," Sy said. "I fully intend to enjoy as many of the sights of Los Angeles as I can. However, we will find a time to have another meeting or two." He smiled warmly at Mae and Neil. "Finding a new talent has always been one of my greatest joys. I have found one in your son." Sy turned to Sid. "I must congratulate you, my boy."

Sid lifted an eyebrow. "Yeah?"

"You, at last, have found your calling."

"I have?" Sid looked more than a little startled.

"Indeed, yes." Sy beamed. "You've done an excellent job of instructing Darby on the piano. We both know you are not a concert pianist, and I don't doubt you haven't the least aspiration to such. But you are an exceptional teacher, much like Stella is."

Sid smiled, utterly bemused. "I never thought of myself as a teacher."

"Ah, but you have the gift for it. If your son and fiancée haven't learned, then you know a great truth. There is no learning where there is no interest."

Sid's eyes flicked over to mine, and I shrugged.

When we finally got around to eating dinner, I checked in with Frank, who looked oddly shell-shocked.

"That's Sylvester Flournoy?" Frank asked, almost incredulously.

"That's the name he gave us."

Frank groaned. "I had no clue! Do you have any idea how big this guy is? His texts on theory and strings are required reading. Thank God, I'm a flautist. How does he know Sid?"

"He and Stella have known each other for a while," I said, although I suspected it was more than a while.

Frank blew out his breath, but I was glad for the comment. If Mae and Neil needed any other reassurance, Frank's angst would help.

I eventually managed to corner Sy, although I suspect that he was expecting it.

"So," I asked as we settled in a corner of the living room. "How long have you known Sid?"

"Eh, most of his life." Sy smiled weakly. "I usually saw him every other year or so, especially after he was around seven. Stella was impressed by his progress on the piano, but worried that she could not be impartial."

"And...?"

Sy chuckled. "Sid is an exceptionally good technical piano player. But his music lacks emotion. It's a subtle difference, but a significant one. Sid's technique and execution have always been almost perfect, some of which he owes to Stella. But that isn't what makes a great concert pianist. That is the emotional element."

I chuckled. "And that's not Sid's strong point. He can get there, but not with the classical stuff." I looked at Sy. "Stella told me about a grand experiment she tried with a young man she'd been at Juilliard with, one who went on to study in Vienna."

Sy sighed and nodded. "Yes, that was me. My darling woman, you have no idea how lucky you are. Sid may have been raised with the notion of marriage as a lie. Stella, alas, lived it. And I have been paying the price." He looked over at Stella, who was talking to Frank and Darby. "I cannot say how much I love that woman. Sadly, she does not understand love. I do not fault her for it. I make do with what I've got. The blessing is that we have both mellowed as we have gotten older. Whether that means we'll be able to live together, I do not know. But I do fervently hope so. You realize she named her music school after me?"

"Now that I think about it, yeah."

"When she met Sid again, which I understand you engineered, I was flabbergasted. She called me that night. She was in shock and utterly terrified that she would mess everything up." Sy gazed unseeing at the wall. "I advised her the best that I could. But you, my darling woman, had gotten through in a way that neither I, nor anybody else, could have. Yes, I was dying to meet you."

"She was talking to you then?" I frowned.

"Of course." Sy smiled. "I suppose that was not immediately obvious."

"No. It wasn't." I still nodded. "But something must have broken through because she did act a little differently."

"Then it was all to the better." Sy sighed deeply. "God, I love that woman."

"I can see you do."

Sy smiled. "I am so glad you see it that way. It is the truth, but occasionally hard to get her to see it."

"I know."

The glory of having Sid, Stella, Sy, Darby, and Frank all in the same house was that after dinner and the music started, it was amazing. Sy and Darby went toe to toe on a Celtic fiddle showdown that blew our minds, as it had us all laughing. Frank and Sid played around with Rhapsody in Blue, with Darby and Sy jumping in. Nick talked Sid into playing his composition class final.

"I'm not really that good a composer," Sid said before beginning.

Still, the tune was quite lovely. I'd heard bits and pieces of it as Sid had sweated it through the quarter. It had gotten an A-minus because there was an awkward break at one point. Sid had titled it, "For my Family," which was probably the only reason he was playing it that night.

"I don't know why you're saying you're not that good a composer," Stella growled after he'd finished. "That was quite nice."

Sid beamed. "Thanks, Stella."

"We do need to work on that one bridge, though," she said.

"Let it alone, my darling," Sy said. "We can do that later."

Then the singing started. Yeah, Sid and I started it with Two Sleepy People, which got a big laugh when I sang, "Father didn't like it at all," and Daddy snarled, "Hell no, I didn't."

Then Mama called for a couple traditional Christmas carols, and given Stella, that had me a little worried. Stella dealt with it okay, though. Mama asked Mae if she wanted to sing "Oh, Holy Night." The three of us had sung it back before Mae and Neil had gotten married. Well, Mae sang most of it. Sid, sitting at the ebony baby grand, asked Mae what key, and she told him, then told him how to go back to the one section where Mama and I knew to join and harmonize.

We had all forgotten just how beautiful Mae's voice really is. Even Mae had. When we got to the harmony part, Mae really went to town, and I couldn't help but let the tears flow. Mama and I both hugged Mae as she gasped afterward.

"Oh, my god," she said. "I can't believe I did that!"

"What?" I all but screeched. "You've always had that voice."

"You're right," Mae gasped. "I guess I need to use it more."

"Damned straight," said Neil. "I've missed it."

She looked at him and the two held each other. The rest of us got totally misty-eyed. Okay, maybe the twins missed it, but they were only five. They still jumped into the family pile on that followed.

It was, altogether, an entirely satisfactory evening.

[You missed the other major event of the night. I'm not sure where you were at that moment. Possibly helping the kids get settled in the rumpus room. I'd gone into the library for some reason, and your mother and Neil were there.

"Sid, honey," your mother said. "You don't have to wait until the wedding."

I blinked and looked at her. "For what?"

It was kind of obvious that we hadn't waited on sleeping together.

"To call Bill and me Daddy and Mama." She smiled.

"I, uh, wasn't waiting," I said slowly.

"What else are you going to call us?"

"What I've always called you. Bill and Althea."

"Stuff and nonsense. We're Mama and Daddy. It's no disrespect to Stella. You can have more than one mama, as Nick likes to say."

"And your husband is okay with that?" I swallowed.

"He'll get used to it." Mama smiled, but I knew then that, yes, Daddy would.

"Okay." I swallowed again.

Mama left the library, and I started after her. Neil clapped me on the back.

"Mama got you, didn't she?"

"Yeah."

"There's a reason we love her daughters."

"I'm afraid so." - SEH]

Sid talked Mae and Neil into staying at the house through Christmas Day. Neil agreed to do a quick run the next morning to make sure everyone had fresh underwear and whatever presents were still waiting at the O'Malley house. Nick and Darby settled in Nick's room. The other kids landed in blankets and pillows in the rumpus room. Mae and Neil had the last guest bedroom. The house was full, and my heart was full. You couldn't ask for better than that.

December 23, 1985 – January 4, 1986

The next morning, Sid let us sleep past our usual five-thirty wake-up time. However, when the phone rang at six-something-or-other, Sid reached for the phone, and I pulled his arm back.

"Please, can we let the machine get it?" I mumbled through my sleep fog.

"Sure." Sid nuzzled my ear, pulled me closer to him, and went back to sleep.

He was awake somewhat after seven, which is sleeping in for him. I was less than awake. I am not a morning person. We still went running, taking the car out to a nearby park to do it. It's not my favorite activity but I do appreciate that we need to stay in good condition. When we got back to the house, everyone was up and either eating breakfast or had just finished. Neil had already taken off to get fresh clothes. When I got downstairs after my shower, Mama, Janey, and Sy were gathered at one end of the dining room table discussing different sights to see. Daddy, Stella, Nick, and Darby were having another intense discussion about baseball, of all things. It turns out that Stella is quite a fan. Ellen and Mae were bringing the dirty breakfast dishes into the kitchen, and the twins were outside in the back yard, playing with Motley. Sid showed up wearing jeans, a sport shirt, and a sweater. He smiled as he got some fruit salad and toast, then nodded at me and glanced toward the office. Nobody seemed to notice that he'd disappeared. I grabbed my plate and fork, some more fruit and toast, then followed him.

"What's up?" I asked, shutting and locking the door.

"I should have picked up that call this morning." Sid sat at his desk, eating. He glared at me briefly and I winced. "I just listened to the message. It was the surveillance team. Apparently, Bolinaro has decided that she's done waiting. She told her brother on the phone early this morning that she was going to take us all out at once after all and wanted a plane ticket to Mexico for later this afternoon."

It's the reason he always picks up the phone no matter what we're doing and expects me to do the same. As soon as we don't, the call turns out to be an emergency.

"I'm sorry." I made a face. "So now what?"

"Henry has Kathy and Jesse watching her apartment, so we'll know when she's on her way. We'll have to get everybody out of the house."

"Except us."

Sid nodded sadly. "We'll have to take her down. The best way to do that is give her what she wants. Or let her think she's getting it."

"Should be fairly easy. Mama, Sy, and Janey were talking movie star maps when I came in here."

"That's a good excuse to stay home."

I frowned. "Do you think we can get everybody to go?"

"The kids will go wherever." Sid shrugged. "Stella will follow Sy. She, apparently, finds his taste for kitsch amusing."

"He is surprisingly entertaining that way."

"What about your folks?"

"Daddy will do whatever Mama asks, and she thought hunting down movie star houses would be fun. Neil just goes along. Mae will probably go for it to keep an eye on the kids."

"Sounds good." Sid unlocked his desk. "I'm going to send Nick out with his pager and, hopefully, a good excuse for him to call us."

When Sid and I returned to the dining room, Neil had already returned with plenty of clothes for the next few days. Mae had disappeared. Movie star homes and the Chinese Theater had been selected as the day's excursion. Sid got Nick by himself and went over the pager again. As everyone got into the O'Malley van and the rental, Nick held me tightly.

"It'll be alright, Nick. You know your dad and I are good at this. Just keep everybody away from here."

"Okay."

As soon as they were gone, Sid and I hurried to the office and got our transmitters on, and our snub-nosed revolvers. In the closed space of the house, that would be all we'd need. Sid went to the library, and I went up the hall on the office side.

"Transmitting," I said softly.

"Got you," said Sid's voice in my ear.

"Big Red, Little Red, this is Red Dawn." Jesse came in loud and clear. "Subject is outside your location. Sorry, but we couldn't raise you sooner."

"Where are you?" Sid asked.

"Behind her. We'll have to wait to approach until she goes inside."

Motley, locked in our bedroom upstairs, started barking his fool head off.

A door in the middle of the hall opened and Mae came out. I whipped my gun behind my back.

"Oh, there you are, Lisa."

"Mae, what are you doing here?"

I could hear Sid cursing.

She grimaced. "I was really sick this morning. I heard you and Sid were sticking around and might meet up with everyone later. So, I stayed behind. I hope you don't mind."

"Yoo-hoo!" A hard female voice blared from the house intercoms. "I'm here. Sid? Lisa? Can't wait to see you."

Mae's face went pale. "The crazy lady. Where's your purse?"

"Upstairs," I said.

Kathy's voice cursed in my ear. "Looks like you got a bomb up in the eave of your second story."

"How the hell...?" Sid cursed as well.

I was so glad Mae couldn't hear Jesse, Kathy, or Sid.

Mae pushed me down the hall toward the office. "Go. Hide. I'll be in my room."

I ran for the front of the house and ducked behind a wing-back chair in the living room. Bolinaro came down the hall on the other side of the dining table, with the rumpus room on the other side. She wore black pants, blouse, and gloves, and carried an automatic handgun in her right hand. Her left hand was clenched around something else.

Jesse cursed in my ear. "You've got a bomb at each corner of the house."

Henry James broke in. "What are we looking at?"

Bolinaro spotted something in the living room and squeezed off a round. A vase on the mantle broke. One of the cats must have been up there. They'd been playing hiding games again.

I could hear Jesse and Henry going back and forth about what kind of bomb it was.

"That sounds like what I've got up here." Kathy suddenly cursed. "And two more in the eaves. I'm fairly sure that's it."

Bolinaro turned suddenly and smiled. "Ah, ah, ah."

She advanced toward what had to be Sid, her gun in front of her. At least she was no longer broadcasting over the intercom.

"You're betting you can shoot faster than I can," said Sid.

Henry gave Jesse and Kathy a quick lesson on defusing bombs.

Bolinaro laughed. "No. You're going to drop your weapon." She waved her left hand. "See this? It's a dead man switch. All I have to do is drop it, and we've got fifteen seconds before everything goes boom. I can get out of here in fifteen seconds. Do you think you can shoot me, grab the switch, and figure out which button to push in fifteen seconds?" She raised her voice. "And, Lisa, I wouldn't try sneaking up on me. This place is just a little too open for that."

"Red Team," Henry's voice said in my ear. "You've got back up coming. Just keep her talking. We don't want to take a chance on that switch. Red Sky, Red Dawn, what's the status on the explosives?"

"Two defused down here," said Jesse.

"I've got one on the second story," said Kathy. "That leaves two more—" She cursed. "Three more."

"We have a civilian on the premises," Jesse added.

Henry cursed.

Bolinaro smiled. "Now, why don't you back up, Sid? Oh, and drop the gun."

"Hold fire, Big Red, Little Red," Henry ordered.

I couldn't say anything. I didn't want Bolinaro to hear me. But I wondered what the heck Henry was thinking. After all, we'd have 15 seconds.

"Drop it!" Bolinaro snapped.

"Fine," Sid said.

Bolinaro advanced on him. As soon as she had gone past the dining room opening and was, presumably, pushing Sid back along the hall, I scuttled around the chair to where I could see the front of the house. Sure enough, Sid backed up and into the library, his hands in the air. Bolinaro took one quick look around.

I suddenly realized I could no longer hear Kathy and Jesse. I wondered about that, but there wasn't much I could do.

"Alright, Lisa, come on out. I don't have to wait to start shooting."

"Hold fire," Henry said, his voice worried. "We need to keep her talking."

"Send Sid out here first," I called.

"Are you kidding? You know where we are."

"No, I don't," I said.

"We're in that front room with the books and another piano. Sheez. Who keeps two baby grand pianos?"

"Go," said Henry. "Keep her talking. We only need a couple more minutes."

I somehow doubted that, but slid out from behind the chair and went into the library.

"Drop your gun," Bolinaro ordered as I appeared in the doorway. "Now, next to lover boy in front of the window."

I slowly did as she asked. "How did—"

"Shut up!" She pointed the gun at me then her face contorted into almost a smile. She moved closer to us. "Oh, I have been looking forward to this. You two have no idea what you ruined."

She raised the automatic, and I swallowed. Gunfire cracked twice, but neither Sid nor I fell. Bolinaro crumpled instead.

"Damn it!" Henry's voice. "We're not clear!"

Sid dove, pushing the automatic further away from Bolinaro and scooped up the switch.

In the library doorway, Mae stood, a small pistol in her hand, gasping and with a glazed look in her eyes.

"Mae!" I screamed.

Sid nodded toward the office.

"You weren't that much better than me at skeet," Mae mumbled.

I started crying and ran to her. "Come on. Let's go to the office."

Mae was clearly in shock, so I held her and gently pushed her in that direction.

"What have I done?" she cried as I shut the office door.

"You saved our backsides, that's what you did," I told her. I knew exactly what she was going through, so I held her close to me. "You didn't kill her. She'll live."

Mae sobbed onto my shoulder. "Please. We can't tell anyone."

"I won't. Don't worry. It's alright, Mae. I'm here. It's alright."

I debated calling Father John, but there was enough going on. I heard Sid explaining to Henry what had happened. Fortunately, the FBI team arrived before the Beverly Hills Police. Sid went upstairs before the team or the police could see him, and Henry talked to everyone. I was still holding Mae in the office, but I heard the minor dust up between the cops and the special agents.

Henry arrived in the office and told Mae that an investigator needed to talk to her. She looked like she was about to face the executioner, but Henry patted her shoulders and went with her. Mae came back to me looking a lot calmer.

"He said I did the right thing," she told me. "I had to give him my gun, but that's okay. I, uh, also told him about your ghost-writing contract. Was that alright?"

"I think it will be," I said.

She looked at me. "She was pointing a gun at you. How come I'm more freaked out?"

"I didn't shoot anybody." Lord, I hoped she'd buy it.

For once, she did. "Oh."

There was a lot more chatter coming through my transmitter, but I tuned most of it out. Jesse and Kathy were well clear by the time the special agents and cops had arrived. It was almost one before Sid muttered to me through the transmitter that we needed to clear the premises, so that the cleanup team could come in and get rid of blood stains and any bullet holes, not to mention bombs. Henry coughed his approval, and I pulled Mae from the office to the back of the house and to the garage. Sid was already there.

"We need to make merry," he told Mae. "Are you up for this?"

"Yeah. I think so. It may even be what I need."

"Good. Nick just called. They're all at the Chinese Theater. There's a really great pizza place near there. I told Nick to tell Neil we'll meet everyone there in about half an hour."

Mae looked at him, still dazed. "Do we have to tell them what happened?"

Sid smiled. "Mae, the less said, the better."

"I can do that." Mae swallowed and nodded.

Having everyone around us at that moment was exactly what Mae needed. The twins, of course, were all over the place and keeping them contained got Mae back into her normal demeanor in a jiffy. My darling sister has a mama bear streak a mile wide, and I had to concede it did anchor her. [As if you don't have a similarly wide mama bear streak. - SEH]

Truth be told, the restaurant was a trashy little joint, with cracked vinyl on the booths, beeping video games in the corner, and some of the best pizza ever made coming out of its ovens. We took over four tables in the center of the restaurant. As the kids ran around, largely thanks to the liberal dispensation of quarters by Sy, Daddy, and Sid, we adults ate and laughed. Okay. Both Sid and I needed it, too.

Sy wanted to eat dinner at Musso and Frank. Mama and Daddy had no clue about the significance, nor did Mae and Neil. But Mae and Neil volunteered to take the kids back to Sid's and my place, and I told Mae where the really good pirate version of the Star Wars trilogy was. I probably shouldn't have, but it is an exceptionally good video.

The rest of that week and a half was no less crazy. Christmas Eve was spent at the house, eating, and singing until time to put the younger kids down for naps so that they'd be reasonably awake for Midnight Mass. Ellen was a little worried that Santa Claus wouldn't know where she was, but Sid assured her that he'd called Santa personally to make sure he'd know that Ellen O'Malley was at Uncle Sid's and Aunt Lisa's.

Right before naptime, though, Mama got out that year's Christmas pajamas. It was a little scary just how pleased Sy seemed to be with the flannel shirt and pants bedecked with cavorting reindeer. Stella accepted the nightgown decorated with lovely cardinal birds all over it with grace. Sid's pajamas were perfectly hideous, as in bright red with little dachshunds wearing multi-colored Santa hats. Sid just shook his head. Sid always gets the ugliest pajamas because he refuses to wear them.

Later, Stella got another chance at the church organ before Midnight Mass and after. The youngest three were out cold by the end of Mass. Nick, Darby, and Janey were glassy-eyed by the time we got home. We, adults, went into assembly operations as soon as Mae had gotten the little ones down. It didn't take long. Even Stella, who was a little worried about lying to the little ones about Santa, helped get the Santa gifts out and the stockings stuffed.

The funny thing was the soundproofing on Sid's and my bedroom was so good that we completely missed the twins' shrieks that Santa had come. Nick had to use the intercom to let us know they were all waiting for us the next morning.

Late that afternoon, as we finished our Christmas dinner, Stella got up and motioned for silence.

"I am not one for sentiment," she told us. "But I want to take this moment to say thank you to all of you for welcoming Sy and me into this celebration. I particularly want to thank you, Lisa, for bringing Sid back to me, then refereeing as the two of us worked things out." She smiled as my eyes filled. "But most of all, Sid, I want to thank you for not walking out. Instead, you chose to reach out and..." She choked just a little. "I have my man child back again. Sid, you may not be the son of my womb, but you are the son of my heart."

That's it. We were all sobbing. Sid got up and pulled Stella into his arms and the two held each other. Then Nick bounced up and joined the hug.

Boxing Day, okay, the day after Christmas, found us all at Disneyland because Sy wanted to see it and had decided that seeing it through the eyes of a bunch of children was the best possible way to do so. And so it went on. Sy was indefatigable. He wanted to see everything, from the historic El Pueblo monuments at Olvera Street, the oldest street in Los Angeles, to the Universal Studios tour, to the Getty Museum. We did a day of skiing. We even got tickets to the stands on the Rose Parade route on New Year's morning - another part of Sid's magic. We also concluded that it was worth doing once, but thanks to the incredible crowds, never again.

Somewhere in there, Sid had called his old high school friend Tom Freeman, who also decided that he wanted to come to L.A. for a couple days. Tom found a hotel room, but the three of us went to lunch with Sy and Stella on the day after New Year's. Tom was a delight and he, Sid, and

Stella had a wonderful time, both reminiscing and talking, in general.

Also, during that week, Sy, Stella, Mae, and Neil had several extended conferences on how best to educate Darby. Somehow, they came to agreement, although, I confess, I didn't really pay much attention.

Mae later told me that if the cops wanted to return her gun, she didn't want it. She was no longer scared, and that made me smile. As for Carla Caponetti, Sid decided to sell the family home after Stella said she didn't want it. However, Sid gave Carla the proceeds from the sale to add to her pension. We didn't worry about it past that.

Mama and Daddy left early on January second. Mae and Neil took their kids home after taking my parents to the airport, while Sid and I went to our aforementioned lunch. Sy and Stella pulled Sid, Nick, and me out on another excursion on the third. We finally put the two of them on a plane back to New York (presumably Stella would find her way to South Florida after that) on Saturday, the fourth. That night, Sid and I kissed Nick good night in his bedroom, then climbed the stairs to ours.

"Do you hear that?" Sid asked as we slid under the covers.

"I don't hear anything."

"Yeah. It's finally quiet."

I giggled. "It is. It's been crazy, hasn't it?"

"In a very good kind of way. Oh. I forgot to tell you. Henry called this morning."

"I saw a call come in. That was him?"

"Yep." Sid nuzzled my ear. He really liked doing that, and I liked being nuzzled. "Bolinaro, aka the former Carol Beldon, is in a maximum-security facility. She has pled guilty to a wide variety of charges and unless she pulls off a miracle, she's there for life."

I shuddered. "I wouldn't count on her not being able to pull off a miracle."

Sid sighed. "I suppose that's possible. I sure as hell hope not."

"Me, too."

"Maybe you can make that God thing work in our favor."

I laughed and kissed him. He tenderly brushed the hair from my forehead.

"Sweetheart," he said softly. "I want to say thank you."

"For what?"

"For my best Christmas present."

I giggled. "So, you really did like the synthesizer?"

"Not that one. You got me my mother."

"I didn't do that. If she weren't willing, it would never have happened."

"If you hadn't pushed her, it would never have happened. I'm so glad you did." He smiled. "And I'm glad you pushed me, too. I love you so much, Lisa."

"I love you, too, Sid."

I couldn't help thinking about the night before. Nick had wanted to sing a Foreigner tune, "I Want to Know What Love Is." He had his amp and electric guitar out. Stella had smiled indulgently, but then got a strangely curious look on her face. She looked at Sy, who took her hand and smiled back. Maybe Stella was figuring it out after all.

Book Ten in the Operation Quickline series, *From This Day Forward*

Come, share the joy...

It's The Big Day. Sid Hackbirn and Lisa Wycherly are getting married. But in the days and weeks before the wedding, the pair discover that there is something very strange going on with their work as ultra-top-secret counter-espionage agents. Courier drops are coming in without the usual processing. The bad guys tailing them are unusually persistent.

Then Sid and Lisa take off for their honeymoon only to find that the nice, relaxing vacation in England that they had planned will be anything but. They're being trained for their new job and will be touring the European continent, instead. Skiing in Gstaad, Switzerland, touring Venice, Italy, doesn't sound so bad, except that the two get sucked into a dangerous plot, with bad guys trying to kill them. Still, trying to figure out what the potential killers are planning might actually be easier than trying to figure out how to be married.

Other books by Anne Louise Bannon

I'm so glad you liked this book! Check out my other novels, available in print or ebook at your favorite retailer:

Freddie and Kathy Series:
Fascinating Rhythm
Bring Into Bondage
The Last Witnesses
Blood Red

Operation Quickline Series
That Old Cloak and Dagger Routine
Stopleak
Deceptive Appearances
Fugue in a Minor Key
Sad Lisa
These Hallowed Halls
My Sweet Lisa
A Little Family Business

Just Because You're Paranoid

Old Los Angeles
Death of the Zanjero
Death of the City Marshal
Death of the Chinese Field Hands
Death of an Heiress

Daria Barnes
Rage Issues

Mrs. Sperling
A Nose for a Niedeman

Brenda Finnegan
Tyger, Tyger

Romantic Fiction
White House Rhapsody, Book One and Two

Fantasy and Science Fiction
A Ring for a Second Chance
But World Enough and Time

And I would be honored if you left a review for this and any of my books on GoodReads or any other retail site. It really helps.

Connect with Anne Louise Bannon

Thank you for sticking it out this long! Please join my newsletter. It's the best way to stay up-to-date on my upcoming projects, blog posts and even games and giveaways.

Sign up here: http://eepurl.com/zH0Ab

Or connect with me on your favorite social media platforms:

Visit my website: http://annelouisebannon.com

Friend me on Facebook: http://facebook.com/RobinGoodfellowEnt

Follow me on Twitter: http://twitter.com/ALBannon

Favorite my Smashwords author page: https://www.smashwords.com/profile/view/MsBriscow

Connect on LinkedIn: http://www.linkedin.com/in/annelouisebannon

Follow me on Pinterest: http://pinterest.com/msbriscow

About Anne Louise Bannon

Anne Louise Bannon is an author and journalist who wrote her first novel at age 15. Her journalistic work has appeared in Ladies' Home Journal, the Los Angeles Times, Wines and Vines, and in newspapers across the country. She was a TV critic for over 10 years, founded the YourFamilyViewer blog, and created the OddBallGrape.com wine education blog with her husband, Michael Holland. She is the co-author of Howdunit: Book of Poisons, with Serita Stevens, as well as author of the Freddie and Kathy mystery series, set in the 1920s, the Old Los Angeles series, set in 1870, and the Operation Quickline series, plus several stand alones. She and her husband live in Southern California with an assortment of critters.